Since wh
couldn't b
to be her dad.

"So what do you think?" Megan asked as she focused on the mirror again. The lace distorted her vision, so she nearly saw it: the beauty of being a bride.

But then a shadow stepped behind her. It was tall and dark in a black tuxedo. The mirror showed only his long legs and his chest until he stepped closer yet. Then she saw his head—the short golden hair, the bright green eyes, the dark stubble on his jaw...

Just how badly had the veil distorted her vision? Who was she mistaking for a dead man?

Her hands trembling, she fumbled with her veil—pulling it back so she could focus on the apparition. She whirled around to face him.

It couldn't be...

Gage was dead. He'd been dead for months. But that hadn't stopped her from seeing him everywhere, every time she'd closed her eyes and tried to sleep.

But she shouldn't be seeing him here—not on her wedding day to another man.

"No..." she murmured. Her knees trembled and weakened, threatening to fold beneath her. "No..."

Be sure to check out the previous books in the exciting Bachelor Bodyguards miniseries.

* * *

If you're on Twitter, tell us what you think of Harlequin Romantic Suspense! #harlequinromsuspense

Dear Reader,

Welcome back to River City, Michigan, and the Payne
Protection Agency. *Beauty and the Bodyguard* is
the fourth book in the Bachelor Bodyguards series.
Blushing bride Megan Lynch has more than cold
feet over her upcoming nuptials. She can't marry her
groom. She doesn't love him. She's in love with a
ghost. Then that ghost shows up at the church.

Gage Huxton has no intention of stopping Megan's
wedding. She's broken his heart more than his
captors have broken his body or his spirit over the
six months he was missing in action and presumed
dead. His only intention is to protect the bride—
which proves to be this bachelor bodyguard's most
dangerous assignment yet. He isn't risking just his
life; he's risking his heart, too.

I hope you enjoy this latest book in the Bachelor
Bodyguards series.

Happy Reading!

Lisa Childs

BEAUTY AND THE BODYGUARD

Lisa Childs

HARLEQUIN® ROMANTIC SUSPENSE

Recycling programs
for this product may
not exist in your area.

ISBN-13: 978-0-373-28145-9

Beauty and the Bodyguard

Ever since **Lisa Childs** read her first romance novel (a Harlequin story, of course) at age eleven, all she wanted was to be a romance writer. With over forty novels published with Harlequin, Lisa is living her dream. She is an award-winning, bestselling romance author. Lisa loves to hear from readers, who can contact her on Facebook, through her website, lisachilds.com, or her snail-mail address, PO Box 139, Marne, MI 49435.

Books by Lisa Childs

Harlequin Romantic Suspense

Bachelor Bodyguards

His Christmas Assignment
Bodyguard Daddy
Bodyguard's Baby Surprise
Beauty and the Bodyguard

Harlequin Intrigue

Special Agents at the Altar

The Pregnant Witness
Agent Undercover
The Agent's Redemption

Shotgun Weddings

Groom Under Fire
Explosive Engagement
Bridegroom Bodyguard

Hotshot Heroes

Red Hot
Hot Attraction

Visit the Author Profile page at Harlequin.com for more titles.

For Kimberly Duffy—with great appreciation for all your years of friendship. Without your support and your wonderful sense of humor, I don't know how I would have survived all the ups and downs in my career and in my life. Thank you!

Prologue

How the hell had he survived? It wasn't possible. It just wasn't possible...

But the proof was in the photo. Sure, he looked different. Then again, who wouldn't, after what he'd been through? He'd been tortured to death. At least Derek had thought he'd killed the man...

Cockroaches were like that, though; they could survive the most extreme extermination attempts. The only thing they couldn't survive was getting crushed.

The picture crumpled in a big fist. He better be enjoying his last moments of life—because he wasn't going to stay alive. And this time when he died, he would damn well stay dead.

Derek Nielsen hurled the wadded-up photo against the bars of his cell. An alarm rang out. He hadn't set it off—directly. But indirectly he had. The alarm was sounding because of him, according to his carefully orchestrated plan.

This was it—his escape.

With a buzz and a clank, the cell door slid open. He slipped through it like other prisoners stepped through theirs. They were confused, though, standing in the hall outside their cells. Derek hurried past them. He knew where he needed to be: the laundry room. He had only minutes to get to the vent leading out from one of the commercial dryers. After his efforts, it was big enough now for him to crawl through and escape.

Derek would be out soon to the vehicle that waited outside for him. The one that would slip through the gates and bring him to freedom.

Derek wouldn't be returning to prison, although he fully intended to commit another crime. He was going to kill the man responsible for sending him to jail.

Chapter 1

Gage Huxton had survived six months in hell for this? Since becoming a bodyguard on his return from Afghanistan, his assignments had been a mixed bag. His first job with the Payne Protection Agency had been to protect an elderly lady with Alzheimer's, who had only been in danger from her disease and not her imagined threats.

But then he had also been assigned to follow the man who was now his brother-in-law. That job had nearly gotten Gage killed. But he had survived being shot at and nearly run down.

He wasn't sure he would survive this: wedding duty. He slid a finger between the bow tie and his skin, trying to loosen the stranglehold it had on him. An image flashed through his mind, of a noose tightening around his neck, squeezing off his oxygen until oblivion claimed him. But, unfortunately, oblivion had never lasted. He grimaced as he remembered other horrors.

"Are you okay?" a soft voice asked him.

He blinked away those horrific images and focused on Penny Payne. She sprang up from her chair and walked around her desk in the office in the basement of her white wedding chapel. It was in River City, Michigan—where his friend Nick had moved and where Gage now lived.

Not wanting to worry her, he jerked his chin up and down in a quick nod.

Her brown eyes warm with affection and concern, she stared up at him. "You look very handsome in the tuxedo."

He probably should have shaved the scruff from his jaw so he'd fit in more with the wedding guests when they arrived. But he hadn't had the time or the inclination. "I must be crazy," he said.

"Why's that?" she asked, and now there was a twinkle of amusement in her eyes.

"To let you talk me into playing a bouncer for your wedding business." Penny was his boss's mother, so he probably hadn't had much choice. But it hadn't been any easier for him to tell her no than it probably would have been for her son.

She reached up, and he reacted as he did whenever someone moved to touch him. He flinched. Sympathy dimmed the usual brightness of her smile. "Gage…"

Instead of pulling back as so many other people did, she gently laid her palm against his cheek. "I'm sorry," she murmured.

He shook his head and dislodged her hand. "I don't want pity," he said. "I just want to do my job."

"That's not what—"

He forced a smile. "It's okay." Nobody had known how

to react to him since he'd been back. So maybe it was good that not many people knew he'd survived.

"Where do you need me?" he asked. "Do I need to make sure the bride and groom's mothers don't get into a catfight?"

Penny's smile dimmed more, and she replied, "The bride's mother passed away years ago."

"That's too bad." He didn't see his mother often since she and his dad had moved to Alaska, but he could call her anytime. He rarely called, though; he didn't want to worry her. "So no catfights between the mothers. What about the bridesmaids?"

Penny's lips curved into a bigger smile. "Why do you sound almost hopeful?"

He chuckled. "Just looking for the upside in this assignment."

"Cake," she told him, and she patted his cheek again as if he was a little boy she was promising a treat if he behaved. Her kids were grown now, but she had raised three boys and a tomboy pretty much on her own. So she knew how to handle kids.

He wasn't a kid, though. He hadn't been one for a long time—not since he'd joined the Marines at eighteen a decade ago. Then there had been that stint with the FBI. But he didn't like to think about those days, because then he inevitably thought about *her.*

The hell he'd endured the past six months was nothing compared to what she had put him through. No. He would rather think about the horrors of his six months in captivity than about Megan Lynch.

He exhaled a ragged breath and shook off all the memories. He had to leave the past in the past—all of it, but most of all Megan.

"So," he said as he focused again on the present. "You want me to guard the cake?"

Dessert was probably all anyone considered him capable of protecting yet. Why else had he been assigned wedding chapel duty?

Penny shook her head. "Of course not. You have the most important job here."

He narrowed his eyes and studied her, wondering if she was patronizing him. "And what's that?"

"Guarding the bride, of course."

"Guarding her?" He couldn't imagine what danger she might be in, but then he had no idea who she was. "Or do you mean making sure she doesn't run?"

He wouldn't blame her if she did. He would never risk his heart on love again. But then he no longer had a heart to lose. Megan had destroyed it.

Penny sighed. "I almost wish she would…"

"The groom's a tool?"

She shook her head. "He seems nice."

So maybe the bride was a bridezilla. "Why does she need protecting?"

"Her father is a very important man," Penny said, and as she said it, her face flushed.

"Who's her father?" he asked. And more importantly, why had the fifty-something-year-old widow reacted with a blush at the very thought of him?

"He's a man who's made some enemies over the course of his career."

Gage should have picked up one of the programs from the basket outside the chapel. He'd passed it on his way downstairs to Penny's office. Then he would know the names of everyone in the wedding party. But he'd wanted to get his assignment before any of the guests arrived.

Now he had it: bridal protection.

"So he thinks some of these adversaries might go after his daughter during her wedding?" The guy had made some seriously ruthless enemies if that was the case.

Penny nodded. "He's the kind of man who wouldn't care what someone did to *him*." Her face flushed a deeper shade of red.

Who was this guy to her? Apparently, someone she knew well. How well? Just how closely did Penny work with widowed fathers of the brides?

She continued, "But if someone hurt his daughter…"

Gage understood. His best friend, Nicholas Rus, had thought that someone was going after Gage's sister for vengeance against him—because Nick loved Annalise and she had always loved him. But that hadn't been about revenge, at least not against Nick or Annalise.

"If this guy has so many enemies," Gage said, "why am I the only one from the Payne Protection Agency here?" Especially when he knew his boss didn't trust that he was at a hundred percent yet. But Logan Payne wasn't the only one who thought that; Gage didn't entirely trust himself.

He was getting better, but it was still a struggle to sleep, to suppress the flashbacks, to forget the pain…

Penny tilted her head and stared up at him. "You're the bodyguard the bride needs."

Gage's stomach lurched as realization suddenly dawned on him. And even without reading the program, he knew who the bride was. Penny had given him enough clues. He should have figured it out earlier. Hell, he should have figured it out when Penny asked him to help out at the chapel. He'd known she was planning a wedding for someone he'd known. Or at least, he'd thought he'd known her.

He guessed the wedding wasn't all Penny Payne had been planning. Nick had warned him that she was a meddler. Her kids might not mind that she meddled in their lives, but he damn well minded.

He shook his head. "No…"

"Gage," she beseeched him.

But he just shook his head again, refusing the assignment. He didn't care if Mrs. Payne went to his boss and got him fired. He couldn't protect this bride—not when he was the one against whom she most needed protecting.

"He's gone," Penny said.

Woodrow Lynch released a ragged breath and closed her office door behind him. "That's probably for the best."

"How can you say that?" Penny asked, her usually soft voice sharp with indignation. "She's miserable."

"She's miserable because of *him*." Anger coursed through him as he thought of the pain Gage Huxton had put his daughter through. Some of it had been inadvertent, like getting captured.

But the rest…

Quitting the Bureau.

Reenlisting.

Those had been Gage's choices.

"Yes." Penny stalked around her desk to stand in front of him. She was so petite despite the heels she wore with a silky bronze-colored dress. Her eyes were nearly that same color bronze. Her hair, chin length and curly, was a deeper shade of brown with red and bronze highlights.

She was beautiful. She was also infuriating as hell. The woman always thought she was right.

And even more infuriating was the fact that she usually was.

"So, it's for the best that she move on," Woodrow said.

It had to be for the best, because the wedding was due to start in less than an hour. And he would rather walk his daughter down the aisle to a man who would not make her miserable.

Penny shook her head and tumbled several locks of hair into her eyes. The curls tangled in her long lashes. Instinctively, he reached out to extract them, but her hand collided with his. Her skin was as silky as her hair. Her fingers trembled beneath his, and she pulled away from his touch and stepped back until his hand fell away from her face.

He'd known her long enough—had attended enough weddings in her chapel—that he'd seen how warm and affectionate she was. With everyone else...

With him she was guarded and skittish. Usually. Right now she was also annoyed.

"Megan can't move on," Penny said, "unless she has closure."

"Are you speaking from experience?" He hadn't meant to ask the question. It had just slipped out, probably because he'd wondered for a while why she had never remarried after her husband died sixteen years before.

Her big eyes narrowed. "We are not talking about me."

She never did. He'd noticed that, too. She only talked about other people: her kids, his agents and now his daughter.

"Our concern should be only about Megan," Penny continued. "I've never worked with a more miserable bride."

Now he narrowed his eyes with indignation and pride. "Are you saying that she's difficult?"

"Of course not," Penny said. She reached out, almost as if she couldn't help herself, and touched his arm. She probably only meant to reassure him about his daughter. But then she added, "She's sad. So sad…"

He shouldn't have been able to feel Penny's touch, not through his tuxedo jacket and shirt, but his skin tingled as if he'd felt the heat and silkiness of her skin against his. What the hell was wrong with him?

Maybe he'd been single too long. Like her, he'd lost his spouse. She had died, more than twenty years ago, when their girls were little. But he didn't need closure— or anything else—but his daughters' happiness. Ellen was older and settled with a good husband and three beautiful little girls.

But Megan…

He'd always worried the most about Megan and never more than when she got involved with Gage Huxton. She'd fallen so hard for him that it was inevitable she would get hurt.

"She's marrying a good man," Woodrow insisted. He wasn't too proud to admit that he'd used Bureau resources to check out the kid. He was a computer nerd— as introverted and shy as she was. "They're perfect for each other."

They'd met in college, in a computer class. They'd been friends for years before they'd started dating. They hadn't been going out very long before Gage had swept her off her feet.

Damn Gage…

Penny shook her head.

"They are perfect for each other," he insisted.

"It doesn't matter how compatible you are," she said, "if you're not in love."

"Love is what made her miserable," Woodrow said. He could relate to that. Love had made him miserable as well. "Compatibility is more important in a marriage—wanting and expecting the same things. That's what will sustain a relationship." And not send one outside the marriage looking for something else.

"Are you speaking from experience now?" she asked.

He wished. He shook his head. "We're not talking about me."

"No," she agreed. "Megan, and her happiness, is our only priority. You need to tell her that Gage is alive."

"Why?" he asked.

Nothing good would come of her knowing the truth; it wouldn't change anything. She and Gage had broken up nearly a year ago—before he'd quit the Bureau, before he'd reenlisted, before he'd gone missing in action.

Penny's grasp on his arm tightened. Her hand was small but strong. He felt her grip and the heat of her touch. "She deserves to know before she marries another man that the man she really loves is alive."

He hadn't seen Gage yet. But Woodrow's former agent and Gage's best friend, Nicholas Rus, had warned him. Gage had come back alive, but he hadn't come back the same.

Woodrow shook his head. "No, the man she loves is gone." And maybe it was better that she never learned the truth.

Megan Lynch stared into the oval mirror, studying the woman reflected back at her. Wasn't she supposed to look beautiful? Weren't all brides?

The gown, while not her style, was certainly eye-catching. With twinkling rhinestones sewn onto the heavy brocade, it sparkled. The lacy veil was beautiful and softened the sharp angles of Megan's face and hid some of the severity of the dark hair she'd pulled into a tight knot to tame. But she didn't look beautiful. She shouldn't have expected that she would; she had never looked beautiful before. Why should her wedding day be any different?

No matter how much makeup the beautician had applied, the dark circles were still visible beneath her dark eyes. Tears brimmed in them, but she blinked them away. She wouldn't feel sorry for herself anymore. She had done enough of that the past several months. She'd nearly drowned in self-pity and guilt.

The knob rattled as someone turned it and began to open the door to the bride's dressing room. She hurriedly tugged the veil over her face to hide the hint of tears she couldn't quite clear from her eyes. They kept rushing back—every time she thought of him.

She had to stop thinking about *him*. He was gone. But even if he wasn't, he wouldn't have ever come back to her, not after what she'd done. She had to stop thinking about the past and focus on the future, not that she deserved one.

Because he didn't have one...

Marrying Richard was the right thing to do. He'd always been there for her. Even after she'd broken up with him, Richard had remained her friend. And when her heart had been broken, he'd tried to piece it back together. Eventually, he had even accepted that there was no patching a heart as shattered as hers. He'd insisted that their friendship was a stronger and safer foundation for a marriage than love.

Safe had sounded good to her. And there was no one safer than Richard. He was quiet and shy and nervous and cautious. He wouldn't put himself or her in any danger for any reason. He would always be there for her—like he'd always been.

Not like Gage…

The door opened fully, but she didn't turn toward it. She suspected it was her matron of honor, who was supposed to have arrived with the beautician an hour earlier. Her sister, Ellen, was always late. She also had three little girls she'd needed to get ready besides herself, though.

Megan's heart swelled with love for her nieces. They and the kids she worked with every day made her yearn to have children of her own. She wanted to be a mom like her sister—loving and fun.

She didn't remember her own mom. Dad had been both a father and mother to her.

Since whoever had entered was quiet—it couldn't be her sister and nieces. It had to be her dad.

"So what do you think?" Megan asked as she focused on the mirror again. The lace distorted her vision, so she nearly saw it: the beauty of being a bride.

But then a shadow stepped behind her. It was tall and dark in a black tuxedo. The mirror showed only his long legs and his chest. He was too thin to be her father. Too tall to be Richard. She had no idea who he was until he stepped closer yet. Then she saw his head—the short golden hair, the bright green eyes, the darker blond stubble on his jaw…

Just how badly had the veil distorted her vision? Who was she mistaking for a dead man?

Her hands trembling, she fumbled with her veil, pulling it back so she could focus on the apparition. She whirled around to face him.

It couldn't be...

Gage was dead. He had died months ago, his body lost in some foreign country. But that hadn't stopped her from seeing him everywhere, every time she'd closed her eyes and tried to sleep.

She shouldn't be seeing him here—not on her wedding day to another man.

"No..." she murmured. Her knees trembled and weakened, threatening to fold beneath her. "No..."

Chapter 2

"So what do I think?" Gage repeated her question. He thought he'd been punched in the gut. The minute he'd opened the door and seen her—sparkling like a vision in white—all his breath had left his lungs. His chest burned, his ribs ached. He felt like he was getting the life pounded out of him all over again.

Her usually honey-toned skin was pale except for the dark circles beneath her enormous eyes. With her sharp cheekbones, small pointed chin and wide dark eyes, she appeared fragile—vulnerable. He knew she was tougher than she looked, though. She'd been tough on him when she'd broken up with him. Then she swayed on her feet, as if she were about to faint.

Instinctively, he reached out to catch her, closing his hands around her waist. She was thinner than she'd been when he'd seen her last. Maybe she was one of those brides who'd been starving herself to fit into her gown, to look good for her wedding photos and her groom. Maybe that was why she trembled in his grasp.

From starvation…

He preferred the sexy curves she'd had over her new svelte figure. She'd been perfect as she was.

Her breath escaped in a gasp. "You're real…" she murmured. "You're alive…"

As he realized what she'd thought, he chuckled. "You're not seeing a ghost."

"I thought—*everyone* thought—that you died in Afghanistan."

"I was presumed dead," he said, "but I was just missing." Missing everyone back home, but most especially her. She had obviously not been missing him at all, though. She'd been dating, getting engaged.

Anger coursed through him, making him shake like she was. His hands tightened around her tiny waist. "So what do I think," he mused again. "I think you make a beautiful bride, Megan Lynch."

He had once planned on asking her to be his; he'd even bought the ring. But he had never gotten the chance to give it to her before she'd broken up with him, before she'd broken him.

She flinched as if he'd insulted her. But she'd never been able to accept a compliment as anything but a lie. She'd actually accused him of lying to her, of using her.

His blood heated. This was why he couldn't protect her—because he wanted to hurt her—like she had hurt him, like her marrying another man was hurting him all over again. "So let me be the first to kiss the bride…"

He gripped her small waist and dragged her up so her feet dangled above the floor. She gasped in shock, her breath whispering across his lips as he lowered his mouth to hers. Her lips were as soft as he remembered, her taste as sweet. He had missed this so much. He'd missed her. He deepened the kiss. Pressing his lips tightly against hers, he slid his tongue into her mouth.

A moan rumbled in her throat. And her hands clasped the back of his head, her fingers sliding over his short hair. She stilled as she touched one of the scars. Those wounds hadn't hurt, though, at least not in comparison to what she'd done to him.

Remembering the pain she'd caused him, he dragged his mouth from hers. Then he lowered her until her feet touched the floor again. When he released her, she swayed and her palm pressed against his chest. His heart leaped beneath her touch, and she must have felt it because she jerked her hand away.

"Gage," she murmured, and she stared up at him as if she still couldn't believe he wasn't an apparition. Then her gaze scanned him, over the tuxedo he was wearing, the damn bow tie choking off his breath.

"*Why* are you here?" She looked both fearful and hopeful, and he realized what she thought.

A chuckle of bitterness slipped through his lips. "Don't worry," he assured her, "I'm not here to stop the wedding."

"Then why are you here?" she asked.

"I work for a security firm now," he said. "The Payne Protection Agency. Penny hired me to make sure nothing stops this wedding from happening." Actually, he suspected just the opposite—that she had imagined some romantic reunion between him and Megan. Since she was a wedding planner, she probably believed in romance and happy endings and all that stuff Gage had given up on nearly a year ago.

There would be no happy ending for him.

Like she had so many times before, Penny tugged the dress over Nikki's head and zipped her into it. "Thank you, honey, for helping me out."

Nikki grimaced. Like she had a choice…

Like anyone could say no to Penny Payne. Even Gage Huxton hadn't been able to, and he could have come up with more excuses than Nikki had.

Her small hands gripping Nikki's shoulders, Penny spun her around to face her. "You look beautiful."

After having three boys, Penny must have been very happy to finally have a girl so she could dress her up like a doll. But having three brothers, Nikki hadn't wanted anything to do with dresses or dolls. She'd wanted to play the sports her brothers had played. She'd wanted to wrestle and fight. She couldn't do that in the dresses Mom had constantly tried to zip her into then—or now.

"Mom…"

Penny's palm cupped her cheek. "I know you don't want to be, but you are beautiful."

Her face flushed, but she couldn't deny that she was beautiful—not without insulting her mother. She looked exactly like Penny.

"I want to be taken seriously," she said. And that was hard when she looked like the doll her mother treated her like she was. She was petite and delicate looking with big heavily lashed eyes. And now her mother had zipped her into a blue satin dress so she looked like a curly auburn–haired Barbie doll.

"I want you to be happy," Penny said.

"I am," Nikki insisted.

But her mother just gave her a pitying smile. Penny didn't think it was possible for Nikki to be happy unless she was all in love like her brothers were. Her brothers had been lucky to find their perfect mates. Nikki didn't think there was anyone out there who would be perfect for her.

She'd once thought another man had been perfect— her father. Of course she only had a child's memories of him, since he'd died when she was nine, so she'd idealized him. When she'd learned that he had cheated on her mother, Nikki had been more upset than Penny had been. Her mother had been able to forgive him. Nikki couldn't.

Nor could she trust any other man.

"Well," Nikki amended her statement, "I'm not happy to be here."

"I appreciate your helping out," Penny said.

"What happened?" Nikki asked. "Why did a bridesmaid get tossed out of the wedding party? Did she sleep with the groom?" And the stupid bride had forgiven him but disowned her friend?

Penny shook her head. "The matron of honor. She's sick. Either food poisoning or…"

"Or? Regular poisoning?"

Penny laughed. "You're hopeless. You'd rather think of the worst than the obvious."

To Nikki, the worst was the most obvious. "What is the obvious?"

"She's pregnant."

Nikki groaned. Fortunately, she wasn't as fertile as the women she knew, like her sisters-in-law and apparently the sick matron of honor. Of course she'd have to actually be involved with someone to have the possibility of becoming pregnant. And she wasn't going to risk that again. She'd had boyfriends, even a fun fling or two. But despite what her mother thought, she didn't need a husband or a family.

"And no one else could fill in for the sick matron of honor?" Nikki asked.

Penny shrugged. "I didn't bother to find out."

That wasn't like the wedding planner who always went the extra mile to make sure the bride's special day was extra special.

But then Penny always enlisted Nikki before any of her other kids to help out at the chapel. She'd probably expected her only daughter to go into the wedding planning business with her instead of into the bodyguard business with her brothers. Even before she'd learned of her father's betrayal, Nikki had never had any interest in weddings.

"Is there any particular reason you want *me* to step in as maid of honor?"

"It's because of the bride," Penny said. "She's Woodrow Lynch's daughter."

Woodrow? The first name basis caught Nikki by surprise. "Do you mean Chief Special Agent Lynch? Nick's old boss?" Her half brother had been an FBI agent before he'd recently quit to join the Payne Protection Agency.

Her mother's face flushed slightly, and she nodded.

How did that make this bride special? And she obviously was to Penny. Nikki had never seen her mother so worried about a wedding, not even the one she'd planned as a ruse to flush out a sadistic serial killer.

"Do you think she's in danger?" Nikki asked. Had her mother enlisted her not as a dress-up doll to play wedding party but as a bodyguard?

Penny's teeth nipped her bottom lip, and she nodded. "I have a *feeling...*"

Nikki's blood tingled with excitement and nerves. Her mother's feelings were legendary, because they were rarely wrong. If Penny Payne thought the bride was in danger, then Ms. Lynch was definitely in danger.

Megan was scared. Even though she lived a relatively boring life as a school librarian, she knew fear well. She had been very frightened when she'd broken up with Gage. She'd had a horrible feeling then that she was making a mistake. And when he'd reenlisted and been immediately deployed...

She'd been scared out of her mind that something would happen to him. Even worse, he'd gone missing and had been presumed dead...

She had nearly lost her mind. She wasn't that scared now, because she knew what she had to do. She was going to thwart Gage's assignment. There was no way she was going through with this wedding.

Minutes ticked away on the clock hanging on the yellow wall of the bride's dressing room. She was still alone inside—although she didn't feel alone anymore. While Gage had been gone for long moments, his presence was palpable in the room, which was another reason she needed to leave it. She needed to find the groom's dressing room and tell him that she couldn't do this. She couldn't marry him.

She shouldn't have accepted Richard's proposal in the first place. While he was okay that she wasn't in love with him, she wasn't. As he had convinced her, it was safer to marry someone you didn't love. There was no chance of getting your heart broken. But then there was no chance of passion, either. She'd had that passion with Gage.

While she'd had boyfriends before—Richard and a couple of high school boys before him—she'd never felt the passion she had with Gage. Only with Gage...

The first moment she'd met him—during a Super Bowl party at her father's house—she'd been overwhelmed by attraction.

He was tall, with broad shoulders and heavily developed muscles. He had looked like a gym rat—then. But not now...

While he'd looked good—damn good—in the black tuxedo, he'd also looked thinner than Megan had ever seen him. What had he endured throughout those long months he'd been missing?

She wanted to know. Most of all she wanted him every bit as much as she'd wanted him that day they'd first met. When she'd closed the refrigerator door to find him leaning against the side of it, she'd thought he was big then, towering over her.

But he wasn't just big physically.

It was his personality that was so big. His voice carried to the point where she'd been able to hear him above the other men gathered in the family room around her father's enormous TV. She and Ellen had bought him that TV for Mother's Day because he'd been both mother and father to them. She'd been invited to sit around that TV, too, but she'd been too shy to join the group of rowdy guys to whom her father had introduced her when she'd come home from a short and boring date with Richard.

Gage Huxton was the rowdiest with his booming voice and his even louder laugh. Or maybe he was the one she heard because he was the one she'd thought the most handsome with his golden-blond hair and smoky green eyes.

She'd never seen a more beautiful man. And, thanks to her father being bureau chief, she'd met some good-looking guys over the years. But they had never noticed her; they'd never sought her out like Gage had in the kitchen.

"Do you need something?" she'd asked him. "More beer?" Her father had a bar in the family room, but the fridge was small. With that many guys, they had probably already emptied it.

He'd shaken his head. "No."

"Food?" she'd asked.

Her father was an excellent cook. He'd had to be, or they would have starved. But maybe he hadn't made enough for the number of guys who'd showed up at their house.

Gage had shaken his head again. And there'd been something in his eyes, a wicked glint that had had her pulse racing.

"Then what do you need?" she'd asked.

He'd stepped closer then, so close that he'd towered over her, until he'd leaned down. His mouth tantalizing close to hers, he'd murmured, "You…"

She'd laughed at him then because she'd thought he was just trying to be funny. Because men like him, men that beautiful, were never interested in girls like her. Chubby girls with unmanageable hair.

"I'm not kidding," he'd told her.

She'd laughed harder then, though it had sounded high-pitched and a little hysterical. "I have a boyfriend."

"Dump him."

"Why would I do that?" she'd asked.

"Because of this…" And then he'd kissed her. For the

very first time in her life she'd experienced real passion. Her flesh had heated. Her heart had pounded so hard and so fast. Other parts of her had reacted, too—like her nipples tightening. Like the pulse that beat in her core, throbbing as pressure built inside her.

She'd never felt anything like it before. She'd felt it every time he'd kissed her or even looked at her. She'd felt it just moments ago when he'd kissed her.

She had never had that passion with Richard, and she never would. No. She couldn't marry him. This wedding was not going to happen.

She had to tell him. Now. Before the wedding began…

She lifted her arms and tried to reach the buttons behind her back. They were too small, though. Penny Payne had buttoned her up before the beautician had arrived. And even she had had to use some kind of tool, which she'd taken with her. Megan couldn't get out of her dress alone. Of course Ellen still wasn't there.

Her sister was beyond late now. Maybe she didn't intend to show up at all. She hadn't agreed with Megan marrying Richard. A loving and biased older sister, Ellen was convinced that Megan could do better. She wasn't a Richard fan. She had been a Gage fan.

But they had thought Gage was dead…

She cursed and gave up the struggle with her dress. It wasn't as if seeing her in it would give her and Richard bad luck in their marriage. They weren't getting married. She'd hoped to slip out of the room and across the church unnoticed. If she wasn't wearing the huge dress Richard had designed and made for her, she wouldn't have been noticed at all. People rarely looked at her. And no man had ever looked at her like Gage had.

Her fingers trembled slightly as she reached for the

knob and pulled open the door. And fear washed over her all over again.

She wasn't afraid of telling Richard she wasn't going to marry him. She was afraid of the gun pointed at her—afraid that it might go off and bore a hole right through that wedding dress and through her.

Of course she'd already had a hole inside her—where she'd lost her heart to Gage.

Now she was about to lose her life…

Chapter 3

Once Gage had realized who the bride was, he hadn't thought about the rest of what Penny Payne had said. He hadn't believed then that the bride could be in any danger aside from making a mistake.

She'd made her biggest mistake nearly a year ago. Or maybe it had been before that, when she'd let him kiss her that first time.

Maybe that had been the mistake she'd made.

Gage had nearly made one himself. He'd started to leave the church. Again.

He'd started leaving once after he'd refused Penny's assignment. But he hadn't been able to walk past the bride's dressing room without looking inside to see Megan. That had been a mistake, seeing her in that sparkling white gown.

Now he couldn't get the image out of his mind. He'd

thought stepping outside would help him clear his head. But he'd been seeking not just fresh air but also an escape. Six months of captivity had made that his first instinct. He'd had no intention of going back inside, either. He'd endured enough torture. Watching Megan marry another man would have been him torturing himself.

He couldn't do it.

But he couldn't leave, either.

Not when he noticed the guns.

They were discreet with them. A man dressed like a waiter carried one in his duffel bag. Another man, dressed like a guest, carried one beneath the trench coat he wore over his suit. There was a woman, too, with a purse that was big and—from the bulge inside it—heavy.

Heavily armed…

After Gage had realized who the bride was, he'd thought Penny's claim about her being in danger had just been a ploy, a manipulation, to enlist him as the bridal bodyguard. But Penny hadn't been lying about Chief Woodrow Lynch. He had a lot of enemies, maybe even more than Gage.

And if those enemies wanted to hurt him, they would go after his daughter. Megan was the one with whom Woodrow had always had the most special bond, and he was so protective of her. So if his enemies really wanted to get to him, they'd go after Megan.

She wasn't his only family at the church, though. A minivan pulled up front and parked between the catering van from which the armed waiter had stepped out, and the long black car from which the armed wedding guests had exited. The side door slid open, and three little blond girls tumbled out. They were dressed in miniature versions of Megan's lacy white dress. The sunlight sparkled off the rhinestones, but they didn't seem to shine quite as brightly as Megan's.

Megan sparkled. But it wasn't just the dress. It was her eyes—those fathomless dark eyes—and her heart-shaped face.

God, she was beautiful.

She couldn't see it herself, though. She had no idea what she actually looked like. Whenever she looked in the mirror, she still saw the chubby girl from her adolescent years with the bad complexion and glasses. Gage had only seen that girl in old photos. There was nothing of her left in Megan the woman.

One of the little girls looked like Megan must have when she was chubby—with rosy, round cheeks. The little girl was cute. She was also heading toward the church, her sisters running after her. Gage didn't want them any closer to the danger. He rushed down the stairs to head them off.

"Wait, girls," he said. "Wait for your parents."

"My aunt Meggie's getting married," one of the girls told him.

No, she wasn't. Now Gage had a reason to stop the wedding. He just hoped he had time. No way could he let Megan's nieces get inside the church. "You have to wait out here," he told them.

The chubby one shook her head. "We're late. Mommy made us late."

The man who stepped from the driver's side hurried after his daughters. "Don't let them inside," Gage warned him. "Get them down here."

While he'd dated Megan, he'd met her brother-in-law. With a headstrong wife like Ellen, Peter was used to doing as he was told. He corralled his kids while his wife came around the front of the van. Her eyes widened when she saw Gage, and a little scream slipped out between her lips.

He hurried toward her. "Ellen, shh…"

He didn't want her drawing the attention of the armed arrivals. He also didn't want her falling on her face, since she looked like death. Ellen was usually so vivacious, with rosy cheeks and bright blue eyes. Now she was paler than her light blond hair, and her eyes were dull. She swayed, and he caught her.

"You look as bad as I do," she murmured.

"You should've seen me a few weeks ago," he replied. He'd finally started to gain back some weight and muscle. And he'd managed to get some sleep.

"We should've seen you the minute you got back," she said. "You're not dead."

"No."

"Does Megan know?"

He nodded.

"So I didn't have to drag myself out of bed to attend a wedding that's not going to happen…" She leaned heavily on the front of the van.

"What's wrong with you?" he asked.

"I thought it was the idea of my baby sister marrying that dweeb Richard that was nauseating me," she replied. "Now I think it's another pregnancy." She shot a glare at her husband.

Gage had no time for congratulations or diplomacy. "You need to leave," he said.

She sighed and admitted, "I would have liked to stay home. I fully intended to bail on my matron of honor duties. But Megan's my only sister."

Ellen had always treated her more like her oldest child than her sibling, though.

"She's not getting married," Gage assured her. "You can go back home. And take your family."

She shook her head. "They want cake. Even if there's no wedding, there is already food here." She gestured toward that catering van.

Gage wasn't so sure that they had brought anything other than weapons. He needed to find out. He also needed to call for backup bodyguards and police. But when he pulled his phone from the pocket, he found no signal. It would've been like Mrs. Payne to have some cell signal jammer so no ceremony would be interrupted in her church.

"And if there is no wedding," Ellen continued, "there will be explanations to make." She narrowed her blue eyes and stared up at him. "What's the reason the wedding is canceled, Gage?"

He had no time for explanations, either. He just leaned closer and whispered, "Something's going on, and you don't want your family in the line of fire."

Her eyes widened now, and her face paled even more. "My family is already in the line of fire," she said. "My dad and baby sister are already in the church."

Gage's stomach lurched. He had to get them out—alive—before the gunmen made their move.

If they hadn't already…

He had no time to drive far enough away that he could get a call out for backup. And he certainly had no time to wait for them to arrive. He had to get back into the church and make sure Megan wasn't in danger.

Megan's heart slammed against her ribs, and she backed up into the dressing room, trying to put distance between herself and the barrel of that gun. She raised her hands. "What do you want?"

The woman holding the gun was dressed in a navy blue bridesmaid's dress. But she wasn't one of Megan's bridesmaids. She had never seen the woman before, although with her curly auburn hair and brown eyes, she looked familiar.

The gunwoman stepped inside the room and shut the door. As she did, she pointed her weapon toward that closed door.

Megan didn't breathe a sigh of relief that it was no longer directed at her. Her breath was stuck yet in her lungs, burning.

"What do you want?" she asked the woman again. And why was she dressed like a bridesmaid? Megan didn't have any besides her sister. She'd wanted to keep the wedding small, probably because she really hadn't wanted one at all.

"I want to protect you," the young woman replied.

"What are you?" Megan asked. "A bridesmaid or a bodyguard?"

"Bodyguard," she replied quickly and emphatically.

"I already have one of those." According to Gage, it was the only reason he was at the church. "And I don't need that one."

The young woman shook her head and tumbled those auburn curls around her delicately featured face. "Yes, you do."

She did. But she wouldn't admit it. She didn't need Gage for protection, though. "I'm not in any danger."

"There are guys coming into the chapel concealing weapons."

Megan snorted. "My father is an FBI bureau chief. All

of his agents were invited to the wedding. They don't go anywhere without their guns."

They had all come armed to that Super Bowl party nearly two years ago.

"I know your dad's agents," the woman replied. "These people aren't them."

Megan's blood chilled. "Then who are they?"

The woman shrugged. "I don't know. Maybe people with a beef with your dad."

Megan bristled. "Why would anyone have a beef with my dad?" He was an honorable man—a fair man.

The only person she could think who'd had a problem with him had been Gage when he'd quit the Bureau. But that hadn't really been because of her father; that had been because of her.

"He's put away a lot of criminals," the woman replied. "Any of them could want revenge."

"Of course…" Megan murmured, embarrassed that she'd been so naive. Of course there were criminals who wouldn't appreciate how good her father was at his job. "But why here? Why now?"

"Your wedding announcement was in the paper," the pseudobridesmaid reminded her. "It provides a great opportunity for anyone looking for vengeance."

"But…"

"Don't worry," the woman assured her. "I'll protect you."

She was armed, but it sounded like the other people might have more weapons.

"How are you going to do that?" Megan questioned her.

The woman's dark eyes narrowed, as if she thought Megan was questioning her abilities.

"If none of those gunmen are my dad's friends, then you're outnumbered." Even if Gage hadn't left...

"I have a plan," the woman replied. "You need to take off that dress."

Megan couldn't agree more.

"No one can know that you're the bride."

She wasn't the bride, because she had no intention of getting married. "You'll need to help me," Megan said. "I can't undo all the buttons."

The woman lifted the skirt of her own dress and slid her gun into a holster strapped to her thigh. "Turn around." But she only fumbled for a few moments before cursing. "Damn it, I should have paid more attention when I've helped Mom out with weddings."

That was why she'd looked familiar. She was the spitting image of her mother. "You're Penny Payne's daughter." Mrs. Payne had said that her sons were bodyguards. She hadn't mentioned that her daughter was as well.

"Nikki," the young woman replied.

"I'm Megan," she said.

"I know," Nikki replied.

She sounded like her mother—like a woman who knew everything except how to get Megan out of the heavy, constrictive wedding gown. She continued to fumble with the tiny buttons, but she only managed to undo a couple of them.

"Cut it off me," Megan urged her. She grabbed a pair of scissors that had been left on the vanity table.

"That won't work."

"Of course it will." She didn't even care if she got cut in the process. She just wanted it off. Now. And it had nothing to do with fear of any suspiciously armed men. It had to do with fear of making a horrible mistake.

Again.

"I won't be able to put it on if it's ruined," Nikki replied.

"Why would you want to wear it?" She turned to face the woman.

Nikki shuddered. "Not because I want to get married. I want to act as a decoy."

"For me?" Megan asked. "You won't pass for me." The other woman was beautiful.

Nikki wrinkled her forehead. "Why not?" she asked. "We have the same coloring and build."

Megan shook her head. Her hair was darker, her body heavier. There was no way she looked like the beautiful bodyguard.

"You're a little curvier," Nikki admitted. "But with how heavy this dress is, no one will notice."

Megan suspected plenty of people would notice. But she didn't care as long as she wasn't the one walking down the aisle. "No one will notice if you snip a few of those buttons off," she said.

"You really want out of this dress," Nikki observed.

"When you came in, I was just getting ready to cancel the wedding," Megan said. "I can't go through with it."

"Gage?"

Nikki Payne might have been like her mother. Penny had pried out of Megan how much she'd loved another man—and how she'd lost that man when he'd gone missing in action and been presumed dead. But she'd lost Gage long before he'd been deployed again.

"Where is he?" Megan wondered.

He'd vowed to make sure no one would stop the wedding from taking place. If he'd noticed the men Nikki had noticed, he might have taken them on—alone. He might have put himself in danger—again.

Nikki sighed. "I don't know. But I could use his help. I left my phone in my mom's office when she enlisted me as your maid of honor."

"Ellen canceled." She wasn't surprised. Her sister hadn't wanted her to marry Richard.

She had no other bridesmaids. She hadn't wanted a big wedding; it was her father who'd convinced her to get married at Mrs. Payne's little white wedding chapel.

Nikki continued as if she hadn't spoken. "So I couldn't call for backup before I hurried in here to make sure you were safe. Do you have a phone?"

Megan shook her head. "Your mom took it from me when I got here," she said. "She wanted to take all my calls to make sure nobody would bother me."

But then she'd enlisted Gage Huxton—who bothered her more than anyone else ever could—as her bodyguard.

Why?

What had the older woman hoped would happen? A happy reunion?

Gage hadn't been happy to see her at all. He was still mad at her. Earlier, that had upset her. But it gave her some comfort now. With as mad as he was, maybe he wouldn't risk his life to protect her. Maybe he wouldn't put himself in any danger.

Nikki cursed. "I need to call for backup."

"Then forget about the dress and let's get out of here," Megan suggested.

Nikki shook her head. "You can't leave this room—not in that wedding gown."

"You can leave," Megan said. "Go—call for help."

Nikki shook her head again. "I can't leave you in here alone," she said, "and unprotected."

Her pride stinging, Megan lifted her chin and said, "I'm not helpless. I can take care of myself." She was Woodrow Lynch's daughter. When she and Ellen had barely been able to walk, their father had taught his daughters self-defense maneuvers as well as other ways to protect themselves.

"Do you have a gun?" Nikki asked.

"No," she admitted. She would have had to carry it in her purse, and she spent too much time at her sister's— with her young nieces—to risk that. They went in her purse all the time looking for gum. But she gripped the scissors. "I have these. I'll be fine. You go call for help."

"A good bodyguard never leaves her subject unprotected," Nikki said.

A good bodyguard would have made certain the door was locked, too. But they both tensed as the knob rattled and began to turn.

Nikki fumbled with her holster, but she didn't have time to draw her gun before the door opened. She cursed and stepped between Megan and whatever danger might be coming through the door.

But Megan doubted the petite bodyguard would be able to protect her from a real threat. Was there a real threat?

Blood had been shed in her wedding chapel before. A groom had been assaulted and abducted. Another man had died.

Brides had been threatened.

Penny's notorious instincts were telling her that there was another threat. Just as she'd told Gage, Megan Lynch was in danger. When she'd told him that, Penny had thought the only real threat had been of Megan making a mistake—of marrying a man she didn't love.

Penny's chapel was so successful because she ran it well. She knew every waiter on the catering staff, so she immediately recognized the one who didn't belong. She also recognized the guests who hadn't been invited. It was obvious none of the other early-arriving guests knew them. If they had ever worked for Woodrow, someone else would have recognized them. And they were armed—just like the unfamiliar waiter.

So who were they? And why had they brought guns into the chapel?

She couldn't tell if any of the other guests who'd arrived early were armed. Most of them were older, though. Probably great-aunts or -uncles of the bride or groom. If any were Woodrow's agents, they probably hadn't thought they needed to bring their weapons. Penny wished they would have.

Because the only person she knew for certain was armed was Nikki. She'd seen the holster when she'd helped her into the bridesmaid dress.

And Gage…

But where was Gage? Had he left like he'd threatened he would? He'd claimed he wanted no contact with Megan again. But if he was that angry and bitter yet, his emotions were still involved. Megan still affected him, hopefully too much for him to have just walked away.

Woodrow hoped he had. But he was an overprotective father. Too overprotective for him to not have noticed the people sneaking weapons into the wedding.

So where was Woodrow?

She scanned the foyer of the church, looking for him

and for Gage. But before she could find either, a strong hand gripped her arm and a deep voice murmured in her ear, "You're in danger."

Chapter 4

Feeling like he'd been sucker punched, Gage gasped for breath. He shouldn't have been surprised. He'd already seen Megan in that damn dress. But it was still a shock—more of a shock than Nikki Payne pulling a gun on him. Everyone knew that Nikki was trigger-happy.

He was damn lucky she hadn't shot him.

"Just your usual amount of jumpy?" he asked. "Or did you notice the armed arrivals, too?"

Her hand shaking slightly, Nikki holstered her weapon beneath the skirt of her bridesmaid dress. He'd had no idea that she and Megan were even friends. But then he'd been gone a long time.

"I'm glad you noticed them, too," she remarked. "So you called for help?"

He shook his head. "Did you?"

"When she asked me to step in for a sick bridesmaid,

I left my phone in Mom's office," she replied. "Where's yours?"

He held up the useless cell. "No signal. Your mom must have a jammer so her ceremonies don't get interrupted because someone forgot to shut off their phone."

Nikki sighed. "What doesn't she think of?"

"Armed gunmen," Gage replied.

"No, she has a plan for those, too."

Gage drew in a deep breath. "That's good," he said. "We need a plan."

"We need backup," Nikki said as she opened the door a crack and peered out into the foyer. "How many did you spot?"

"I made three," he said. "But there could be more." If they were seeking revenge against Woodrow, there would be more. They would know that they'd need an army to take down Chief Special Agent Lynch. "I told Megan's sister to call Nick."

Maybe she'd been frozen with fear. Maybe she'd just been confused by the exchange between Gage and Nikki. But Megan finally spoke, her voice raspy as she asked, "Ellen is here?"

"Not anymore," he assured her. "I told her and her husband and the girls to leave."

"The girls…" Her soft voice cracked with fear, and she trembled.

He found himself reaching for her, his hands lightly grasping her shoulders so she didn't fall. "They're gone," he said. "They're safe."

She peered up at him, skepticism in her dark eyes. "Ellen listened?"

He hoped like hell she had. He'd warned her that if

she didn't follow his instructions, she would put her sister and dad in more danger.

Ellen wouldn't have wanted that. Gage didn't want Megan in any danger. Hell, he just wanted her. His palms heated and tingled from the contact with her shoulders. Only thin lace sleeves separated her skin from his. He stepped back and dropped his hands back to his sides.

"She wouldn't put the girls in danger," he reminded her. She had definitely left with her husband and kids. But he didn't know if she'd listened to him, if she'd called only Nick.

If she had called 911 like she'd mentioned, she risked getting them all killed. When the gunmen heard sirens wailing, they might just open fire. Hopefully, she would do as he had directed: call Nick and tell him to do nothing until Gage contacted him.

Nikki's face had paled, too. "I hope Nick doesn't call Logan. If they all rush in…"

Gage shook his head. "I told her to have him sit tight until I—or someone else from inside the church—make contact with him. So we need your mom to shut off that damn cell jammer."

Nikki nodded. "Yes. You need to find her."

Gage's heart constricted as fear squeezed it. "No. You need to." He wasn't leaving Megan, not when he was certain that she was in danger now.

"I have to stay here," Nikki said. "I have to get her out of that dress."

"Why?" he asked.

"Because nobody can know she's the bride," Nikki said, as if he was an idiot. And maybe he was, because getting her out of the dress was pretty obviously the easiest way to protect her. They had to disguise her.

"I would be out of it," Megan said, "if you would have used the scissors."

Nikki shook her head. "Then I won't be able to put it on and switch places with you."

Gage already knew Nikki was smart. She'd helped Nick figure out why someone was really after him and Annalise. He was impressed as hell that she'd already come up with a plan to protect Megan. His only instinct had been to get to Megan and get her out.

But just like police couldn't come in with sirens wailing, he couldn't sneak Megan out in that damn sparkling gown without drawing attention, either. And if, as he suspected, the armed people were here for her, they wouldn't let him just walk out with her without one hell of a fight.

"You get word to Nick," he said. "I'll get Megan out of the gown."

Nikki nodded in agreement before opening the door and slipping out into the foyer. She disappeared before Gage fully realized what he'd agreed to do: he was going to undress Megan.

"Wait," Megan called out, her voice a faint croak in her suddenly dry throat. But Nikki Payne was already gone, leaving her alone with Gage.

She would rather have taken her chances with the armed gunmen. After all, there were only three of them. That wasn't nearly as dangerous as one Gage Huxton.

"She'll be okay," Gage assured her.

She flinched from a pang of guilt. Of course she should have been concerned about Nikki's safety. "She seems pretty tough," she said. Despite her petite size.

"She has three older brothers," Gage said. "Four, actually, with Nick."

"I know," Megan said. "Mrs. Payne—" The wedding planner was insistent that Megan use her first name. "Penny has told me all about her sons. And she counts Nick among them."

Even though she hadn't given birth to him. While Megan knew someone else who'd loved a child that wasn't really his, she still considered Penny Payne to be very special. Megan had realized that the first time they'd met. Penny was intuitive and empathetic. She'd understood Megan's pain—her grief over thinking Gage was dead—because Penny had lost her husband. But Gage wasn't Megan's husband, and she doubted that he would ever be.

"Penny's great." Gage's mouth curved into a faint grin. "And her sons, they're good guys. They'll come with Nick for backup. It's going to be okay."

Megan released a breath she hadn't realized she'd been holding. Of course everything was going to be okay. She wasn't even convinced that they were really in danger. Nikki and Gage could have been overreacting.

But she somehow doubted that.

"You'll still be able to get married today," Gage continued.

Maybe she would be able to, but she had no intention of exchanging vows. She couldn't promise to love any man but Gage. He didn't want her love, though. He apparently didn't even want to touch her.

But then his hands were on her shoulders again. He didn't hold her, though. He only turned her so that her back was to him. Then his fingers skimmed down the line of buttons on her back. "Nikki didn't undo many of these," he mused.

Just enough that she could feel the brush of his fingertips across an inch of her spine. She suppressed a shiver of reaction. She had always reacted to his touch.

"They're tiny," she said. Every fitting with the seamstress had taken so long, just getting her in and out of the dress.

"They're also slippery as hell," he said with a grunt.

They were clear, either crystal or glass, like the sparkling rhinestones on the bodice of the gown.

"And it's like the holes are too small for them," he mused. "I can't get them through."

Her hand shaking, she held up the scissors again. "I think you just need to cut it off."

He stepped around her, his brow furrowing as he stared down at her. "Why would you want to destroy your wedding gown?"

Because it wasn't really her gown...

She never would have chosen anything so ostentatious for herself. She'd wanted simple and elegant, like the gown her mother had worn. Her father had even taken it out of storage for her. Megan hadn't wanted lace. And certainly no rhinestones. In the elaborate, sparkly gown, she felt more like a beauty contestant than a bride.

"I just want it off," she murmured as panic began to overwhelm her. She didn't care about the possibility of armed gunmen in the church. She just didn't want to get married. Now or ever...

It wasn't as if she needed a husband to have children. She could be a single parent. Like her father had been. Like Penny Payne.

"Don't worry," Gage assured her. "Nikki and I won't let anything happen to you. She has a good plan, switching places with you."

She wasn't as convinced as they were. "Putting her in danger in my place—that's not a good idea."

"Nikki's tough," he reminded her.

"We don't need to go to all that trouble," she said. "We can just cancel the wedding."

He shook his head. "I told you that I'd make sure the wedding happened."

She shivered now, but it wasn't in reaction to his touch; it was because of the coldness in his eyes and his voice. He hadn't changed his mind. He wanted her to marry another man, probably any man but him.

"But if those people brought guns in here to stop the wedding…"

His brow furrowed more. "We don't know why they brought guns in here."

"Nikki thinks they want revenge on my father and that they intend to use me to do it," she said.

Her stomach clenched with dread at the thought. She never wanted to cause her father any pain. He'd already been through too much when he'd lost her mother so many years ago.

"We don't know that for certain," he said.

Maybe they didn't intend to hurt her. Maybe they intended to hurt her father when they figured his guard would be down—when he'd be distracted with his daughter's happiness. But he already knew his daughter wasn't happy. He'd been so worried about her.

Now she was worried about him. Where was her father? Was he okay?

"You need to find my dad," she urged him.

Gage shook his head. "I'm not leaving you."

She would have been touched had she thought he actually cared. But he was only doing his job. She tried to remind herself of that when he turned her around and attacked the buttons of her gown again. She tried to remind herself that he wasn't undressing her for the reason he'd undressed her so many times before.

He didn't want her naked. He didn't want her at all.

"Why would you say I'm in danger?" Penny Payne asked as she closed her office door behind Woodrow.

"You saw the gunmen." He'd been watching her when she'd noticed them. That was why he'd pulled her aside before she could confront them. He wouldn't have put it past her. She was that protective of her chapel and her brides.

But this particular bride was his responsibility. He would keep Megan safe. The only other person he would trust to protect her was Gage Huxton. While his quitting the Bureau and reenlisting had hurt Megan, Gage would never consciously cause her harm.

When Woodrow had seen Gage slip into the bride's dressing room a little while ago, he had breathed a sigh of relief. Then he had guided Penny down the stairwell to the basement and the safety of her office. While Gage protected Megan, he would protect Penny—from herself.

"You don't know them?" she asked. "You didn't plant the waiter among my catering staff?"

"Why would I?"

"For additional security."

"I didn't think I'd need security for my daughter's wedding." And maybe that had been naive of him. There'd been an announcement in the paper, which had probably been like an advertisement for anyone harboring a grudge against him. *Want revenge against Woodrow Lynch? Hurt his daughter on her special day.*

"We need it now," Penny said. "There's only Nikki."

"And Gage."

Her thin shoulders slumped, and the corners of her mouth dipped down in a frown. "He left, remember?"

"He's back."

Despite the situation, she smiled that all-knowing smile that both infuriated and fascinated him. "I knew he wouldn't be able to let her marry another man."

Woodrow sighed. Now he understood what a hopeless romantic was. There was no hope of changing Penny's mind about who she thought belonged with whom. "I think it's more likely that he spotted the weapons, too."

Penny was undeterred and smiled even brighter. "And he came back to protect her."

"It's not personal," he insisted. "Gage was a soldier and an agent and now a bodyguard. It's not in his nature to walk away from danger."

For once Penny didn't argue with him. Her mouth curved down again. "And that nature nearly got him killed. You need to call for more backup," she said.

He held up his blank cell phone. Trying to get a signal had drained its battery. "I couldn't get any reception. Now it's dead."

Penny stared at its black screen. "Why not?"

"You tell me," he said. "I assume you have a cell signal blocker so no calls will interrupt weddings in your chapel."

Color streaked across each of her delicate cheekbones. "I have one," she acknowledged. "But I didn't turn it on today."

"You wanted Megan's wedding to be interrupted." He narrowed his eyes and studied her flushed face. "Is that armed waiter yours?"

"Of course not," she said. "I didn't want to disrupt Megan's wedding. I would have turned on the signal jammer if she decided to go through with the ceremony."

"But you were hoping that she would decide not to."

"I don't want her to make a mistake she'll regret the rest of her life."

"Have you?" he wondered.

"Have I what?"

"Made any mistakes you still regret?" He didn't expect her to answer him since she never talked about herself.

But instead of changing the subject as she always had whenever he'd asked her something personal, she stared up at him, her usually warm brown eyes cool and guarded. And she replied, "Not yet."

Was he a mistake she was considering making? He wanted to ask, but he couldn't risk making a mistake of his own. Not now...

Not with his daughter and other innocent bystanders—and Penny—in danger. He had to act and quickly before more guests arrived at the church. There had only been a few early arrivals, besides those armed people. Unfortunately, they'd been aunts and uncles and cousins of his late wife, unarmed civilians who wouldn't be able to help him protect the others.

If only some of his agents or Penny's sons had arrived already...

"Where do you keep your signal jammer?" he asked.

"Nobody's been in my office," she said.

"Where do you keep it?" he persisted. God, the woman was stubborn. It was good that he'd decided not to ask her out—despite all the times he'd thought about it since meeting her. He'd picked up his phone a million times to call her. But something had held him back.

Fear. He was not good husband material. His late wife had told him that often enough. He had been consumed with his career, had spent so much time away. Of course that had ended when she'd gotten sick. His job was still just as important to him, though.

Like Penny's job was to her…

She pulled a charm from the bracelet on her wrist—a tiny key—and slid it into a lock on a drawer built into the wall perpendicular to her desk. Instead of the drawer opening, the wall slid forward revealing a space behind it large enough for a glass case full of guns and the signal jammer. The industrial-style box jammer was closed and inactive.

"What the hell?" he murmured, in awe of the hiding place and the equipment and guns she'd stowed inside it.

"This church has a lot of history," she said.

He suspected not all of it had been good. She'd been married there. He wasn't sure if that had been a good or bad union.

"There are other hiding places," she said. "And a secret passageway that leads to the little courtyard out back."

"That's good," he said. "You can leave that way." But were there other armed gunmen outside? Would they see her if she escaped that way?

She shook her head. "I'm not leaving."

"We need backup," he reminded her. "And since you're not the one jamming the signals, someone else is." Someone who'd planned to cut off communication to the church.

She turned back toward her desk and opened a bottom drawer. "I have a landline, too," she told him.

He was surprised. Smartphones were more useful, especially for businesses.

She had an old-school kind, the console with the cord attaching the receiver to it. No wonder she put it in a drawer, so it didn't take up too much of the surface of her whitewashed oak desk. When she put the receiver to her ear, her brow furrowed. "There's no dial tone."

That didn't surprise him. If the gunmen had gone to the trouble of jamming the cell signals, they would have made certain to cut the landline, too. And they probably had reinforcements stationed outside. He couldn't send her out alone to the courtyard.

He needed reinforcements of his own.

Penny's eyes widened—looking even bigger and darker—as her face paled. And the woman who usually had all the answers asked, "What are we going to do?"

Something shifted in Woodrow's chest, squeezing his heart. He reached for her—intending to offer her only comfort from the fear gripping her. But her lips parted on a soft gasp, and he had the sudden urge to taste them.

To taste her...

Before he could lower his head to hers, the doorknob rattled. Someone had found them. Would he have time to draw his weapon and protect them?

Chapter 5

Frustration knotted Gage's stomach muscles. The damn little buttons were driving him crazy. His fingers were too big to grasp them, let alone push them through the little loops wrapped tightly around them. The edge of the glass or crystal was sharp, scraping his fingertips. He glanced at the scissors she'd set on the vanity table.

"I should cut it off," he said.

"You should," she eagerly agreed.

But he liked Nikki's plan to change places with the bride. Hell, maybe he just liked it because Megan would no longer be the bride. He shouldn't care that she was going to marry another man. While he'd once considered asking her to marry him, he never would again. She'd said she hadn't loved the man he'd been. She certainly wouldn't love the one he had become. "We can't."

He'd been at it for long moments and had only undone

one button. They were spaced so closely together that even with the couple that Nikki had undone, only a little more than an inch of Megan's skin was visible through the slight opening.

Megan was never comfortable showing much skin. She always dressed in layers. Skirts with tights beneath and tall boots. Blouses buttoned to her throat with sweaters over them. She dressed like the librarian she was. For some reason Gage had found that super sexy. Just like he'd always taken his time unwrapping presents, to draw out the anticipation and excitement, he'd taken his time getting Megan out of her clothes.

He'd toyed with the zippers on her boots before lowering them and pulling them off her curvy calves. He'd taken his time with the buttons on her cardigan sweaters and on her blouses beneath them. Even with the layers, she'd never had as many buttons as this, though.

And at least then his efforts had been rewarded. He'd been able to stroke and taste all that honey-colored skin he'd exposed. He'd been able to elicit soft moans and cries from her as she'd pressed her hot, naked body against his.

Remembering the sensations—the heat, the tension, the pleasure—had a groan slipping from his throat.

"Use the scissors," she told him.

But his frustration wasn't with the buttons. It was with the fact that even if he managed to undo all those buttons, he wouldn't be able to kiss and touch the skin he exposed. She wasn't his anymore.

She'd never really been his, because she'd never trusted him. She'd never trusted what they'd had. Or she wouldn't have accused of him using her.

"I can't…" he said.

She tilted her head and peered over her shoulder at him. "Can't cut it off?"

He couldn't keep thinking about what they'd had, what they'd done to each other. How he hadn't ever been able to get enough of her.

Heat rushed through him, making his blood warm, his skin tingle. He'd bared less than an inch of her silky skin, but he wanted her as obsessively as he'd always wanted her.

Maybe it was her shyness that had appealed to him the first time they'd met. When her father had introduced them, she hadn't met his gaze, and she'd ignored his outstretched hand, hers shoved deep into the pockets of her skirt. Used to women seeking his attention, flirting with him, he'd been intrigued by the novelty of Megan Lynch. She'd challenged him.

And Gage had never been able to walk away from a challenge…until the end. Until he'd realized there was no way he would ever win her trust or her heart.

He just shook his head.

And her face paled. "You're giving up again?"

"Again?" he asked. "When did I give up before?"

Unless she was talking about them. But she'd given him no choice then.

Now color flushed her face. "You quit the Bureau."

After they'd broken up, he hadn't been able to work for her father. Not only would it have been awkward but it would have killed his pride. He'd learned what everyone thought of him—that he was doing the boss's daughter in order to get ahead. Megan had believed those vicious rumors. So maybe that was another reason he'd quit, to prove her wrong.

"I had my reasons," he reminded her.

She jerked her chin up and down in a nervous nod. "I thought it was my fault. The reason you quit, the reason you reenlisted, the reason you..." Her voice cracked, cutting off whatever she'd been about to add.

"The reason I what?"

"Got killed," she said. "I thought you were dead."

And she'd blamed herself. He shouldn't have been surprised, though. He'd blamed her, too. Getting mad at her had eased some of his pain.

"I didn't die there," he said. He wasn't so certain that he wouldn't here, though. He glanced to the door, wondering if those armed people were out there yet, waiting to force their way inside.

"Do you think it's that dangerous?" she asked.

He didn't have Penny Payne and Nick Rus's notorious instincts or he wouldn't have fallen for Megan in the first place. Nor would he have spent six months in captivity in Afghanistan. But maybe those six months had helped him develop some kind of sixth sense as well.

Because he knew Megan Lynch's wedding day wasn't going to end well—for anyone.

She expelled a shaky breath. "You do..."

"Nikki has a good plan to switch places," he said. But Nikki had been gone a long time. Had one of those gunmen taken her out?

He pulled his cell from his pocket and glanced at his blank screen. She hadn't gotten the jammer turned off yet. They still had no backup. No way of knowing if Ellen had even been able to reach Nick.

Gage flashed back to those six months that he'd spent wondering if anyone was going to come to his rescue, if they knew where he was or even that he was alive.

They hadn't. There had been no help coming. So he'd had to rely on himself. Then. And now.

"We need to get you out of here," he said. Maybe it was time to cut off the wedding dress. He reached for the scissors.

But she caught his hand, her fingers sliding over his. "No."

"It was your idea," he reminded her.

Her face flushed. "I know. But now I don't think it's a good idea…"

He thought he understood, even though it knotted his stomach, this time with dread. It was still her wedding gown. She must have been having second thoughts about destroying it.

"You want to wear it again," he said. "For Richard."

"Richard." His name slipped through her lips on a gasp. "Richard—what if he's in danger?"

Gage didn't give a damn. But then guilt flashed through him. Richard Boersman had never done anything to him. It had been the other way around. Gage was the one who'd stolen Megan from Richard. But he hadn't been able to keep her.

"You really think anyone has a beef with Richard?" he asked with disbelief. "I'm sure he's perfectly safe." There was no doubt why she'd agreed to marry him. Richard was safe and boring and dull, and she didn't have to worry about him breaking her heart like she'd constantly worried Gage would.

The irony was that she'd broken his instead.

She squeezed Gage's hand around the scissors. "Please make sure he's okay."

"I'm not leaving you," he said. If he walked away and

left her alone and unprotected, he might never see her
again. And he couldn't risk that.

Couldn't risk never seeing her beautiful face again,
never touching her soft skin…

His free hand moved up to cup her cheek. He skimmed
his thumb along her chin and tipped up her face. Then
he began to lower his head…just as the doorknob rattled.
Someone was trying to get inside.

Déjà vu. Nikki wasn't like her mother or half brother
with all their premonitions and instincts. She hadn't ever
experienced any psychic phenomena until now. Now
she had that weird sense of déjà vu. Walking inside the
bride's dressing room gave Nikki the exact same feeling
she'd had walking inside her mom's office just moments
ago. And she murmured, "I keep interrupting."

Gage tensed, and his hand tightened around the
weapon he'd drawn from beneath his tuxedo jacket before opening the door for her. "What did you interrupt?
Are they making a move?"

She suspected that Woodrow Lynch had been thinking
about making one on Penny before Nikki had burst into
the basement office. But Penny hadn't been very happy
with the man for drawing a gun on her only daughter.
She'd been even unhappier with him when he'd agreed
with Nikki's plan to switch places with his daughter.

If something happened to her, she doubted her mother
would ever forgive the FBI chief. So she had to make sure
nothing happened to her.

She shook her head. "Not yet."

"What do they want?" Megan asked.

Nikki exchanged a glance with Gage. They were both

pretty sure they wanted the bride. Even Woodrow and Penny had agreed about that.

"It doesn't matter what they want," Gage said. "We're not going to let them get it." He held up his cell. "It's completely dead now. Didn't you find your mom's jammer?"

"It's not hers."

He sucked in a breath.

"Her landline was cut, too."

Still standing guard at the door, he opened it a crack and peeked out. "Where are all the guests?"

"The wedding isn't supposed to start until noon," Megan said. "We have a half hour yet."

"People usually arrive a half hour early," replied the daughter of the wedding planner. Nikki had grown up knowing about weddings—and never planning to have one herself.

Even before she'd learned about her dad's betrayal, she'd never wanted a husband of her own. She'd had enough males in her life with her overprotective brothers. Occasionally, she got lonely, though…

Occasionally, she missed that kind of tension she'd felt in her mother's office and when she'd walked into the bride's dressing room. Then again, she wasn't certain she'd ever felt *that* kind of tension herself.

"Do you think they have someone posted outside the doors?" Gage asked. "Turning guests away?"

"They've planned this out," Nikki said. "So yeah, probably."

"Wouldn't that draw suspicion?" Megan asked.

"They're probably telling everyone the wedding was canceled," Nikki said. "And the guests who know about your past—" she jerked her thumb at Gage "—and his return from the dead probably wouldn't question it."

"But how would those gunmen know about that—" her face reddened as Megan asked "—about us?"

Unless…

Maybe this siege on the church wasn't about revenge on the bride's father. Maybe it was about revenge on the bride's ex-lover.

Because it was clear that hurting Megan would hurt Gage. Nikki narrowed her eyes and studied Gage's face. He was even tenser now than when he'd opened the door to her, his handsome features so tight his face looked like a granite mask—hard and sharp—like his green eyes.

He'd obviously considered the same thing she had. And he didn't like it.

"It doesn't matter," Nikki told them both. "What matters is everyone getting out of here alive."

Gage looked at her then, his glance one of pity for her naïveté. She wasn't so stupid that she hadn't considered the other alternatives. She already knew there was a strong possibility that they wouldn't survive.

Then she would never experience that tension she'd felt in her mom's office and in this room. But you couldn't miss what you'd never had.

She held up the one useful item she had retrieved from her mother's office.

Gage stared at the small tool. "What the hell is that?"

"Crochet hook," she replied. "This'll get those buttons undone."

"That's what your mom used to do it up," Megan said. And she released a ragged breath, as if the dress was constricting her lungs. Maybe it was. It looked tight and heavy and uncomfortable as hell.

Nikki couldn't wait to get it on and put her plan into motion, even though it could quite possibly be the last thing she would ever do.

Megan jerked away as Nikki reached for her. Sure, she wanted out of that dress—so badly that she hadn't even cared if Gage was the one to cut it off her. But it was different now, different since he'd nearly kissed her again.

Wasn't that what he'd been about to do before Nikki had started turning the doorknob? He'd been lowering his head, and his eyes had gone dark, the pupils dilating as he'd stared down at her. He'd looked like he'd wanted to kiss her, just like he'd looked that first day in her father's kitchen.

Now that all the old memories and feelings and longings washed over her, she couldn't bear it, couldn't stand to have him watch her get undressed and know that he wouldn't touch her—wouldn't kiss her.

Not that she wanted him to.

She didn't want to put herself through all that pain again, no matter how much she probably deserved it. She'd hurt Gage. And now she was about to hurt another man, if he hadn't already been harmed.

"You said you'd check on Richard," she reminded Gage.

"I said that I couldn't," he corrected her.

"Because you couldn't leave me alone," she said. "But I'm not alone." Nikki had a gun. And Megan had the scissors. Gage had pressed them back into her hand before he'd drawn his gun and opened the door.

Nikki nodded. "I'll protect her and get her out of the dress," she said. "You should check on the groom. We don't know what the hell could have happened to him."

Megan's stomach lurched, and a gasp slipped through her lips.

And Gage's jaw tightened. He thought she loved Richard. And she did—as a friend. Nothing more. But he was a friend and had been one for a long time. So she was worried about him.

His blond head jerked in a sharp nod. "Sure, I'll check on him."

"Gage…" She wanted to call him back, wanted to explain that she didn't love her groom. She didn't love anyone but Gage. She never had.

But the door slammed behind him.

Nikki jumped. "So much for not drawing any attention to himself."

It wouldn't have mattered if he'd slammed the door or quietly slipped out. Gage Huxton was the kind of man who drew attention with his height and his handsomeness. He wasn't like Megan, whom people rarely noticed.

Why had he ever been interested in her? It was no wonder she'd doubted his feelings. She couldn't believe even now that he'd ever really wanted her.

Richard claimed he did, that he wanted to be her husband, wanted to build a life with her. He'd anticipated that this day would be the first of the rest of their life together. And now the man who'd stolen her once from him was about to take her away again…

Only for her own protection.

But she wasn't sure he would tell Richard that. She wasn't sure what Gage would say to the other man. She only knew that she was the one who should tell Richard that she couldn't marry him. "I need to get out of this dress," she told Nikki.

"I know," the other woman replied. But even with the tool, the buttons weren't opening easily.

During the long moments Nikki struggled with the dress, Megan imagined Gage walking toward the groom's dressing room. Now she didn't worry about what he would say to Richard. She worried about what could happen to him before he got there. She worried that he would take on those gunmen alone.

"No," she said, as she jerked away from the other woman. "We're wasting too much time."

"We still have a half hour before the wedding is supposed to start," Nikki said.

But Gage had already been gone too long, long enough for Megan to worry that he would never come back. She'd lived through that nightmare once. She didn't want to live through it again.

Panic filling her, constricting her lungs even more than the heavy dress, she rushed toward the door and pulled it open. And just like the last time she'd tried to leave, the barrel of a gun stopped her.

Unlike last time, this barrel pushed into her abdomen. And she had no doubt that this woman, who stared at her with cold blue eyes, would pull the trigger and bore that hole right through her.

Chapter 6

Just as Nikki had remarked, the church was too empty for a wedding that was less than an hour away from beginning. Gage didn't know much about weddings, but he knew that people usually liked to get to them early so they could get the good seats. As he passed through the vestibule, he noticed that some of those front pews were occupied by little gray-haired people.

Older people were always early. It was the younger ones that weren't on time. Like the Paynes. Where was Logan or Parker or Cooper? Or had any of them even been invited?

They were Penny's kids. Not Woodrow's agents. Of all the Payne Protection bodyguards, only he and Nick had worked for the Bureau.

What about the agents, though? Where were they? Woodrow would have invited them for certain. Sure, Dalton Reyes hated weddings. But Gage had heard that after finding a bride in a car trunk, the agent had gotten married himself, so he must have changed his mind.

And what about Agents Campbell or Stryker or Bell? They were all close with Woodrow. They wouldn't have missed his daughter's wedding.

But the only one Gage saw from the Bureau was the ass kisser. The young guy had been even more of a rookie than Gage. But he'd been desperate to get ahead and jealous that Gage had. He was the one who'd spread the lies that Gage was only dating Megan for a promotion.

Because it didn't matter how much ass Tucker Allison kissed, he would never make special agent. There was nothing special about him. He didn't have the guts for the job. Or to help Gage and Woodrow take down the armed suspects.

Where the hell were they? He hadn't noticed any of them as he'd crossed the vestibule. But as he stepped through the doors at the back of the church, a man straightened away from the wall. He wore a suit that didn't fit him well. Even as big as it was, it couldn't conceal the bulge of a weapon.

Acting oblivious, Gage forced a smile. "Hi. Bride's side or groom's side?"

He'd like to know who the hell the guy was here for. But he had a sick feeling that he already knew. It had to be for the bride.

But why? Because of Woodrow?

Or because of him?

Keeping the grin plastered on his face, he studied the stranger. The guy's hair was nearly shaved, just stubble showing on his skull. He could have been military. But what army? And more importantly, what side?

"Are you an usher?" the guy asked. His thin lips curved into a faint, mocking grin. "I thought you were the *best* man."

Did he know Gage? And how? Had they met on opposite sides of the law or a battlefield?

He could have been a supporter of the group that had taken him. He and the other gunmen could have been determined to carry out what the others had begun. For some reason his captors had thought he'd had information they'd wanted. But no matter how badly they'd tortured him, he hadn't been able to tell them what they'd wanted to learn.

That didn't mean they'd given up, though. He resisted the urge to reach for his weapon and drop the guy. For one, he didn't know if he would be fast enough, and for two, he didn't know where the other armed people were.

"It's a small wedding," Gage replied. "We're all pulling double duty."

The guy nodded as if he believed him. But he doubted he'd taken him at his word any more than his captors had.

"So which side?" he asked again. "Bride or groom?"

He shrugged. "I'm the plus one, just waiting for my wife. She went to the restroom."

With her big purse with her heavy gun inside? Gage hoped like hell that was really where she was. The guy had answered easily, as if he were speaking the truth.

Some people believed their own lies. Like the little FBI agent who nervously glanced back at him...

Tucker had believed the lies he'd spread. Maybe that was why Megan had believed them so easily as well.

But if she'd trusted Gage, if she'd loved him like she'd once claimed she had, she never would have doubted him. Like Gage doubted this guy.

"Well, I hope your wife returns quickly," Gage said. "The wedding will be starting soon."

The guy arched a brow as if skeptical of Gage's claim. "Really?" he mused. "I've never known a wedding to start on time. Usually brides take longer to get ready than they plan for, especially if they're nervous."

How did this guy know that Megan was nervous? Because he was giving her every reason to be?

"You must have never attended a wedding here," Gage said. "Mrs. Payne's events always start on time. She has a way of quelling every fear of even the most nervous bride." Or at least that was what he'd been told. But knowing Penny, he didn't doubt it.

It was clear she had her doubts, though. She and Woodrow stepped into the vestibule from the basement stairwell. His arm was around her waist, as if he'd had to help her up the steps. But her body was stiff—not trembling—and she pulled away from him. Penny was proud and tough. She had raised her kids alone and had survived her fears over all their brushes with death.

And he knew they'd had many just since he'd met them.

"Well, if you won't let me usher you to a seat, I better assume my best man duties and check on the groom," Gage said.

"That's who should be nervous," the man remarked beneath his breath.

Gage turned back. "What? Why would you say that?"

The guy shrugged again, and a small, mocking grin curved his thin lips. Gage didn't recognize the man but he recognized the look: condescension. Like he thought Gage was an idiot because he didn't know what he knew.

What the hell did he know?

The guy shrugged again. "In my experience the guy always has more reason to be nervous when he's getting married, especially when the *best* man keeps going into the bride's dressing room."

Innuendo joined the condescension now. The man's dark eyes gleamed.

Anger coursed through Gage, making him tense. He didn't give a damn that the guy was armed and had armed friends. He stepped closer to him.

But then a small hand gripped his forearm. "Gage, you need to make sure Richard is ready. The ceremony will be starting soon."

His stomach lurched at the thought of that actually happening, of Megan actually marrying her old boyfriend. But Richard wasn't her old boyfriend anymore.

Gage was.

He stepped back and turned to Penny, who was smiling at him. But unlike all the times she had before, the smile didn't warm her brown eyes, didn't dispel the fear widening them.

"Hurry up," she urged him.

But then his stomach lurched for another reason, at the thought of leaving her alone with an obviously dangerous man.

"Go," she said and her tone brooked no argument. She was stubborn.

And he knew better than to argue with a stubborn woman. Annalise—his sister—had taught him that. So he turned and headed down the aisle toward the front of the church. The groom's dressing room was behind the altar. Sun shone through the stained glass windows, sending a kaleidoscope of colors dancing around the room with its sparkling marble floor and whitewashed oak pews.

It really was a beautiful chapel—a beautiful venue for a wedding. Too bad there would be no wedding today. He only hoped there would be no funeral, either.

Penny lifted her chin and stared into the stranger's cold eyes. She was good at pretending to be brave when she was actually quavering with fear. When her husband had died in the line of duty, she'd had to pretend to her kids that she was fine, that she wasn't scared of raising them alone. That she had everything under control when she'd actually had no idea how she was going to manage.

"Well, you're obviously the one running the show," the man replied.

She wished that were true—then her daughter wouldn't be intent on using herself as a decoy. And her bride would be marrying the man she really loved, the one who was so stubborn he was probably going to get himself killed. That was why she'd intervened. She'd seen the anger course through Gage. She'd worried that he was about to lose more than his temper.

She tilted her head. "Show?"

He gestured around the chapel. "The wedding. This is your place, right? You're Penny Payne."

She held out her hand, proud when it didn't tremble. "Nice to meet you…?"

"D," he said. "Everyone just calls me D."

"The initial?"

He nodded.

It could have been for his last name. Or his first…

"Are you here for the groom or the bride?" she asked.

His mouth curved. "Everyone keeps asking me that."

And he obviously had yet to give an answer.

"And what is your response?" she asked.

His grin widened. "I'm here for my wife."

She glanced around. "Where is she?"

"Powder room," he said. "She wanted to touch up her makeup. Hope she doesn't outshine the bride."

Penny doubted that was the threat this man and his wife posed to the bride. But they definitely posed a threat—to everyone in Penny's chapel. No, she had never been more afraid than she was now.

But she smiled. "Well, it was nice meeting you, D. I have quite a few details to see to before the ceremony begins. I hope you and your wife enjoy it."

He smiled back at her. "I certainly plan on it. Now as for my wife... I can't imagine what could be keeping her..."

"What do you want?" Megan asked. She doubted it was to protect her, as Nikki had professed when she had walked into the bride's dressing room with a gun in her hand.

Nikki obviously didn't know her. She didn't greet her at all, but just quietly studied her.

The woman tossed her long black hair over her shoulder and smiled. "Just wanted to give the bride my best regards."

What was that? A euphemism for a bullet? The way she pointed the gun at Megan certainly implied as much. She swallowed down a lump of fear as the woman stepped even closer and pulled the door closed behind her, trapping Megan and Nikki inside with her.

Nikki was armed, too, though she hadn't drawn her gun. She'd had no time to react because Megan had been the stupid one—the one who'd opened the door without checking to see what danger might be lurking on the other side.

"I don't know you," Megan said. "And I don't know why you have that gun. Who are you?"

The woman uttered a pitying sigh. "That is a problem when you have a big wedding. You have no way of knowing all your guests. You don't know who the groom has invited."

"Richard invited you?" she asked. She doubted that. Richard had invited very few people to the wedding. An only child of only children who were now deceased, he had no family. And because he worked so much at his IT job, he had few friends, either.

The woman continued as if Megan hadn't spoken. "You probably have no way of knowing who all your own family invited. Friends or acquaintances of your parents."

Fear clutched Megan's stomach. This was about her father. He was out there in the chapel somewhere. Hopefully, Gage was with him, protecting him.

"It's much better to marry like I did," the woman said. "It was just me and my husband. The only two people who really matter in a marriage."

Megan nodded in agreement. "That's true. You're right. I didn't want this wedding."

She didn't want this marriage.

"The chapel is beautiful," the woman said, almost wistfully. She had claimed her wedding was better, but she wasn't as convinced as she'd tried to make Megan. "The flowers." She jabbed the gun into Megan's bodice. "Your dress." Her dark eyes narrowed as she studied it. "Your dress…"

That damn dress. Megan wanted it off. Despite the

few buttons Nikki had freed, it was still too tight—too constricting, too heavy...

"It's a mistake," Megan said.

"The dress?"

"The wedding," she said. "You didn't need to come in here with the gun to stop it. I have no intention of getting married."

The woman's face paled, and she emitted a nervous laugh. "Oh, no, stopping the wedding is not my intention at all."

"Then why the gun?" Nikki finally spoke, repeating Megan's earlier question that the woman had already ignored.

The woman glanced down at the barrel as if she hadn't realized she held it. "This isn't to stop the wedding," she said. "This is to make certain that the wedding goes exactly as planned."

Megan shook her head. "No."

"That doesn't make sense," Nikki said. "You and your gun are disrupting the wedding, not making it come off smoothly at all."

The woman snorted. "She just admitted she has no intention of going through with it."

Megan silently cursed her admission. She'd just assumed the woman intended to stop the wedding. That was why she'd admitted she had no intention of getting married.

"You couldn't have known that," Nikki prodded her. "Unless..." She glanced around the room as if looking for cameras.

When they'd hidden the cell jammer, they might have planted a camera, as well. It made sense, or as much sense as any of this did.

"The man who keeps traipsing in and out of this room," the woman said, "is not the groom."

"Do you know Richard?" Megan persisted. Or was it Gage she knew?

"I know you are to marry your groom today," the woman said. "And you're not going to let any other man dissuade you from doing that."

Megan's brow furrowed. "Gage isn't trying to dissuade me."

Disbelieving, the woman snorted again. "A man like that…" She emitted a lustful sigh. "He doesn't have to *do* anything to distract a woman."

"He's not distracting me," Megan said. But for the first time she lied to the woman. She realized now it was what she should have done in the first place. Honesty had only put her in more danger.

She'd only really lied once in her life, and that had had horrible consequences. Gage had quit his job and reenlisted because of it.

So Megan had vowed she wouldn't lie anymore. She saw now that had been a mistake, though.

"Then why were you chasing after him?" the woman asked.

Sticking with the lying, Megan protested, "I wasn't!"

The woman struck her—thankfully not with the gun—but with the palm of her hand. Megan's cheek stung, and her eyes teared at the pain.

"Don't lie to me!" the woman said. "That's what you were doing when you opened the door."

And that must have been why she'd drawn the gun. She hadn't wanted Megan to leave the bride's dressing room unless she was heading down the aisle.

"You really want this wedding to take place," she

mused in confusion. What the hell could this stranger hope to gain from Megan's marriage?

"It will," the woman replied, her dark eyes wild with a determination so fierce it almost appeared to be madness. "Or you will die right here."

And Megan realized that maybe she would rather die than marry a man she didn't love, whom she would never be able to love because another man had already claimed her heart.

Chapter 7

Gage glanced to the back of the church to reassure himself that Penny Payne wasn't in any danger. She'd slipped away from the gunman. And he had let her leave.

The man stared back at Gage, then slowly, mockingly nodded his head. Who the hell was he?

Gage should have taken him down. But it was too great a risk when he didn't know where the other armed people had gone. Where was the guy's date, really?

Gage's blood chilled and pumped heavily through his quickly beating heart.

If Megan was in danger…

Even though Nikki was with her, he shouldn't have left her. But she'd wanted him to check on Richard. After the cryptic remark the guy in the back had made—and the mocking nod he'd just given him—Gage realized he needed to check in with the groom. He lifted his fist and pounded hard on the door behind the altar.

"About time my best man got here," a male voice remarked as the door opened. "What the hell…"

Richard Boersman's mouth fell open, and his already pale face paled with shock. "You came back from the dead?"

Stepping forward, Gage shoved Richard back into the room and closed the door behind them. He grunted in reply. When he'd finally escaped captivity, he had felt as if he'd returned from the dead.

Richard uttered a shaky sigh and murmured, "I did that once myself."

"What?" Gage narrowed his eyes and studied the shorter man. Like Gage, he wore a tuxedo, but his hung even more off his skinny frame. His thick-framed glasses had slid down his long, narrow nose. His whole face was thin and unremarkable, like his bowl-cut brown hair and pale complexion. He looked like he had probably spent most of his childhood being bullied. But maybe he wasn't the harmless geek Gage had always thought he was. "What the hell does that mean?"

He shrugged his thin shoulders. "Nothing…just had a close call myself a few years ago."

Megan had said something about it before, about Richard surviving a house or apartment fire. If Gage looked close enough, he could see a few thin scars along the man's hairline. But those scars were nothing compared to the ones Gage had now.

He remarked, "I think you're about to have another close call."

Richard stepped back, and his Adam's apple bobbed as he swallowed nervously. "What are you doing here? Dressed in a tux? You're not my best man."

"I am now," Gage said. "Not that this wedding's gonna happen anyway."

"You son of a bitch," Richard said, and now his face flushed a mottled red. "How dare you come back from the dead to stop my wedding?"

A laugh slipped out of Gage. He couldn't help it. Richard was that damn ridiculous. "I had no intention of stopping your wedding."

Spit dribbled out of Richard's mouth when he sputtered, "But—but you said it's not going to happen…"

"That isn't because of me," Gage said. "It's because the church is under siege."

Richard laughed now. "That's crazy. Under siege—what the hell are you talking about?"

"Guys—and a woman—with guns," Gage said, "have infiltrated the church."

"Megan's father is the Chicago FBI bureau chief," he patronizingly said, as if Gage wasn't already aware. "Of course there will be men and women with guns at his daughter's wedding."

"These people are not Woodrow's agents," Gage said. "They're strangers. And they're dangerous."

Richard's skin paled again. "What—what are you saying?"

"This isn't random," Gage said. "They've planned this out. Someone has a cell signal jammer. We can't call out, and only a few guests were able to get into the church. They have us surrounded."

"Why?" Richard asked. "What did you do?"

Gage laughed again. "This doesn't have anything to do with me." At least he hoped like hell that it didn't.

Richard snorted. "You've been nothing but trouble

for Megan since the day you met her. This has to be your fault."

Gage laughed again. "I've been nothing but trouble for her?"

She was the one who'd destroyed his life. She'd broken his heart and made it impossible for him to work for her father, the man he'd respected more than any other.

"Why couldn't you have just left her alone?" Richard asked.

"I don't want her," he said. But it was a lie.

And Richard knew it. "That's bull! You're behind this. You've put some sick plan into action to stop our wedding!" Despite the guy's smaller size, he launched himself at Gage.

Gage easily held him off with his hands on Richard's thin shoulders. "I wouldn't have had to go to this much trouble," he said. He was angry, too, so angry that he taunted the groom. "All I would have to do is kiss her, just like I did the last time I stole her from you."

Richard lost it, cursing and swinging. He wasn't able to get in a good punch. But his arms were long enough that he reached for Gage's holstered weapon.

Hearing the tussle from outside the door, Woodrow burst into the room with his gun drawn. He'd expected to find one of the armed strangers inside. Unfortunately, he knew the two men inside, but maybe he didn't know them as well as he'd thought. He had never thought Richard would have had either the courage or the stupidity to take on Gage Huxton.

He'd nearly grabbed Gage's gun—until Gage had shoved him back against the wall, his arm pushing against Richard's throat until the guy struggled for breath.

"Let him go, Gage," Woodrow said. He spoke softly and calmly.

He knew what Gage had been through. After Nicholas Rus had told him that Gage had survived all those months he'd been missing in action, Woodrow had reached out to guys he knew from his own days in the corps. And he'd found out the hell Gage had endured, the kind of hell few other men could have survived. The kind of hell from which nobody ever fully recovered.

That was why Woodrow hadn't told Megan that Gage was alive. He knew his daughter loved the man, so much that she would want to be with Gage again. But with the PTSD that Gage had to have, he wasn't safe for anyone to be around, as evidenced by how tightly he held Richard.

Maybe Woodrow had spoken too softly, because it didn't look as though Gage had heard him. Instead of loosening, his arm momentarily pressed harder. Behind his huge glasses, Richard's eyes began to roll back into his skull.

"Gage!" Woodrow spoke sharply now, making the younger man's name sound like a command.

And like the soldier he was, Gage obeyed. He stepped back.

And Richard slid down the wall, gasping for the breath Gage had momentarily denied him.

"You're crazy," Richard murmured, his voice raspy. Then he turned toward Woodrow. "He nearly killed me."

"You're damn lucky he didn't," Woodrow replied. And with no sympathy for the fool, he added, "You *never* reach for a man's gun." Not unless you were certain you could take it from him without getting killed.

Or Woodrow would have already taken on the armed wedding guests.

"But he's threatening to stop the wedding," Richard said.

Woodrow shook his head. "He's not the threat."

Impatience flashed in Richard's pale eyes. "Of course he is. He put this whole sick plan in motion."

"What the hell are you talking about?" Gage asked, his voice very deep and raspy despite not having had anyone strangling him as he had nearly strangled Richard. Not only did he not look the same, he didn't sound the same, either. The boy Woodrow had known was gone.

His heart ached for the loss. Gage Huxton could have been the best agent he'd ever had.

Through his thick lenses, Richard glared at Gage. "I'm saying you staged this whole scenario just to stop the wedding."

"And I told you I wouldn't have had to go to any of that trouble *if* I wanted to stop it," Gage said.

Richard's face flushed again. And now Woodrow understood why he'd gone for Gage's gun. Huxton could be damn infuriating. As his former boss, Woodrow knew that too well. Maybe there was more left of the boy he'd once known than he'd imagined.

"There is no time for fighting between ourselves," he told them. "We need to work together."

In unison, they snorted.

"We have to," Woodrow said. "We don't know how many of them we're dealing with."

"Ask him," Richard petulantly said.

This wasn't the first time Woodrow had noticed the man's petulance. Maybe it was because Richard Boersman was an only child that he was used to getting his own way all the time. Like that damn dress. Megan had wanted to wear her mother's dress. But Richard had pouted until she'd agreed to wear the gown he'd had designed for her.

Realizing now that Richard had manipulated her—the way Megan's mother used to manipulate him—made Woodrow feel a little better about the wedding being canceled. Maybe Penny Payne was right again—damn her—and Richard wasn't the right man for Megan.

But Penny was wrong about Gage. Woodrow didn't believe he was the right man for Megan, either, at least not anymore. It was doubtful he could ever recover fully, physically and mentally, from what he had endured.

Gage seemed focused now, though. Ignoring Richard, he said, "I only saw the one guy in the back of the church."

"The one Penny stopped you from killing." Letting her be the one to intervene in their tense exchange had nearly killed Woodrow. But Penny had pointed out—rightfully—that two men approaching the wedding crasher might have forced his hand and the hands of whoever else was working with him.

Richard snorted again. "There's only one guy?"

Gage continued to ignore him. "I didn't see the woman or the man who's dressed like a waiter."

"Me neither," Woodrow said, and his stomach muscles knotted tighter than they'd already been.

"We need to make sure Megan's safe," Gage said. He wasn't as muscular as he'd once been, but he easily moved Woodrow away from the door so he could rush out of it.

"Gage…" Woodrow hurried after the younger man as he started down the church aisle. But before he could catch up to him, someone grasped his arm and jerked him to a halt.

While it was something Penny would have done, she

wasn't the one who stopped him. His skin would have tingled, his pulse would have quickened—with attraction. He felt only irritation now.

The man who held his arm was also armed, a gun bulging beneath his jacket. But unlike the others he knew this man. Although with his smooth face, wide eyes and slight build, Tucker Allison looked more like a child than a man. "I don't have time—"

"I see you've thrown out Gage Huxton, sir," the young man said, his voice high with excitement. "I was going to do it earlier myself—"

Woodrow nearly laughed. Him and what army? Because apparently even another army hadn't been able to permanently take out Gage Huxton.

"Gage isn't leaving," he said. Even when he'd said he was, he hadn't been able to walk away from Megan, not when he'd realized she was in danger.

"Do you want me to help you get rid of him again?"

Woodrow narrowed his eyes. "Again? What are you talking about?"

The young man's face flushed. "I—I—uh…"

"Spread some vicious rumors," Woodrow finished for him as he shook off his hand. He hadn't had the time or the patience for the agent's nonsense and gossip then, and he had less time now.

"I—I didn't say anything that wasn't true," the kid nervously insisted.

"You had no idea what was the truth." Then or now. The problem was that neither did Woodrow.

What the hell was going on at his daughter's wedding? Could Gage have staged everything to disrupt the ceremony just as Richard suspected? Or were the gunmen here for revenge against Woodrow?

If that were truly the case, then no one was in more danger than Megan. He had to get to her—before it was too late.

Megan stared at the gun clasped so tightly in the woman's hands. "Are you going to walk me down the aisle with that shoved in my back?" she asked.

The woman chuckled, but her ivory complexion flushed slightly. "That might be noticeable."

"It would be," Megan agreed. "You can't force me to go through with this wedding."

"Maybe not," the woman admitted. "But if you don't, you'll be sending all your guests home in body bags. Is that what you want?"

"Of course not," Megan said. All she'd really wanted was Gage. Even when she thought he was dead, she shouldn't have accepted Richard's proposal, shouldn't have agreed to a loveless marriage. Sure, she wanted children, and she'd thought she could raise them with a man she liked and respected. But it was very clear to her that she'd made a mistake. Another mistake. The last had nearly cost Gage his life. This one would probably cost hers.

"You only have one gun," Nikki said. "How can you kill us all?"

The woman laughed again. "You think I'm here alone?"

No. They all knew better. But Nikki sounded clueless and young and scared as she asked, "You're not? You have a partner?"

"I have more than *a partner*," the woman replied. "So unless you want everyone inside the chapel to die, you will walk down that aisle. You will pretend everything is perfect. And you'll marry your groom."

Megan had already decided she had no intention of doing any such thing. But she didn't want to put innocent lives in any more danger than they already were. But if she were going to be forced into doing something she didn't want to, she had to know. "Why?"

The woman's smooth brow furrowed slightly. She was young—probably only Megan's age or maybe a little older. "Why what?" she asked.

"Why do you care about my wedding?" Megan asked. "Why would you be willing to kill in order to make sure I go through with it?"

"And how do we know you won't kill everyone even if she does?" Nikki asked. She stepped closer to Megan, almost as if using her as a shield.

What kind of bodyguard was Nikki Payne?

Then Megan realized, when she heard the whispering rustle of silk, why Nikki was using her as a shield. She was drawing her gun from the holster on her thigh. Megan reached behind her back, but instead of the gun, Nikki pressed the scissors into her hand. As a weapon, she would have preferred the gun. But she tightened her fingers around the scissors.

"Nobody will get hurt," the woman assured them, "as long as nobody interferes with the plan."

"Plan?" Megan repeated. She hoped like hell Nikki had one, too, for their immediate situation. But she asked the woman instead, "What plan?"

The gunwoman chuckled again. "Your wedding…"

"My wedding is part of some plan? A plan for what?" Revenge?

Against whom? Megan's father? Or Gage? Or had Megan done something that had made someone angry enough to want vengeance against her?

The only person she knew for certain whom she'd really hurt and who didn't seem able to forgive her was Gage. But he wouldn't go to such extremes to hurt her. He hadn't cared enough to fight for her—for them—a year ago. Why would he care enough now?

The woman's face flushed. "I've said too much. You don't need to concern yourself with anything but walking down that aisle and saying 'I do.'"

Megan shook her head. "No. I can't."

"You will," the woman insisted. "Unless you want to get hurt."

Megan was counting on the woman not wanting to hurt her because if Megan couldn't walk down the aisle, she would mess up their plan—whatever the hell it was. So she drew in a deep breath of air and courage, tightened her grip on the scissors, and lunged at the woman.

She didn't hear the gunshot, but she suspected there had been a silencer on the barrel of the gun. It had looked funny when the woman had pressed it into her stomach earlier. And now she felt the blood, thick and sticky, as it oozed from the wound.

Chapter 8

What the hell kind of bodyguard was she?

Nikki had frozen in place with the gun grasped in her hand. She hadn't even disarmed the safety. She stared down at the women lying on the floor in front of her. One minute Megan had been standing—strong and defiant—before her. The next she'd been gone.

Was she gone?

Knowing the other woman who lay on the floor with Megan might still be armed Nikki thumbed off the safety and put her finger near the trigger. She would kill her if she needed to. She had killed before. Or so she thought. Her brothers had never confirmed it.

But even if she pulled the trigger now, she would only be saving herself. She worried that she might be too late to save Megan.

Her veil had fallen off, and some of her dark hair had

slipped free of the knot on the back of her head. It was tangled over her face, covering it and the woman who lay beneath Megan.

"Are you okay?" Nikki asked as she knelt beside her.

A gasp slipped free of Megan's lips. Either she'd had the breath knocked out of her or she'd been holding it. Then she rolled over and held up a hand covered in blood.

Nikki cursed. No, she wasn't all right. "Where are you hurt?"

Megan glanced down at herself. There was a smear of blood on the gown, too. But just a smear. Surely if she'd been shot, blood would have saturated the heavy fabric.

And Nikki hadn't heard a gun go off. Then there had been a silencer on the woman's weapon. She could have fired it. But Nikki smelled no telltale scent of gunpowder.

Megan released another unsteady breath. "I don't think I am."

They both turned to the other woman. She lay on the floor, her face pale again, her eyes closed. She might have struck her head on the edge of the vanity table behind her. Or she might have been dead, as blood oozed beneath her.

"D-did I kill her?" Megan stammered. She was more afraid now than when the woman had been threatening their lives and the lives of everyone in the church.

Woodrow Lynch's daughter had guts. Nikki had been impressed. She moved forward and felt the woman's neck. A pulse pumped steadily beneath her fingers. "No."

She examined the woman. "Looks like you stabbed her shoulder with the scissors." The wound appeared to be the source of the blood.

"Did I hit an artery?" Megan anxiously asked.

Nikki inspected what appeared to be a shallow wound.

The scissors weren't sharp enough to have gone very deeply into the woman's flesh. "No. It's not a bad injury. The blood is already clotting and drying up."

"But she's unconscious," Megan said.

Nikki felt the woman's head. A knot swelled on the back of it. "She hit the table when you knocked her down."

Megan released a shuddery sigh now. "I'm such an idiot."

"No, you're not," Nikki said. She'd acted faster than she had. And Nikki was a trained bodyguard. Megan Lynch had great instincts.

"I could have gotten us both killed."

"You did everything right," Nikki assured her. "You disarmed her without anyone hearing anything. You're awesome."

A giggle, albeit a little hysterical, slipped from Megan's lips. "I just really don't want to go through with this wedding."

Nikki laughed, too. She'd loved growing up with all brothers, and always wanting to be one of the guys, she hadn't ever yearned for a sister. Now she had sisters-in-law and some great female friends. For the first time, she wondered what she might have missed if she'd had a sister, one as kick-ass cool as herself or Megan Lynch.

"I thought you just wanted out of that damn dress," she teased. "But now I see how desperate you are to cancel this wedding." She shuddered at the thought of being a bride herself. "Not that I blame you."

The woman murmured and shifted on the floor as she began to regain consciousness. Megan hadn't knocked her out nearly hard enough. She still posed a threat. But she wasn't the only one. The dressing room door began to open. Nikki grabbed for the woman's gun and turned toward that opening door with the barrels of that gun and hers pointing at the intruder.

Gage cursed. "What the hell!" He'd known he might have been walking into a dangerous situation when he entered the dressing room. He hadn't thought the women he'd left there earlier would pose the threat, though. "Don't shoot me."

"You keep surprising me," Nikki said, as if it was all his fault. But then that was what Richard thought, that Gage had orchestrated the whole scenario. Nikki shook her head. "You're just like your best friend."

"Best friend?" Megan asked from where she lay on the floor. Half of her thick dark hair had tumbled down around her thin shoulders.

"My brother—Nicholas Rus," Nikki replied.

Gage swallowed a gasp, still surprised that Nikki had finally accepted her illegitimate half brother.

She smiled. "I've almost shot him more times than I can remember."

"I'm not entirely sure that was by accident, though," Gage said. "What the hell happened here?"

He doubted it was an accident, either. His heart beating fast with the fear he'd felt that Megan might be in danger, he stepped closer to her. That was when he saw the blood—on her hand and smeared on her dress. He dropped to his knees beside her. "Are you all right?"

She nodded. But her usually tan complexion had paled, making her dark eyes look even bigger and more vulnerable. He'd been so furious with her for so long. His anger now dissipated, leaving only concern and something he refused to acknowledge.

"She's great," Nikki said. "She took down this bitch who had a gun pointed at us."

Gage felt all the blood drain from his face.

"You wouldn't let me use the scissors on the dress," Megan said. And there was that little teasing lilt in her voice—the one she used to use when she'd flirted with him.

The blood rushed lower in his body. Then he realized what they were saying. "You two overpowered her?"

"No," Nikki said. "It was all Megan. She's a badass."

Megan smiled with a pride Gage had never seen in her before. Then the smile dimmed as the woman moaned and shifted on the floor again. "I didn't want to hurt her, though..."

Seeing that Nikki had her hands full with the two guns, Gage grabbed the measuring tape that either Mrs. Payne or a seamstress must have left in the room. He bound the woman's hands and ankles. Then he reached for something to use as a gag. Her eyes were beginning to flutter. She would be fully conscious soon and probably screaming.

But Megan tugged the gauzy fabric from his hands. "You can't use that," she said. "That's my veil." Then she gasped as she glanced down at the blood she'd smeared on it.

"Why do you care?" he asked. It wasn't like she was going to be able to wear it.

"Use this," Nikki said. She'd put down one of the guns on the vanity table and had found a roll of duct tape. "I think Mom keeps a roll in every room, here and at home."

Gage ripped off a piece of tape and fastened it over the woman's mouth just as her eyes opened fully. Her eyes widened as she stared up at him in shock.

"What the hell did she want?" he asked. "To stop the wedding?"

"Just the opposite," Nikki replied. "She wanted to make sure it happened as if nothing was wrong."

"Why?" Maybe he shouldn't have put the tape over her mouth. But he doubted she would willingly give up her reason, especially with her cohorts free and able to carry out whatever their plan was.

"There's only one way to find out," Megan said while trying to wipe the blood from the veil and her hand.

Gage's blood chilled as he noticed the expression on her beautiful face. Her chin was pointed, the skin taut over her cheekbones. It was her stubborn look. And he knew from experience that there was no changing her mind when she was that determined.

He hated to know but he had to ask, "What?"

"I get married exactly as planned."

His stomach lurched. "No, no. It's too dangerous..."

"She's right," Nikki said. "I have to tell my mom and Woodrow that we have no time to waste. The wedding's supposed to start soon." She pulled the door open a crack, peeked out—then opened it fully and stepped out, closing it behind her.

"You really want to do this?" he asked Megan. "You really want to marry Richard?"

She glanced down at the woman who struggled against the measuring tape binding her wrists and ankles. "She's still bleeding," she said with concern and guilt.

Gage pulled the torn edges of her jacket away from her wound. "It's shallow," he said. He ripped off another piece of tape, squeezed her skin together and pressed the tape over it. And as he did it, the woman thrashed around in pain. "That'll stop it from bleeding."

For extra reinforcement, Gage wound a length of duct tape over the measuring tape bindings—to make sure she couldn't get free—because from the way she was glaring at him, with such hatred, he knew he wouldn't be safe from her wrath.

But she was the least of his concerns.

He reminded Megan, "You didn't answer my question. You really want to do this?" Marry another man?

"I *have* to do this," she said. "Please go get my dad for me."

"So he can give you away?" He shook his head. "It's not going to happen." There was no way that Woodrow Lynch would willingly put either of his daughters in any danger.

Megan reached for him, her small hand clasping his forearm. "It has to happen."

"I don't understand why you're so determined." Did she love Richard? Just because she hadn't really loved Gage didn't mean that she wasn't capable of love. She and Richard had much more in common than Gage and she had ever had.

Her hand slipped from his arm, and she pointed at the woman. "She is. She threatened that if the wedding didn't take place as planned, that nobody would get out of the church alive."

Gage uttered a ragged sigh. He'd thought the gunmen were there to stop the wedding, not make sure that it took place without a hitch. Apparently, he was the only one who didn't want Megan to marry Richard.

"She's hardly in a position to carry out that threat anymore," Gage pointed out. He had made certain that she wasn't able to get free.

Megan shivered. "You already know and she admitted that she's not here alone."

He glanced down at the woman again. She glared back at him. It might help things if he questioned her. He reached for the tape over her mouth, but Megan caught his hand.

"Please, get my father," she urged.

"And leave you alone?" He shook his head. "Look what happened the last time I left you alone." He pointed at the woman now.

"And like Nikki told you, I took care of her." She reached for the gun Nikki had left on the vanity table. "And with this, I can take care of myself."

She could shoot. Woodrow had bragged about how good a shot his youngest daughter was. Or maybe he'd only done that because he'd been warning Gage to stay away from her.

It was a warning Gage should have heeded.

"Please," she implored him. "Get my father for me."

Was it Woodrow she wanted? Or Richard? After her close brush with death, had she realized she couldn't live without her groom?

"We already told Richard that the wedding is canceled."

She gasped. "You shouldn't have done that."

"You told me to," he reminded her.

"I told you to check on him," she said.

And Gage had to know. "Does he mean that much to you?"

She glanced at the woman who stared hatefully at them. "I don't want anyone to get hurt," Megan said.

He snorted in derision. She'd hurt him—like hell. But apparently she'd forgotten all about that. "You're right,"

he said. "You can take care of yourself." He headed toward the door.

But she reached for him again. Her hand grasping his
arm, she swung him back around to her.

"What do you want, Megan?" he asked her.

"Gage…"

"You don't want *me*," he said. "You made that clear
months ago. And you've made it very clear today. I'll go
get your father for you so you can marry the man you really want." But before he could turn back to the door, she
stepped forward and closed the distance between them.

With her free hand, she tugged his head down, and
after rising up on tiptoe, she pressed her mouth against
his. She kissed him deeply, sliding her lips back and forth
across his. He wanted to grab her and jerk her body up
tightly against his. But he resisted the urge and kept his
arms at his sides. Finally she stepped back, her breasts
pushing against the bodice of that sparkling dress as she
panted for breath.

He'd stopped breathing entirely. He wasn't even sure
his heart was still beating.

She said nothing.

Was that kiss supposed to be a message for him? Was
he supposed to think that he was the man she wanted?
He knew better. She only wanted him to do as she'd
asked: bring her father to her so Woodrow could give
away the bride.

Derek "D" Nielsen felt sweat trickle down the back
of his neck to run between his shoulder blades and soak
into the waistband of his dress pants. The suit was hot.
But that wasn't why he was sweating.

Andrea had been gone too long. Since his escape a

few days ago, she had rarely left his side. So she would have been back…if she was able.

Had something happened to her?

Of course she could have just been checking in with the other members of the crew she had put together. She was determined that nothing go wrong with the plan. She wanted this wedding to take place probably more than the bride did.

Derek understood how important it was for every element of a plan to come off precisely. The prison break had been his plan—plotted from the inside—but Andrea had made certain that plan had been carried out exactly as he'd ordered. If it hadn't been, he would still be behind bars.

More sweat trickled down his back. He didn't want to go back to prison. Ever.

But it wasn't like anyone would expect an escaped convict to show up here. Except maybe one person.

If he'd heard about the escape…

But Derek suspected he'd been a little preoccupied lately. Right now he was preoccupied himself.

"Andrea," he murmured. "Where the hell are you?"

He needed to check in with the others to find out if they'd seen her or if she'd used her walkie-talkie to contact any of them. But before he did that, maybe he needed to check first where he'd seen her last, heading through the vestibule to the back of the church.

The guy with the military haircut, scars and attitude had just been back there again. He also had a gun. Derek had seen the bulge of it beneath his tuxedo jacket. That guy wasn't the only one armed in the wedding party. The gray-haired guy had a gun, too, and at least one of the guests.

More and more people had permits to carry concealed weapons. But Derek suspected something else was at stake, that these guys weren't just carrying because it was their constitutional right to bear arms. They weren't civilians who'd taken a weekend firearms class. These guys were trained. And they wouldn't be easy to take down.

Andrea had hired all those reinforcements for them. Derek felt he would need every one of them. Most of all, he needed Andrea. If anything had happened to her, the plan be damned. He would finish this now, and he didn't care who died in the cross fire when he went down shooting.

Chapter 9

Nerves fluttered in Penny's stomach. It wasn't just because of the people with guns who'd crashed the wedding. It wasn't just because of the danger they were all in. It was because of Woodrow Lynch.

He had looked like he was in such a hurry when he'd started down the church aisle a short time ago. After speaking with one of the guests, he'd joined her in the vestibule where she was checking the basket for programs and making sure the flowers weren't wilting yet. Then he'd guided her through the door leading into the coatroom off the vestibule. It had a stained glass window dividing it from the church. But she doubted anyone could see them through the colored glass.

"Where were you going?" she asked, keeping her voice low in case the stranger with the gun was hovering nearby yet. "I saw you following Gage from the groom's dressing room." Maybe the better question was: "Where was he going?"

"Like you need to ask," he said.

And she smiled. "To Megan." Gage hadn't been able to stay away from her since finding out this was her wedding. Maybe the gunmen and the danger were just an excuse. "I'm proud of you for letting him talk to her alone."

"I doubt he's talking," Woodrow said then shook his head when her smile widened. "That's not what I meant. I'm not matchmaking. He thought she might be in danger and wanted to make sure she was safe. And there was no way to stop him."

"We didn't need his help," Nikki said as she joined them inside the coatroom. She must have seen Woodrow guiding her mother through the door. Hopefully, she hadn't overheard them because then someone else—like one of the gunmen—could have as well. "Megan and I overpowered the woman."

The color drained from Woodrow's handsome face, and he sputtered, "Wh-what? Overpowered what woman?"

"The one who forced her way into the bride's dressing room with a gun."

Penny reached out and clasped Woodrow's arm for support, since he looked like he was about to keel over with shock and fear. "She's all right." She turned toward her daughter and scanned her. Not even a curl was out of place, which was unusual for Nikki when she hadn't been in a fight. "You're both all right?"

"Yes," Nikki said. "Thanks to Megan. She's amazing. She took the bitch out with the scissors before I even had a chance to pull the trigger of my gun."

Penny had hoped Nikki and Megan might bond. But she hadn't wanted it to be over an encounter with a dangerous woman with a gun. She wasn't even sure why she'd wanted them to become friends. It wasn't like they would see each other again. Nikki lived here in River City and Megan lived in Chicago. She had only decided to get married in Penny's chapel because her dad had suggested it.

Why had he?

Sure, Penny had done a few weddings for his agents. But this was his daughter whose special day he'd entrusted to her. And she was failing him.

Why hadn't Penny realized she would need more security? Woodrow had been a lawman for so long that he must have made enemies—criminals who wanted revenge for their incarcerations.

"Is Megan really all right?" her father anxiously asked.

"She's fine," Nikki assured him. "She's very smart and strong. She's also determined to go through with this wedding."

"That's out of the question," Woodrow said. "I won't allow it."

And Penny couldn't help but think that was what he should have done from the beginning instead of bringing Megan to her to plan this wedding. He should have told his daughter that marrying someone she didn't love was out of the question. She must have let out a soft snort or something, because Woodrow looked at her as if he knew exactly what she was thinking. From the way his dark brows lowered, he wasn't pleased.

"If you won't allow it," Nikki said in a tone her mother knew too well, a mixture of stubbornness and defiance, "then you'll be getting everyone killed."

"Nikki!" Penny admonished her daughter.

"Hey," her daughter replied. "That's what the woman swore would happen if Megan canceled the wedding."

Woodrow looked at Penny again, his blue eyes wide with alarm. Penny's heart began to pound quickly and heavily, too. "No. There has to be another way."

"There isn't," Gage said as he stepped into the coatroom doorway.

Woodrow glanced around Gage, and his voice sharpened with concern when he asked, "You left Megan alone?"

"She's not alone," Nikki said. "The woman's with her."

"She's tied up," Gage said. "And Megan has her gun."

Obviously unappeased, Woodrow shook his head. "You still shouldn't have left her."

Penny silently agreed. How could Gage and Megan realize that they still loved each other if they kept running from each other?

"She won't be alone long," Gage said. Maybe he intended to return to her immediately. Then he added, "She wants to see you."

Woodrow's face paled. "Of course after what she's been through…" A girl would want her father.

Penny glanced at Nikki. She'd been so young when she'd lost her dad that she'd never looked for him to comfort or rescue her. She'd never looked to anyone for comfort or rescue. Not her three big brothers or even her mother.

"Megan wants to see you," Gage reiterated, "because she wants you to walk her down the aisle. Just like Nikki said, she's determined to get married today."

But Penny suspected it wasn't for the reasons Gage obviously thought. His face was grim, his green eyes dark, his mouth drawn into a grimace. He was hurt thinking that she wanted to marry someone else.

Woodrow shook his head again. "It's not going to happen."

Nikki shushed him as she glanced nervously around. "It has to... That woman isn't here alone. They are determined that this wedding takes place. I don't think her threat that everyone would die was an idle one."

Gage nodded grimly in agreement.

Penny's stomach lurched. She felt sick. Maybe she'd been wrong. Maybe Gage didn't love Megan anymore if he could let her marry another man.

Megan's lips tingled yet from the contact with Gage's. She wasn't sure what she'd been thinking to kiss him like she had. But he'd looked so upset with her, like he'd looked that day she'd broken up with him. Just like that day, he'd looked betrayed.

She hadn't cared back then, because she'd thought she was the one who'd been betrayed, who'd been used. But when Gage had quit the Bureau and reenlisted with the Marines, she'd been afraid that she might have been wrong. Now she was all but certain.

"Gage," she murmured, hoping he would come back.

She doubted that he would. He didn't understand why she wanted to go through with the wedding. He thought it was because of Richard, but it was because of him. She didn't want anyone else getting hurt but most especially not Gage. He had already been through too much.

Was that her fault? Had he reenlisted because of her? She would never forgive herself if she'd caused him that much pain. And the way he'd snorted when she'd said that she didn't want anyone getting hurt...

She must have hurt him. She couldn't go back. She couldn't change the past. But she could make certain no one else got hurt because of her.

Over the tape covering her mouth, the woman narrowed her eyes and glared at Megan. She struggled against the tape binding her wrists and ankles, flinching as she aggravated her wound.

Guilt flashed through Megan. But she'd needed to disarm the woman before she'd shot someone. If she managed to get loose, someone was certain to get hurt. But she wouldn't get loose, Megan assured herself.

She wouldn't...

A knock at the door startled Megan, and a gasp slipped through her lips. She'd locked the door behind Gage. So it was probably her father. Hopefully, he would understand why she had to go through with the wedding. She had no choice.

Before she could unlock the door, a deep voice called out, "Andrea?"

That wasn't her father's voice. It wasn't her father at the door, rattling the knob as he tried to force it open. Megan's heart rate quickened as fear gripped her. She tightened her grasp on the woman's weapon.

"Andrea, are you in there?" the man asked.

The woman struggled harder and murmured against the tape over her mouth. Megan pressed her free hand over the tape, making certain that no sounds could escape it.

"Sweetheart," Megan said, pretending that she knew the man, that she thought he was her groom. "I know you're anxious but you'll have to wait until our wedding night. It won't be long now." Like never. While the wed-

ding had to happen, there would be no wedding night—
no honeymoon—no real marriage.

She held her breath, waiting to see if she'd fooled the
would-be intruder. But the door rattled as the guy twisted
the knob again. It was locked, but it wasn't a dead bolt.
It wasn't going to hold out someone who really wanted
to get inside.

Megan gripped the gun more tightly and made certain
the safety was off. She knew how to shoot—at targets.
She'd never pointed a gun at someone and fired. She wasn't
certain that she would be able to do it, to take another life.

Megan had only been able to overpower Andrea with
Nikki's help. On her own, she had no hope of protecting
herself from Andrea's very determined male friend, unless she found the courage to pull the trigger. And then
she wasn't certain she would actually hit him. Targets
didn't move, didn't fire back. She suspected that this
man, being a friend of Andrea's, would. And he probably wouldn't miss...

Woodrow tightened his grasp on his gun handle before releasing it—reluctantly. The guy wasn't alone in
the chapel. If Woodrow took him out, he would force
the others to react. So he called out instead, "Hey, that's
not the restroom."

His hand under his jacket, the guy tensed. But like
Woodrow, he didn't pull his weapon. He turned to Woodrow, his lips curved into a forced smile.

His hair was buzzed so short that Woodrow couldn't
tell what color it was. His eyes were dark and cold. He
seemed vaguely familiar. But that was probably because
he looked like a thousand other perps Woodrow had either personally arrested or had arrested.

Was he here because of that—for revenge?

The guy betrayed nothing. No recognition. No flicker of emotion, of anger or of fear.

Woodrow gestured down the hall. "The men's room is down there. But you better hurry. The wedding is about to start soon."

The guy narrowed his dark eyes and skeptically asked, "Really?"

Woodrow nodded. "Of course. Everything is right on schedule."

The guy nodded. "Yeah, I heard Mrs. Payne puts on the perfect wedding."

Woodrow hoped that was true this time, too, that the wedding ran perfectly according to the plan they had quickly concocted just a short while ago in the coatroom.

"So you better use the restroom and take your seat in the church," Woodrow urged the man.

The guy hesitated and glanced back at the door to the bride's dressing room. "I was actually looking for my plus one," he replied. "I thought my wife went into that room."

Woodrow forced a laugh. "Not likely. My daughter has been obsessive about no one seeing her in her dress yet. She wouldn't have let anyone in there."

The guy chuckled. "The best man has been in and out of there since I arrived."

"Best man?"

"The grim-looking blond guy."

He'd described Gage perfectly, but he didn't reveal whether or not he knew him. He hadn't mentioned his name. If he wasn't here for revenge against Woodrow, he could have been seeking revenge against Gage.

But if not...what the hell did he want? Why were he

and his female friend—or wife or whatever she was—
determined that the wedding take place?

The guy's mouth curved into a smirk as he continued,
"The bride has let *him* inside that room."

Woodrow narrowed his eyes now. "Any reason you've
been watching that room?"

The guy glanced around then stepped back. "No. Just
anxious for the wedding to start."

"It will," Woodrow said. "So you better…"

The guy chuckled. "I know, take my seat." And finally
he moved back toward the chapel.

Woodrow knocked on the bride's room door.

"Go away," she said, her voice pitched low. "Please,
go away…"

"Megan, it's Dad."

The lock clicked, the knob turned and the door
opened. As soon as he'd stepped inside and closed the
door again, she threw her arms around him and held on
tightly, trembling against him. "I thought I was going to
have to shoot him."

He doubted his softhearted little girl would have actually been able to pull the trigger. Like Nikki had claimed,
she had obviously overpowered the woman who lay tied
up on the carpet. But taking a life… He didn't think she
could have. He hoped she was never put in the situation
where she had to or risk losing her own life.

He would make certain she was never put in that situation. "It's okay," he told her as he held her like he had
when she was a little girl frightened after a nightmare.
"It's okay, my beauty."

While he had made certain to teach her and Ellen
how to protect themselves, he had also tried to shield his

daughters from the ugliness of his job, of his life. Now he'd brought that ugliness to her.

Or maybe Gage had. Again.

She pulled back and stared up at him, her eyes glistening with unshed tears and irritation. "Don't lie to me, Daddy," she said.

He didn't know if she was talking about his assurance that everything was okay or that she was beautiful. She'd always argued his nickname for her. She had no idea how beautiful she was.

"We have a plan," he said. "It's going to be okay." He hoped.

Megan shook her head. Her hair had fallen down around her shoulders, the curls springing free for once. She looked even more beautiful than when she wound it into a tight knot on the back of her head. She also looked scared.

"They're the ones with a plan," Megan said, gesturing at the woman.

If there was time, Woodrow would have tried to get the plan out of the woman. He'd once been a master interrogator. But now he only supervised and left the interrogations and fieldwork to younger agents. There wasn't time for him to try, though.

The music began. "That's our cue," he told her.

If everything didn't go according to plan, there was a good chance that none of them would make it out of the wedding chapel alive.

Chapter 10

Gage stood uneasily at the front of the nearly empty chapel. He had never been anyone's best man before, not even for his best friend, Nicholas Rus. Nick had chosen his half sister, Nikki Payne, to stand by his side while Gage had walked his sister, Annalise, down the aisle to the man she had loved almost her entire life. At least Gage hadn't had to give Megan away. But he hadn't imagined—even in his worst nightmares—that he would be the best man at *her* wedding.

Richard wasn't thrilled, either. He probably would have refused had it not been for Mrs. Payne.

Nobody told Penny no, not even Woodrow. But the bureau chief had won one argument with the stubborn wedding planner. Gage would have wondered what the hell was going on with the two of them if he wasn't more concerned about what the hell was going on at the church.

Why would gunmen crash a wedding, not to stop it but to make certain it happened?

None of it made any sense.

The only one who had anything to gain by making sure the wedding took place was Richard. He gained Megan as his bride, as his wife. But that was good for Gage, too. He'd wanted the wedding to happen, too. He'd wanted Megan off-limits, so he wouldn't be tempted to forget the pain she'd caused him. But her kisses tempted him. And her beauty. And her strength.

She was much stronger than he'd ever realized. He'd once been furious with her for not trusting him. But then maybe she hadn't known him any better than he'd known her.

Even if he could forget the pain, he couldn't forget what he'd been through the past six months. He couldn't forget how it had changed him. Megan was stronger than he'd known, but she wasn't strong enough to deal with what he couldn't even manage himself.

The music began, an organ playing from the balcony above the pews. Everyone stood and turned toward the back of the church, where the veiled bride appeared on the arm of the debonair-looking father of the bride.

Gage and Richard were already standing next to the minister in the front. Richard was ahead of him but so much shorter that he didn't block Gage's view. He could see the back, but he studied Richard instead. Sweat trickled down the guy's neck to wick against the collar of his tuxedo. His face was flushed, his skin red and blotchy.

Having never been a best man before, Gage wasn't certain if Richard's nervousness was normal. Or was it the knowledge of the gunmen and the plan that had freaked out the groom?

Richard had been opposed to more than Gage being his best man. He'd been opposed to the entire plan, almost violently opposed. But Woodrow had cut off his argument. If Richard really loved Megan, wouldn't he be willing to do anything to protect her?

Gage was willing to do anything to protect her, even pose as Richard's best man. He'd never liked the guy before, but now suspicion joined his dislike. The comment he'd made earlier, about coming back from the dead, and his reaction to their plan…

What the hell was the real story about Richard Boersman? He certainly wasn't the harmless computer nerd everyone thought he was.

As Woodrow and the bride started down the aisle toward them, Richard began to shake. He wasn't just nervous, though. He was scared.

If he had anything to do with the gunmen being in the church, he should be scared—not of the gunmen but of Gage.

Her mom had forced Nikki into a lot of different dresses over the course of her twenty-five years. But this was a dress Nikki had promised herself that she would never wear. If only there'd been time to get Megan out of hers.

But they had been too busy overpowering a crazy woman with a gun to use the tool Mom had given her. Nikki suspected there would have been time after they'd all agreed to the plan, though. Her mom could have helped Megan out of her gown and Nikki into it. Penny had insisted it would be easier for Nikki to wear this one.

Her gown…

It was beautiful, with its intricate lace and beading,

but it was also a joke. A farce. This dress hadn't brought good luck to Penny and Nicholas Payne's marriage. It hadn't stopped him from betraying his bride or from dying in the line of duty.

Nikki just hoped it didn't cause her to die, too. Her fingers trembled slightly as she clutched Woodrow Lynch's arm. Her knees trembled, too, as they started down the aisle. Not only had she vowed to never wear this damn dress, she'd vowed to never do this—have a man walk her down the aisle to some guy who would make empty promises. Like her father had made empty promises to his bride.

She wasn't being forced to do any of this. In fact she'd had to argue for the right to switch places with Megan. Eventually, she had convinced everyone else that this was a good plan, such a good plan that it would work.

She had only been able to convince them because Logan wasn't in the church. Her oldest brother would have nixed her plan for certain. Maybe she was so used to his doing that, though, that she hadn't considered all the consequences of what she had plotted to do. Like her either getting married or killed...

Megan's stomach churned with nerves and guilt. She should have been upstairs, walking down that church aisle on her father's arm. Instead she'd slipped out of the bride's dressing room and down the back stairs with Penny Payne.

The wedding planner hadn't taken the time to help Megan out of that damn dress. Instead she'd thrown Woodrow's trench coat around Megan's shoulders to cover up her and the gown. Then she'd hustled her down the stairs to the hallway leading to her office. But they'd passed the door to it.

They were heading to a hidden door to a secret underground tunnel to the courtyard outside the church.

Penny held Megan's hand to lead her down the dimly lit corridor. The reception area, with its stone walls, rafter ceiling and twinkle lights, was at the other end of the basement. This area looked even older. It was also eerily quiet except for the faint echo of the organ music drifting down from the chapel above them. The traditional wedding march...

Megan's nerves and guilt increased. She squeezed Penny's hand. "I'm sorry," she murmured. "I shouldn't have let Nikki take my place."

Penny stopped walking and turned back toward Megan. With her free hand, she gently patted her cheek. "Don't feel bad," she said. "You had no choice."

That was what she'd thought—that she'd had no choice, that she would have to go through with the wedding. But then they had all come up with another plan, one to protect Megan. She and Mrs. Payne were the only ones who would be safe. Everyone else was in danger.

"But I shouldn't have let her risk her life for mine," Megan insisted.

Penny sighed. "I know my daughter. There is no one more stubborn than she is."

"Gage." The name almost unconsciously slipped out of Megan's lips. He was always on her mind, though. He had been since that day she'd met him in her father's house. "He's more stubborn than Nikki."

Too stubborn to ever forgive her.

Penny squeezed her hand now. "That may be true. He

is an obstinate man. But in Gage's case, that's a good thing."

Megan gasped in surprise that the older woman would say such a thing.

"Being stubborn is probably what kept Gage alive those six months he was missing," Penny explained. "But Nikki..." She was clearly worried that her daughter's stubbornness would get her killed instead. "Gage wouldn't be here, he wouldn't have come back to you if he wasn't stubborn."

"Gage hasn't come back to me," Megan said. "He would much prefer that I was the one getting married right now." Earlier he'd promised her that he would make certain nothing disrupted her wedding. But he'd broken that promise. He'd agreed to Nikki's dangerous plan.

Penny chuckled. "I think Gage would only prefer that if you were marrying him."

That wasn't likely to happen. But being a hopeless romantic must have been an occupational hazard of being a wedding planner, like being in danger was an occupational hazard of being a bodyguard.

A librarian really had no occupational hazards, except maybe reading all those books had made Megan a bit of a dreamer. She found herself wistfully asking, "Do you really think..."

But she couldn't even complete the thought. It was too ridiculous, not after their horrific breakup.

Penny finished the thought for her. "That Gage loves you?"

"No." Her face flushed with embarrassment. She'd broken up with Gage because she hadn't been able to believe he'd loved her then. He had even less of a reason to love her now. "No. I know that isn't a possibility."

She listened to the music drifting faintly down from the chapel. "Do you really think the plan will work?"

Mrs. Payne didn't need to answer. The reply to Megan's question stood at the end of the hallway ahead of them. A man, dressed as a waiter, blocked their way out with his burly body. He also held a gun, pointed at them.

Megan raised the weapon she held, the one she'd knocked out of the woman's hands. She hadn't been certain before that she could fire it to protect herself. But now she wasn't protecting just herself.

She had to protect Mrs. Payne, too.

Before she could fire, she heard another trigger cock as a cold barrel pressed hard against the side of her head.

No, their plan was *not* going to work.

Chapter 11

As the music wound down, fear clutched Gage's heart. The plan wasn't going to work. They'd known that once Woodrow pulled back Nikki's veil, the gig was up. So the plan had actually been just to buy enough time for Megan and Penny to get to safety and call Nick and the rest of Payne Protection to rush to the rescue.

But as Gage scanned the chapel, he realized they hadn't bought themselves any time. They hadn't fooled anyone. The armed man he'd spoken to, the one Woodrow had caught outside the bride's dressing room, wasn't present, but he had representation. There was a guy in the back and another near the front who were fidgety, their hands sliding too frequently beneath their jackets as if to assure themselves that their weapons were ready. Gage hadn't noticed them earlier, so they must have recently sneaked into the chapel.

Something had definitely been planned to go down

during the ceremony. So why would the smug guy, who'd looked like the ringleader, be missing? Unless he'd already figured out the bait and switch, which meant Megan and Penny were in danger.

Gage began to cough, as if he was choking. Everyone turned toward him, but he waved off the attention and rasped, "Water." Then he headed quickly for the back of the church.

His ruse must have worked because no one followed him. Of course they were all focused on the bride whom the father had yet to give away. Her veil hadn't been lifted; the gig wasn't up yet.

Once it was, Nikki and Woodrow would be in danger. But Gage knew Nikki could take care of herself. He was more worried about Megan.

And Penny, too, of course.

He hurried toward the stairwell leading to the basement. He had to get to Megan and Penny before the smug gunman found them. He just hoped like hell he wasn't too late to save them.

Megan held her breath, afraid to move even a fraction of an inch with the cocked gun pressed to her temple. The weapon she held was snapped from her hand.

"This is Andrea's gun," the man said. "How the hell did you get this?"

Still holding her breath, Megan had no air to answer him.

The barrel moved from her head as the guy jerked her around to face him, pulling her father's jacket from her shoulders. It dropped onto the concrete floor. "Did you kill her?"

With the barrel gone, Megan shook her head. "N-no…"

"That's crap," the waiter said. "The only way someone would get Andrea's gun away from her is if she's dead."

"I knocked her out," Megan explained.

The guy narrowed his eyes and looked her up and down as if he doubted her claim. "What the hell really happened?"

"I knocked her into a table—" she swallowed the nerves choking her in order to continue "—when I stabbed her with a pair of scissors."

The guy sucked in a breath.

"She hit her head. Hard," Megan said.

And then the man hit her hard, so hard that Megan's head snapped back and she tasted blood inside her mouth. She must have bitten her tongue or the inside of her cheek.

"Don't!" Mrs. Payne exclaimed as she tried to step between the man and Megan. She wasn't a bodyguard like her children, but she had the tendencies.

Nobody could protect Megan from being too honest, though. How had she managed to lie so easily to Gage that once? Because she'd been trying to protect herself. She needed to do that again.

"You bitch!" the man yelled at her. "You stabbed her? You really stabbed her?"

"Yes," she admitted. Now she had a reason for being so forthcoming.

The man reached for her again, but Penny caught his arm. He lifted his other hand—with the gun—to swing toward the older woman.

"No!" Megan yelled. "Your friend needs your help. She's wounded, but she's alive. For now."

He drew back his arm. "Where is she?"

"In the bride's dressing room," Megan replied. "You

need to get her medical attention." Gage had taped her wound to stop the bleeding. But she was probably in pain, especially if she'd continued her struggles to free herself.

The guy glanced at the waiter. "Shoot them if they move." Then he turned to leave.

But Megan called out to him. "No!"

He turned back, his eyes narrowed again and hard with anger. "What?"

"Unless you're going to call 911, you're not going to be able to get her the help she needs alone."

"Now you want to help her?" the man scoffed. "You've left her bleeding while you're playing a runaway bride." He peered around the hallway. "Where the hell were you running?"

She shook her head. "Not running. Hiding."

"If she's not alive," he began, his voice cracking.

"She won't be if you keep wasting time," she warned him, surprised that she'd finally managed to refrain from being honest. "But if you want to help her, you're going to need your friend. One of you will need to carry her, the other drive…" Or hold a gun.

The guy smirked. "So the two of us should just leave you alone?"

"No," Megan said. "Have him tie us up, so we can't get away."

The smirk widened. "You're pretty sure that'll buy you time for someone to rush to your rescue, huh? The big blond guy with the chip on his shoulder? The gray-haired guy who looks like a retired Marine?" He chuckled. "They won't get out of that chapel alive. No one will."

Panic clutched Megan's heart. Thinking Gage was dead had been like living a nightmare, but this was worse.

She was going to lose him all over again and her dad, too. Probably her own life as well.

"Your friend certainly won't," Megan said. "With every minute you waste here threatening us, she loses more blood. And she's in more pain."

He flinched as if she'd struck him. Then he gestured at his friend. "Tie them up and stash them in a closet or office where no one will find them. Then meet me upstairs." He pointed one gun at Penny and the other at Megan. "Don't make me regret letting you live."

As soon as he disappeared down the hall, the waiter expelled a shaky breath. He was nearly as afraid as they had been.

"He's not going to let us live, is he?" Penny asked, her voice tremulous, as if she were overcome with fear.

Maybe she was. Megan wouldn't blame her. She was scared, too. But she wasn't ready to give up yet.

The guy's face flushed. "D's a dangerous dude. I heard he tortured and killed his best friend."

"Why would you work with him, then?" Penny asked. "Why would you trust that he won't do the same to you?"

The guy shuddered. "I don't trust him. But I don't work for him," he said. "I work for Andrea. She controls him."

And apparently everyone one else, as well.

Penny sighed. "But if Andrea dies…"

"You better go," Megan urged him. "You need to make sure he gets her help."

The guy shook his head. "I have to tie you up."

Megan glanced around the hall. It had widened after passing the office and now doubled as storage space. Boxes lined one stone wall. Ribbon dangled from one of them.

"Let me tie us up," she offered. "That way you won't have to juggle the gun."

The guy studied her face, his skeptical as if he worried that she was tricking him. But he was probably more worried about how D would react if they got away.

"You'll check," she said. "You'll make sure we're tied tightly."

"You can't tie up each other," he said.

"Of course not," she agreed. "I'll tie up Mrs. Payne." She unwound some of the ribbon and tied Penny's delicate wrists and ankles together as she'd been taught. Then she handed the ribbon to him.

"Now you tie me up," she said. When the ribbon cut into her wrists and ankles, she almost regretted the offer. But the discomfort would be worth it—if her ploy worked.

He glanced around for a hiding place. "I need to put you out of sight."

Megan tried to move, but with her ankles bound, she stumbled forward and fell to her knees. The thick gown should have cushioned her fall, but one of the sparkling rhinestones ground through the fabric, scratching her skin. She cursed. God, she hated this damn dress.

"We can't walk," she needlessly pointed out.

"This is just a storage area, for things I probably should have thrown out years ago, at the end of this hall," Penny said. "Nobody will come back here."

The waiter snorted. "Unless you yell for help…"

"We won't," Megan said.

The guy glanced around the space again. Then he walked around them to inspect the boxes.

Penny sucked in a breath as if afraid that he might find

something—probably the opening to that secret passage. If he knew it was there…

He would never leave them.

He pulled a few cloth napkins from one of the boxes. "Now you won't," he said as he shoved one of the cloths in Penny's mouth and then another in Megan's.

"Don't screw me over," he threatened. "Or you won't need to worry about D. I'll kill you myself."

Megan knew then that there was no use appealing to the better nature of any of the gunmen. None of them had a conscience. None of them would hesitate to take a life—any life.

Penny's throat dried of any moisture, and she struggled not to gag on the cloth shoved so deeply in her mouth it nearly choked her. She had only to wait until the fake waiter disappeared down the hallway before the cloth was gone.

After spitting out her cloth, Megan had twisted around and used her teeth to pull out Penny's. "You can untie yourself now," the younger woman told her.

Penny lifted her hands, which Megan had tied in front of her, unlike how the man had tied Megan's behind her back. "How?"

"Pull on the end of your ribbon with your teeth," Megan directed her.

Following instructions, Penny leaned forward, and with one tug, the ribbon easily unwound from around her wrists. Using her newly freed hands, she tugged loose the ribbon around her ankles. "How did you do that?"

"My dad taught me and my sister when we were little," Megan replied as if it was a perfectly normal part of childhood to learn how to tie slipknots.

"Didn't that scare you?" Penny asked, worried about how that single dad had raised his little girls. Not only had he been a single parent, but he was also a lawman.

"He made a game of it," Megan said nostalgically. She smiled then added, "Kind of like hide-and-seek on steroids."

Penny laughed. "Nikki would have loved that."

"Yes, she would have," Megan agreed.

So Penny hadn't been the only one who'd raised her kids in fear that something horrible could happen to them. Woodrow had been out there, fighting criminals despite knowing his work could make his family a target for revenge. So he'd obviously done his best to provide them with the skills to protect themselves.

"Unfortunately, the waiter didn't tie me up the same way I tied you," Megan said.

Penny inspected the ribbon binding Megan's wrists and ankles. The fake waiter had bound her so tightly that the edges of the ribbon were cutting through her skin. Penny sucked in a breath, unable to bear the thought of a bride—but especially this bride—being in pain.

While Penny didn't carry a weapon like her children, she did always have a small knife on her person. She pulled it from the pocket of the silk jacket that matched her dress. The blade was narrow but sharp. Being careful of Megan's skin, she sliced through the ribbon.

Megan expelled a shaky little sigh and rubbed her wrists. "Thank you."

"Thank you," Penny said as she hugged the young woman. "You were brilliant, the way you manipulated those men."

This Megan was nothing like the miserable bride Penny had worked with on her wedding plans. But then the young woman had been grieving the love of her life. Now, knowing Gage was alive, Megan Lynch was once again the woman she must have always been, the one her father had raised her to be: strong and savvy.

Megan pulled back and humbly replied, "I just bought us some time. We need to get out of here before either or both of them return. Or worse yet, Andrea comes back with them." She shuddered with fear.

Penny shuddered, too. When she'd gone back to the bride's dressing room to help Megan downstairs to the secret passage, she'd seen the other woman lying on the floor. Andrea had radiated hatred and resentment. Penny had no doubt that she was probably the most dangerous of all the wedding crashers.

"Yes," she heartily agreed. "We need to get out of here and get help."

She was actually surprised that Nicholas hadn't arrived yet. Even if Woodrow's daughter Ellen hadn't been able to reach him, he would have been on his way to the church anyway. He had been invited. And if the men outside the church had tried turning him away, he would have known something was wrong. He knew all Penny's staff and Woodrow's agents. He wouldn't have been fooled.

Her stomach pitched as fear unsettled her. If Nick had been here, he wouldn't have left without making sure they were all right. He would have put himself in danger for them. She hoped that he hadn't. He had a baby due soon. Annalise and their unborn son needed him.

Annalise had loved the boy who'd grown up next door to her too long to lose him now, when he'd just finally admitted he'd always loved her, too.

But they needed Nick here, too. Hopefully, he had left without incident and called his brothers, her sons. Logan,

Parker and Cooper would help them. But she had to make certain they knew what was going on, that they were all in danger but no one more than Nikki.

Penny headed toward the stack of boxes. They were only being stored at the end of the hallway in order to hide the door to the secret passage to the courtyard. When the fake waiter had rummaged through them earlier, Penny had been afraid that he might see the door.

There was no way he would have left them here if he had. But he'd been worried about Andrea. When they found her and discovered that her injury wasn't serious, they would be back.

The same thing must have been on Megan's mind, because she said, "We need to hurry."

Before Penny could reach for the first box, a dark shadow dimmed the already faint light at the end of the hallway, making the glint off the metal object he held even more noticeable.

They hadn't moved fast enough. One of the gunmen had found them.

Chapter 12

The minister spoke softly and slowly. "Who gives this woman in marriage?"

Just as slowly and softly, the father of the bride replied, "I do."

Nikki hoped like hell she wouldn't have to say those words herself. She had no intention of marrying anyone. Ever. Most especially not this guy. FBI bureau chief Woodrow Lynch pulled back her veil, leaned down and kissed her cheek. Something twisted inside Nikki, making her heart twinge. Her father would never be able to do that, never be able to give her away. She drew in a shaky breath. It wasn't a big deal since she never intended to marry anyone.

And knowing now what she knew about her father, about his cheating, Nikki wasn't sure she would have wanted him to give her away even if he had been alive. He'd been dead for nearly sixteen years, though. When she'd found out about his betrayal, it had been like losing him all over again.

Woodrow stared down at her, his eyes dark with concern. For her. He had wanted to protect his daughter, but he'd made it clear, maybe more for her mother's sake than Nikki's, that he hadn't wanted to sacrifice her in order to do that. She knew that. She'd convinced him and everyone else that this was the only way to buy enough time for Megan and her mom to get out of the church.

They must have had enough time to make it to safety now. They had to be out in the courtyard where they could get help for everyone else. She nodded at Woodrow and whispered, "Go."

He had to make certain that they were safe. For some reason Gage must have thought they weren't. Or he wouldn't have staged that coughing spasm in order to slip out before she and Woodrow had even made it down the aisle to the front.

With a wink she turned away from Woodrow to focus on the front and her groom. It was the first time she had seen Richard Boersman, and disappointment washed over Nikki. But her disappointment was more with the woman she'd begun to consider a friend than with the man. How had a feisty woman like Megan ever considered marrying such a dweeb?

His face was pale, and he visibly trembled as he stood alone next to the minister. She doubted his best man would return from his coughing spasm. And now the father of the bride was slipping toward the back of the church, as well. That left her alone at the front.

Or relatively alone. The minister was secretly armed. He'd performed enough weddings at Penny's chapel to understand the value of protection. But the groom was more likely to be a hindrance than a help.

"Act like I'm Megan," she whispered to him.

But he didn't look capable of acting anything except confused and scared. Not that anyone probably would have been fooled, even if he'd been capable of an award-winning performance. Murmurs were already moving through the pews as the guests realized Nikki was merely a substitute for the real bride.

She didn't see any of the gunmen she'd spotted earlier, and yet there were replacements. A guy near the front reached beneath his jacket where she'd already noticed he had a bulge.

No, Nikki wasn't worried about having to say "I do." She was worried about not making it out of the chapel alive. If that happened, at least she wouldn't have to listen to Logan tell her *I told you so.*

Her oldest brother had never believed she had what it took to be a bodyguard. So maybe she had concocted this plan to subconsciously prove him wrong. Even if she didn't make it out alive herself, she could still prove him wrong—if Megan and Penny had made it to safety.

They had to have gotten out of the chapel unharmed. Then even if Nikki lost her life, it would have been worth it. She would have done her job.

"Gage!" Penny exclaimed as she pressed a hand over her heart. "You scared me. I thought you were one of the gunmen returning."

Gage had nearly run right into the armed waiter after he had quickly descended the stairs and rushed down the basement hallway. Luckily, he'd been able to duck into the shadows of Penny's office before the guy had noticed him. As soon as the guy was gone, Gage had retraced his steps, his heart beating fast, his hand not quite steady on his weapon. He'd dreaded what he might find: injured women or, worse yet, dead bodies.

He didn't know how he would have handled finding Megan like he'd found so many other people over the years: lifeless, staring helplessly up at him as if berating him for not making it in time, for not being able to save her…

His breath shuddered out with relief that instead he had found them untying each other and getting ready to escape. And he'd thought about just letting them go. He probably would have just let them go if Penny hadn't noticed him.

"He might be back soon," Gage warned. "So you need to leave now."

But instead of moving the boxes away from what must have been the doorway to the underground tunnel, she paused and turned to him. Her face so pale it looked almost ghostly in the dim light, Penny asked him, "What are you doing down here? You're supposed to be in the church. You're supposed to be the best man."

"We all know that's not true," he said. Richard hadn't chosen him. But more importantly, neither had Megan. "I noticed the guy with the gun was missing," he said. "The one you stopped me from pummeling earlier." Penny had been right to stop him, though. He hadn't even noticed the other guys in the church. They could have been there earlier. And he could have started a shoot-out then.

"D," Penny replied. "He calls himself D. He was down here, too, with the waiter impostor. Megan tricked him into going up to check on the woman."

"Andrea," Megan supplied.

"She's fine," Gage said.

"Exactly," Penny said. "As soon as he unties her, all hell is going to break loose."

He didn't doubt it. The woman was furious that Megan had overpowered her and that they had tied her up. Releasing her would like releasing a wild animal from confinement.

Penny moved to walk around him, but he caught her arm and stopped her. "You need to leave with Megan," he insisted, "just like we planned."

She smacked his hand like he was a boy trying to sneak a cookie from the jar before dinner. "We also planned that you would be right at the altar with my daughter, that you would protect her."

"Woodrow is up there. And the minister is armed," Gage reminded her even though he felt a twinge of guilt that he had abandoned his assigned post. "And Nikki is armed. She can protect herself."

Penny shook her head. "No, she can't. She only thinks she can."

Gage resisted the urge to laugh. Penny Payne was legendary for her almost telepathic powers, for always knowing everything about everybody but most especially about her kids. How could she not know her own daughter? How could she have no idea how strong and resourceful Nikki was?

"I'll go back up there and make sure nothing happens to her," he promised. "You leave with Megan."

But he could see that it was too late. Penny didn't trust him anymore to protect her child. Before he could stop the wedding planner, she pulled away from him and hurried down the hall.

Megan tried to pass him to follow her. But he wasn't

taking any chances with her getting away from him like Penny had. He wrapped his arms around her and held her tightly. He wasn't about to let her put her life in danger again.

Megan gasped at the sensation of being pressed against the hard length of Gage's muscular body. Even through her heavy dress, she could feel his heat. And his tension...

"We need to hurry up," she said. "We need to help."

"You need to get the hell out of here," he told her. "That was the plan. To get you to safety. That's why I came down here—to make sure the man hadn't caught you and Penny before you escaped."

"He did, but we got away—"

"Only to try to rush right back into his clutches," Gage said.

"I might be safer in his," she murmured. She hadn't meant to say the words aloud, but they'd slipped out. And now they hung in the air between them.

Gage flinched like she'd slapped him. "I don't want to hurt you," he said.

"And you told me you would never lie to me." At least that was what he'd tried to tell her when she'd broken up with him. He'd tried to convince her that he hadn't been using her to get ahead at the Bureau like she'd been warned. But she hadn't listened to him. Maybe she'd been right not to. "I know you wanted to hurt me when you first showed up in the dressing room today."

"I did," he admitted. "But that was before I knew you were in danger."

She had been in danger then—in danger of making a horrible mistake. Then again, she hadn't known that

Gage was alive. It had taken her long moments of thinking she was seeing an apparition before she'd even believed that he was real and not a figment of her wishful imagination. But if she'd conjured him up, he wouldn't have looked at her like he had, like he'd hated her.

"*You* want to hurt me," she said because she didn't believe that he'd changed his mind. She didn't believe that he would ever forgive her. "But you don't want anyone else to hurt me?"

He groaned as if overcome with frustration. Then he kissed her. His mouth slid over hers, his lips tugging gently on her bottom one before he deepened the kiss. The tip of his tongue touched hers before retreating.

Her heart pounded, and her blood heated as passion overwhelmed her. But he pulled back, just slightly, just enough for her gasp for breath.

She had tried to communicate her feelings with a kiss. Now so had he. But she didn't understand what he was trying to say any more than she suspected he had understood her. She lifted her hands and slid them between their bodies, over his chest. Her palms tingled. She wanted to touch him, but instead she pushed him back. "We need to go upstairs to help them."

"You going up into the chapel will not help anyone," he said. "It will only put you in danger, too."

"I don't care," she said. And she didn't. "Not when the person who matters most to me is in danger!"

Gage flinched. Did he think she was talking about Richard? After their kisses, could he still think she cared about another man?

"My dad," she clarified.

And Gage's head bobbed in understanding.

Her dad had been always been everything to her, both

father and mother. Nurturer. Protector. He was the one whose shoulder she'd cried on when Gage had broken her heart and when she'd thought he'd died.

Gage might have been the one who mattered most to her if she thought he could ever love her again—if he ever had.

"I can't leave if my dad's in danger," Megan said. "And you know he is. The gunmen might be here because of him, because they want revenge against him."

"They might," Gage admitted. "Or they might have a whole other agenda…"

Him? Did he think they were there because of him? But why? Why would anyone think she mattered to him? She didn't even think that, even after that confusing kiss.

"It doesn't matter why they're here," she said. "It just matters that people I care about are in danger."

"People," he murmured.

"Nikki, Mrs. Payne…" There were other guests in the church, extended family. "And Richard." Richard had never done anything to her but be her friend.

He flinched again. He obviously thought she had agreed to marry Richard for love. But all she'd wanted was family. She'd hoped having one of her own might fill the hole in her heart that losing Gage had left in it.

"And how do you think you're going to help them?" he asked as he caught her hands in his. "You don't even have your gun anymore."

"The man—D—took it," she explained, her face heating with embarrassment that he'd snapped it from her grasp so easily.

He groaned again. "By now Andrea has it back, and you're the first person she'd use it on given the chance. You need to get out of here."

She shook her head. The curly hair she always fought so hard to tame tangled around her face. "I can't." Her voice cracked. "If I lose my dad…"

She didn't know what she would do. She couldn't imagine a world without him in it when for so much of her life, he had been her and her sister's whole world. No. She couldn't lose him.

Strong arms closed around her, and Gage pressed her against his body again. His hand stroked over her back, offering comfort. "He'll be fine," he assured her. "Woodrow Lynch wouldn't be bureau chief if he hadn't been a badass agent first."

But it had been years since he'd been in the field, years since he'd fired his weapon at anything other than targets. She knew her father missed it. But he'd given it up and accepted all his promotions and desk jobs because of her and Ellen, because he had wanted to be there for them and now for his granddaughters.

"I can't *not* do anything," she murmured into Gage's chest as tears sprang to her eyes.

"You can do something," he said. "You can go through that passageway and get help."

She pulled herself, albeit reluctantly, from his arms. "Of course."

But when she turned back toward the boxes Penny had begun to move, Gage caught her arm. "No, I'm wrong. That's a bad idea. You can't go out there alone. We don't know what might be waiting for you outside."

"Help."

"Or more people with guns," he said. "If not, there would be more guests upstairs. Somebody is keeping them out."

"I'll be careful," she promised. "You need to go back upstairs. You need to help my father and Nikki."

He sighed. "And stop Penny from taking them all on alone." But he didn't release her; his hand held her wrist yet—his fingers overlapping it. He stroked his thumb across her leaping pulse.

He looked like he was thinking about kissing her again. And she wanted his kiss even now, even when she knew they were all in danger. Maybe more now because she didn't know if she would be able to kiss him ever again.

But she pushed aside her selfishness and told him, "You better go." The music had stopped some time ago. The gunmen already knew that she wasn't the bride in the church. "We have no idea what's happening up there."

But then a shot rang out, echoing from above. And they knew nothing good was happening.

Chapter 13

Crazy bitch! Derek had been incarcerated long enough that he'd forgotten how mercurial Andrea could be. He tightened his grasp on her wrist, making sure the gun stayed pointed at the domed ceiling of the church in case she tried to fire again. She struggled against him, but fortunately she wasn't that strong, thanks to the stab wound in her shoulder.

"Calm down!" he yelled at her.

Eventually her anger subsided. But the moment he relaxed his grip, she tried to point the barrel down again.

"No!" she screamed. "That bitch deserves to die!"

"It's not her," he said.

She leaned closer to the bride she'd just tried to shoot and studied her. Her brow furrowed with confusion. "It's the other one, the bridesmaid."

The young woman shook her head, tumbling her curls

around her face. "No, no, I'm the bride," she insisted. Stubbornly. Stupidly.

"Where's the real bride?" Andrea demanded to know. "She's the bitch who stabbed me!"

Derek replied, "Ralph has her and the wedding planner tied up downstairs."

"Get her!" she ordered.

And his temper flared. His grasp on her wrists tightened until she flinched. "You are not in charge," he reminded her. Maybe he'd given her too much to do, because she obviously thought she was. Unfortunately, so did most of the men she'd hired to help them. They answered more to her than they did to him. And that just wasn't going to do. Maybe he should have left her tied up.

Then again, it might not be a bad thing if she were the one to pull the trigger. Then she would be the one going down for murder. He'd only be returned to jail for escaping and to serve out the last of his sentence for armed robbery. He could claim he had no idea she'd intended to take the wedding party hostage. But even if he faced new charges of kidnapping, the sentence wouldn't be as long as for murder.

During the five years he'd already spent in prison, he had been smug, thinking that he'd gotten away with murder…until he'd seen that picture. Then the joke had been on him when he'd realized that the son of a bitch had survived.

But Derek had been careful not to betray any recognition when he'd looked at him. He didn't want the bastard to know—until it was over—that Derek had gotten his revenge. Better he have no idea what the hell was really going on.

Unfortunately, with the way Andrea was acting, Derek

wasn't certain he was entirely aware of everything going on himself. He'd been attracted to the woman because she was smart. If not for her, he wouldn't have pulled off the robberies he had all those years ago. She'd helped him then. And she'd helped him escape.

But he wasn't sure she was helping him now.

She smiled at him, though it didn't quite reach her cold eyes. She was manipulating him with that smile and with her body, which she rubbed against his. "Please, D, tell Ralph to get her. I want her up here."

And neither of them could leave the chapel now in order to retrieve her. They had just taken everyone inside hostage. He hated sending Ralph downstairs. They needed all the guns they had because as he glanced around the chapel, he realized some guys were missing.

The rough-looking blond best man was gone, as was the gray-haired father of the bride. Where the hell were they?

He wouldn't have expected either of them to leave without a fight. They didn't look like the kind of guys who ran from danger but rather into it. They had to be planning something—something that was going to raise hell with their plan.

He shook his head. "This isn't right…"

"Please get her, D," Andrea implored him. Then she lowered her voice and reminded him in a whisper, "We need her—for the plan."

He wasn't sure if they'd be able to pull off the plan anymore. But he wasn't willing to give it up yet. So he nodded at the guy dressed like a waiter. Ralph started down the aisle toward the back of the chapel.

"Thank you," she said with a smile. She'd gotten what she wanted—or she soon would.

He released her wrist. And she swung the gun right back toward the substitute bride.

"You were there, too," she said, "when that bitch attacked me."

"Andrea!" He reached for her again. But this time he wasn't sure he would be able to stop her.

Her voice shaking with fury, she yelled, "You're going to die, too!"

Gage caught Megan again before she could slip past him and race down the hall to danger. She was struggling too hard for him to hold her tightly.

"Someone's been shot!" she said. "We need to go. Now. We need to help them."

"We don't know that anyone's been shot," he pointed out. "It could just be a trick." A ruse to draw them out. He knew the tricks dangerous men played to get people to do or say what they wanted.

"Or someone could be hurt and needs our help," she argued.

"Then we'll help them," he said. "But we can't do that if we get ourselves killed first."

Megan's safety was his top priority. She was the one in the most danger, for some reason. But the reasons didn't matter at the moment. All that mattered was keeping her safe. "You can't go up there with me," he said. "You need to—"

"I'm not leaving!" she said. "I can't—not until I know…"

If she'd lost someone she loved.

But was her fear for her father or for her fiancé?

That didn't matter, either. Sure, Gage had kissed her, but he would never make the mistake of trusting her with his heart again. He wasn't sure if he should trust her at all. Maybe he needed to drag her out through that tunnel himself to make sure she escaped.

But that shot reverberated inside his head. What if it had been Nikki or Woodrow or Mrs. Payne who'd taken a bullet?

He couldn't just leave them. He wasn't even sure what awaited them in the courtyard. If there were more gunmen outside, he wouldn't be able to get help.

No, he had no backup. Just like during those six months he'd spent in captivity, he could count on no one but himself. "I'll go upstairs," he said. "But I won't be able to help anyone if I'm worried about you."

Her face paled, and she drew in a shaky breath. "Of course."

"So you'll hide," he told her. "You'll hide so well that no one will be able to find you."

She nodded as if he'd asked her a question. But there was no question about it. He wasn't leaving her if he thought she would be in any danger.

"I'll hide," she promised. "Don't worry about me." Her brow furrowed slightly, as if she didn't understand why he was worried.

Did she believe, even after his kiss, that he wanted to hurt her? Even when he'd been furious with her, he hadn't wanted her hurt. He still wanted her...

Damn, maybe those six months had conditioned him for pain—because that was all she would bring him. In order to protect himself and not reveal how vulnerable he was to her, he said, "I'm worried that your father will kill me if anything happens to you. I promised him that I would keep you safe."

She nodded as if his explanation made sense. But then she said, "You don't work for my father anymore."

Giving up the job he'd loved working for a man he'd respected had been one of the hardest things he'd ever done. Losing her had been harder.

"I work for Payne Protection," he said. But that might not be for much longer if anything had happened to Nikki or Penny. His boss wouldn't just fire him; he'd kill him. "It's my job to keep you safe."

"I'll be fine," she assured him. "I'll hide—like you said. I'll make sure nobody finds me."

He nodded and turned to leave. Before he could walk away, she grabbed his arm. Maybe she'd changed her mind; maybe she wanted him to bring her to safety.

"If you're scared, I can get you out of here," he said.

She shook her head. "I'm not scared for me."

"Of course." And she wasn't, or she wouldn't have considered going up to that chapel where Andrea probably waited for her with a loaded weapon and a pair of scissors. "You're worried about your father. And Richard." He couldn't help the resentment that slipped into his voice with that last word. She shook her head again, and that curly, sexy hair tumbled around her shoulders. She was so damn beautiful.

"I'm scared for you…" She rose up on tiptoe and pressed a kiss against his lips. He couldn't help himself; he clutched a handful of that soft hair and held her mouth against his as he deepened the kiss. Passion pooled in his stomach, knotting muscles that were already clenched with adrenaline. Finally, he pulled back. And panting for breath, he rushed down the hall. He wasn't sure now if he was running to danger or away from it.

Because he knew Megan Lynch was the greatest threat to him. No one had ever been able to cause him more pain.

An elbow jabbed his ribs. A heel stomped on his foot. A woman struggled in Woodrow's arms, too, like the gunwoman had just struggled with her partner inside the chapel.

"Let me go," she mumbled against the hand he had clamped over mouth.

"Shh," he cautioned Penny.

They couldn't afford to draw any attention to where they hid in that coatroom just off the vestibule. He had pulled her into the room with him just as she'd tried to storm into the chapel. "You can't go in there."

Bursting in there, surprising already nervous gunmen, was certain to get her shot. "It's too dangerous," he said.

Maybe he'd gotten through to her, because she finally stopped struggling. But the second he released her, she headed for the door. He caught her shoulders and dragged her back into his arms.

"You think I'm going to stand in here and watch my daughter get killed?" she asked, her body bristling with outrage while it also trembled with fear.

He held her more closely, so that he felt her furiously beating heart against his. "She's not getting killed." At least not yet.

"The guy stopped his wife from shooting her," he pointed out. And as they watched through one of the lighter colors of the stained glass window between the coatroom and the church, the guy stopped her again. "If Nikki thought she was going to shoot her, she would draw her weapon."

But she'd left it holstered beneath her dress. Of course if she'd reached for it, Woodrow doubted the man would have stopped his wife. D would have let the woman blow her away. Nikki was so smart that she would have realized that, too.

"I also have a couple of other guys in there," he said. He wasn't certain how much help the minister or Tucker Allison would be. Neither of them had reached for their weapons yet, either, and he suspected it had nothing to do with Nikki's reasons.

They were just scared. Nikki, on the other hand, was fearless. She would make a damn good agent, a far better one than Tucker. She just had to survive this damn wedding. Concern for her was why he'd stopped himself from going any further than the coatroom. He could trust Gage to make sure Megan stayed safe; he needed to protect Penny's daughter.

"I need to go in there," Penny said as she renewed her struggle, pushing her breasts against his chest, her hips against his.

He swallowed a groan. How the hell could he even think about how good she felt now? When they were all in so much danger?

"You can't go storming in there," he said. "You'll get everyone shot—most especially yourself."

"So what am I supposed to do?" she asked, her voice cracking with raw emotion. "Just let my daughter die?"

"Penny…" Her pain reached inside him, twisting his heart around in his chest. And even though he had no way of knowing if he could keep it, he promised her, "Everything will be all right."

She shook her head. "That's easy for you to say. It's

not your daughter in there." Resentment joined the fear in her voice.

"No," he agreed. "It's not my daughter in there."

"Is that why you don't want me going in there?" she asked. "You know that when they see that I got loose, they'll realize she did, too?"

Panic stole his breath for a moment. "What? You two were caught?" Of course that explained why Penny wasn't out in the courtyard. Probably neither was Megan. "You didn't get outside?"

She turned toward him, and her eyes warmed. "Megan probably is now, though. Gage would have made her go."

He expelled a slight breath. "Thank you." Even as upset as she was, she had offered him reassurance. She was that sweet a woman.

But then her resentment returned as she turned away and peered through the stained glass window. "I never should have let Nikki act as a decoy."

"Our children don't always do what we want them to," he said. "Or what we think is best." And as he said it, his stomach lurched, because he knew Megan wasn't out in the courtyard.

Megan wasn't safe yet.

While Penny was focused on the chapel, Woodrow studied the door from the coatroom into the vestibule. He wasn't worried about anyone discovering them. The guy dressed like a waiter walked right past the room without glancing once in their direction.

Gage nearly passed, too, until Woodrow jerked him inside and demanded to know, "Why the hell did you leave her?"

"We heard the shot," Gage said. "And she wanted me to make sure you were all right."

Dread churned Woodrow's stomach. She wouldn't have left, then. She would be waiting somewhere, waiting to find out how he was. Or worse yet, knowing his loving daughter, she was probably on her way up the stairs to check herself because she had never trusted Gage.

Apparently, Woodrow shouldn't have trusted him, either.

Chapter 14

Megan tilted her head and listened. She could hear no sounds emanating from above the storage area where she stood frozen with fear and indecision. The chapel was almost eerily silent after that one startling gunshot.

Who had been shot? Or was it just like Gage suspected, a trick to draw them out? But it had only drawn out him—at her urging. Had she sent Gage alone into danger?

And worse yet, she hadn't told him how she felt about him. What if something happened and he never knew?

She'd spent those six months thinking that she'd missed her opportunity to let him know how much he really meant to her. And that last argument had echoed inside her head all those long months.

"I know you were just using me, trying to get ahead with my father," she'd said. "But that's okay. I was just using you, too."

"You were using me?" he'd asked. And his obvious surprise had made her angrier. She'd figured he'd thought her too ugly and stupid to be able to use anyone. But now she wondered if he hadn't just been confused.

"I used you for sex," she'd explained. "I knew you really didn't want a chubby, unattractive girl like me..." Or she'd thought she should have known. It had taken a few people pointing it out to her before she'd realized and accepted that a man like him would never want a woman like her unless he was getting something else out of it.

Like a quick promotion...

"Megan." He'd murmured her name and reached for her, like he'd intended to comfort her.

She'd jerked away, unable to let him touch her when she'd been hurting so badly. And out of that pain, she'd hurled those hateful words at him. "I never really loved you."

Only with her whole heart. But she'd lied, out of pain and wounded pride. Even then she'd seen that it had hurt him.

"Why?" she murmured.

Why would it have hurt him if he hadn't cared about her, if he'd only been using her? Wouldn't he have just laughed off her declaration like it hadn't mattered? He'd gotten the promotion he'd wanted—or she'd been told he'd wanted it. But if that was all he'd wanted, then why had he quit? Why had he walked away from a job he'd been willing to do anything—even romance her—to get ahead in?

Unless he hadn't been using her...

Unless he really had cared, maybe even really loved her. And she'd tossed that love back at him, unwilling to accept that it was real and that he'd been telling the truth. She'd wounded not only his pride but his heart as well.

Was that why he had reenlisted and put his life in danger? Because of her?

Just like he'd done now. He'd put his life in danger again because she'd asked him to check on the others. If anything happened to him… Guilt and fear overwhelmed her. It was a miracle he'd survived. She shouldn't have convinced him to tempt fate again.

She turned toward the boxes that Penny had begun to move. The door to the secret passageway was back there. She had promised Gage that she wouldn't risk going outside alone in case there were more gunmen in the courtyard. If only she hadn't lost Andrea's gun. Or even the scissors she'd used to stab the other woman. Maybe Mrs. Payne had something in her office that Megan could use as a weapon. Knowing Mrs. Payne and the fact that all of her children were bodyguards, maybe she even had a real weapon that Megan could use.

It was still eerily quiet upstairs. No more gunshots had rung out. So Gage hadn't fired at anyone or been fired at, unless someone had used Andrea's gun with the silencer on the barrel.

If that gun had been used, they all might be dead. Pain and panic gripped her heart over the thought of losing the men she loved: her father and Gage. Or the women she'd already come to care about: Penny and Nikki. She wasn't certain who else was in the chapel, who else could be in danger. She needed to know, so if she found a weapon, she would definitely head upstairs to help the others.

She hurried down the hall to Mrs. Payne's office. Despite living in Chicago, she had made the trip to the wedding planner several times, not because she'd wanted everything to be perfect but because Mrs. Payne had given her something she'd never had.

Sure, Dad had tried. He'd been the best mother he could be. But he was no Penny Payne. He wasn't capable of giving her the maternal understanding and female perspective that Penny had.

That was why she'd kept making the trip to meet with the wedding planner. So she knew which door opened off the hallway into Mrs. Payne's office. Before she could close her hand over the knob, someone grabbed her arm.

Even before she looked up, she knew it wasn't Gage. Her skin wasn't tingling. But her heart was racing. With fear. The man's grip was punishing.

"How the hell did you get free?" he asked her, his voice gruff with anger. He glanced down the hallway. "Where's the other woman?"

"I don't know." Megan breathed a slight sigh of relief. At least *he* hadn't caught Mrs. Payne. That didn't mean that she hadn't been caught, just as Megan had been caught.

"Where are you taking me?" she asked as he dragged her along the hall. His fingers pinched her arm, hurting her. But she held in a cry of pain.

He gave her an almost pitying glance. "I'm taking you to Andrea."

And Megan knew what that meant. He was taking her to her death.

As if he had a noose tied around his neck again, Gage couldn't breathe. There was too heavy a pressure on his chest, too much panic.

His gun drawn, he started forward, but a strong arm caught him and hauled him into a room down the hall from where the gunman had caught Megan outside Penny's office. Gage knew several ways that he could have broken that arm and the man to whom it belonged. But he knew it was Woodrow. So he didn't fight him.

"Shh," Woodrow cautioned him.

Needlessly. Gage knew how to be quiet. His life had depended on it. Now Megan's life depended on it. If the gunman realized he wasn't alone, he would kill her. Immediately. Before they had a chance to rescue her.

Gage shouldn't have left her. He should have known that she wouldn't hide. She wouldn't protect herself, not when she was so worried about her father.

Probably about Richard as well.

And knowing her, Penny and Nikki, too.

"We can't let him get her upstairs," Penny said, her voice soft but cracking with panic. "That woman will kill her for certain." She hadn't wanted to leave the chapel where her daughter was being held. But she'd been concerned about Megan. And Woodrow had insisted that they all stick together. There was safety in numbers.

Gage only needed the guy to get a little closer to him. Then he would act. He would do what he'd learned in the Marines—what had saved his life.

Megan struggled with the guy, fighting against the hand gripping her arm. The guy was big and he had to be hurting her. But she betrayed no pain. Only fear, her dark eyes wide with it. She knew, too, that if he delivered her to Andrea, she wouldn't live long.

Until that day Megan had broken his heart, Gage had had no idea how feisty she could be. She'd always been so sweet and loving with him. Then she had told him that she'd never loved him at all. And she must not have, otherwise, how could she have believed he'd only been using her? Why had she listened to that resentful Tucker? Why had she believed the petulant young agent over Gage?

Of course he had realized today that she hadn't known him any better than he'd known her. He had never guessed the depths of her strength. He saw it now as she continued to struggle with the man.

When the guy raised his hand to strike her, Gage started forward, but Woodrow held him back again. How could he let his own daughter get hurt?

Megan cringed in anticipation of the blow, but it didn't come.

The man tensed. Then Gage heard what Woodrow had heard—the crackle of static. As the guy reached for the walkie-talkie in his pocket, Megan pulled from his grasp and ran.

She was definitely stronger than he'd known. Was she fast enough to get to the secret passageway?

Gage moved to step into the hall again, but Woodrow held on to him, motioning for him to be quiet as a female voice emanated from the walkie-talkie.

"Ralph, did you get her?"

"Yeah, Andrea, yeah, I did," he quickly replied. He obviously feared the woman.

So did Gage. He'd already seen the hatred in her cold eyes.

"Then why haven't you brought her up here yet?" she demanded.

"I'll—uh—be up in a little while," he nervously stammered. "I'm—uh—just having a problem with the wedding planner." The problem obviously being that he had no idea where she was.

Fortunately, he was completely unaware that she was only a few steps away from him.

"Don't waste your time with her," Andrea replied. "The bride's the one we want."

And there was something ominous in her tone, something that insinuated she didn't just want Megan for revenge for the stabbing.

Megan was the key to whatever the hell their plan was.

Derek snapped the walkie-talkie out of Andrea's hand like he had snapped her gun out of the bride's hand. He couldn't believe Andrea had lost her weapon, that she had been overpowered.

Andrea flinched and glared at him.

Where was the love she'd professed when she had visited him regularly at the prison? He wasn't certain he could trust her now.

But she had helped him escape, and she had planned how to crash the wedding. She was the reason the plan had gone awry, though. She never should have forced her way into the bride's dressing room. Maybe the bride had been about to back out of getting married. There could have been another way to convince her than threatening her with a gun, one she'd lost in a struggle anyway. Then once Derek had freed her, Andrea had rushed into the chapel and fired his gun, the one without the silencer.

He pressed the button on the walkie-talkie for the man in charge of the reinforcements posted outside. Once the guy answered, he asked, "Do you see any sign of police?"

Someone must have reported the shot. The police would have to send at least one car to investigate. So he didn't have much time now, not if he wanted to avoid going back to prison.

"Not police," the guy replied, "but the landscaping crew showed up."

"Landscaping crew?"

"Yeah," the guy replied with a mixture of confusion and amusement, "a bunch of guys that all look alike. Gotta be a family business."

"Did you turn them away?"

"Yeah, I told them the wedding couldn't be disrupted." Not any more than it had already been.

Derek had thought about pulling a guy off perimeter duty to help him inside the church. But he had an uneasy feeling about the landscaping crew. If the wedding planner was as legendary as the blond guy had mentioned, why would she have scheduled a crew, with mowers and Weed eaters that could have disrupted the service, during a wedding?

She wouldn't have. That damn sure hadn't been a landscaping crew that had showed up.

"Don't let anyone near," he cautioned the guy.

"That's what Andrea told us."

Derek clicked off the radio.

"What's wrong?" Andrea asked.

Everything. But he just shook his head. "We need to get out of here."

"Ralph's bringing up the real bride," she said.

"If she's the only one you want," the substitute bride said, "can't you let the rest of us go?"

Andrea pointed her gun at the petite brunette. "You're not going anywhere!"

"That's fine," she replied without fear. "But what about the rest of the guests?"

Derek shook his head. "Nobody's going anywhere." If the police showed up, as he suspected they soon would thanks to Andrea's gunfire, he would need hostages.

He saw that realization in the brunette's eyes. Despite switching places with the real bride, she was smart. Maybe too smart…and way too courageous. He narrowed his eyes and studied her.

Who or what was she really?

"We need to search everyone," he said. "Make sure nobody's armed." He knew at least two men were: the best man and the father of the bride.

Where the hell were they? A movement in one of the pews drew his attention. Sunlight shining through the stained glass windows glinted off metal. Instincts kicking in, he turned and fired—once, twice, three times…

But he had Andrea's gun—with the silencer. No shots were heard. Only screams as the hostages reacted.

"Anybody else want to be a hero?" he asked as he swung his gun around, looking for any other shooters. At least nobody else had drawn a weapon. The bride started forward, though, trying to push past him. He shoved her back hard enough that she fell onto the floor.

Certain Andrea wouldn't let her move again, he started down the aisle to where the guy had fallen out of his pew onto the white paper runner which was now spattered with his blood. He leaned down and grabbed the gun the guy had dropped without ever having fired. The barrel was warm and slick with his sweat. He must have been holding it for a while, waiting for the opportunity to use it.

He should have waited longer. But the guy was young, probably early twenties or maybe older and he just looked like a kid. He moaned and shifted on the ground. Derek kicked his side, and the kid cried out.

"Who are you?" Derek demanded to know.

But the young man was too hurt to talk, his consciousness slipping away as the pain overwhelmed him.

Derek leaned down and patted his pockets. He found a billfold and pulled it out. It wasn't a wallet. It was a badge with credentials. He cursed.

Andrea, unwilling to the let the fake bride out of her sight, dragged her down the aisle with her as she hurried to Derek's side. "What? What is it?"

"He's an FBI agent." He'd just shot, probably mortally, an FBI agent. If the guy died, Derek wouldn't just go back to jail; he'd go to the electric chair.

"Why are you surprised?" the substitute bride asked as she dropped to her knees next to the young agent. She checked his wounds. Derek had hit him in the shoulder and the side. If he hadn't hit any organs, the kid might live if he didn't bleed out.

"Why wouldn't I be surprised?" he asked, although he noticed that Andrea wasn't. She hadn't reacted at all to the presence of a federal agent.

"If you somehow hadn't stopped guests from coming into the church," the young woman replied, "this place would have been crawling with FBI agents."

Alarm gripped Derek. "What? Why?"

She wadded the kid's jacket against his side and secured it there with his belt. Was she an EMT or an FBI agent, too?

She glanced up at Derek, and a slight smile curved her lips. "The father of the bride is Chief Special Agent Woodrow Lynch. Every agent in the Chicago Bureau was invited to his daughter's wedding."

In his mind, Derek heard the buzz of the cell door as it opened and then whistled closed behind him. He was going back to prison. That hadn't been part of the plan— at least not his plan. This felt like a trap. He glared at Andrea.

And she stepped back. "D—"

No. He wasn't going back to prison.

He would die first, but he damn well wasn't going out alone. He would take everyone in the whole damn chapel straight to hell with him.

Chapter 15

"The bride's the one we want." The words ringing in her ears, Megan ran for her life. The heavy dress hampered her movements. She tripped on the train and nearly fell, catching herself against the stone wall. The rough stone scraped her palms, but she held in a cry of pain.

The man wasn't running after her. He probably thought she was trapped in the dead end of the hallway. The hallway was her best chance of escaping, if she could find the door to the secret passageway.

She began knocking down boxes, hopeful she would find the door and be able to get inside before the guy caught her again. Her breath shuddered out as she discovered the wooden frame. She shoved the last box aside and reached for the door handle just as a shadow blocked her already faint light.

"What the hell is that?" the man asked.

Megan sucked in the breath she'd expelled and turned to face him. "N-nothing…"

"It's something," the man said. "Where does the door go?"

To freedom. To help. Both of those were eluding Megan now.

He pushed her aside and shoved open the door to see for himself. Peering into the dark hole behind the door, he remarked, "It's a tunnel. Is that where the wedding planner went?"

If only she had…

Megan nodded. "Yes. She's getting help."

He laughed off her bluff. "All she's going to get is killed. The church is surrounded with our guys. Andrea thought of everything. Nobody's getting inside this place and nobody's leaving."

"What do you want?" Megan asked. "Why are you doing this?"

The guy shrugged. "I don't know, lady. I just do what I'm paid to do."

"What are you paid to do?" she asked. "Kill? How much do you charge for that?"

He just glared at her.

"It can't be enough," she answered her own question. "Not enough to risk your freedom. To risk your life."

He shook his head. "Knock it off. You're not getting to me again."

She had to—it was her only chance of escaping him. "I won't have to get to you," she said. "The police will be here soon."

He snorted. "There's no way you were able to contact them. Andrea jammed the cell signal."

Of course Andrea had. Damn the bitch.

Megan offered him a condescending smile. "I heard that gunshot down here. You don't think anyone else heard it and reported it?"

His throat moved as he swallowed. And he tilted his head, as if listening for sirens.

Megan thought she'd heard screams just a little while ago, while she'd been running. She'd thought they might have been her own. She'd wanted to scream. Now she wanted to cry.

The guy shrugged again. "If the cops are coming, then we damn well better hurry."

"Yes," she agreed. "Let's you and I go out through the secret passage. Let's get out of here!"

He snorted. "Lady, that would get me killed for sure. if I double-crossed Andrea."

"Please, don't do this," she implored to his conscience, hoping that he had one. "You know if you bring me upstairs, Andrea will kill me."

"I don't care what she does to you."

Megan did, and she wasn't going to make it easy for him to do his job. Remembering another one of the games her father had taught her and Ellen—deadweight—she dropped to the floor.

"Get up!" he yelled at her. "Get the hell off the ground!" With his hand not holding the gun, he reached for her. Even though she lay flat on the concrete, he got his hand in her hair.

Tears streamed from Megan's eyes as the guy fisted his fingers in her hair and pulled. It hurt like hell, but she refused to budge until he pointed the gun right at her head. "Get up or I'll blow you away right here."

"But Andrea—"

"Andrea wants you dead," he said. "I'll just save her

the trouble of pulling the trigger. I'll kill you right here."
And he cocked the gun.

Megan closed her eyes and waited for the gunshot.

The barrel was so damn close to her head Gage was
worried that the gun might accidentally go off. But he had
no choice. If he did nothing, the guy would pull the trigger and kill her—right in front of him. And he couldn't
let that happen.

He moved quickly like he'd been taught in Special
Forces. The guy never heard or saw him coming. He
probably didn't feel a thing as Gage slid his arm around
his neck, caught his chin in his hand and twisted. He
heard the telltale snap. And the guy went limp in his
arms. Gage let his lifeless body slide down to the floor—
next to Megan.

Startled, she opened her eyes. Staring into the dead
face of her assailant, she let out a soft cry of surprise
and fear. Was she afraid of the man? Or would she be
afraid of Gage because of what he'd done? Of how easily he'd killed?

She turned toward him, and the fear left her dark eyes,
which widened with surprise. He extended his hand to
her, wondering if she'd take it after how he'd just used
it. But her hand closed over his. She pulled herself to her
feet before he could even help her.

And she threw her arms around his neck, clinging
to him. "Thank you!" she exclaimed. "Thank you! You
saved my life."

Before he could close his arms around her, she pulled
away. "But you shouldn't have come back," she said. "You
should be helping upstairs." Then her face paled, and she

began to tremble. Maybe it was shock. Her voice cracking, she asked, "Was it my dad? Was that who was shot?"

Gage had nearly forgotten about that gunshot—the reason she'd convinced him to go upstairs and leave her in the first place.

Before he could answer and ease her fears, another man replied, "I'm okay, sweetheart."

And Megan dodged around Gage to throw herself into her father's arms. "Are you really?" she asked. "You didn't get hurt?"

"No, no," he assured her. "I'm fine. But I'll be better when Gage gets you out of here." Over her head, Woodrow met Gage's gaze. There was so much in his expression: gratitude that Gage had saved her but also recrimination that he hadn't already gotten her to safety.

Guilt churned in Gage's empty stomach.

He wasn't the only one feeling guilty. It was on Megan's pale face when she tremulously asked, "Was it Nikki? Did she get shot?"

"No," Woodrow said. "Nobody got shot. Andrea fired one into the ceiling. That was all."

That had been all. They had no way of knowing what had happened since they'd come downstairs. A few moments ago, Gage had thought he'd heard the faint echo of screams, like someone had briefly opened a door to hell.

After the captivity he'd endured, Gage knew exactly what hell sounded like, the fear and pain of tormented souls. He didn't want the hostages in the chapel to have to endure the torture he had.

They had to rescue them.

But how? If the guy had been telling Megan the truth, it wasn't safe to slip out of the church, either. They were

outnumbered and surrounded. But then, he'd been outnumbered and surrounded before and had survived.

"I'm the one Andrea wants," Megan said.

Her father offered a grim nod. "Yes, you are. That's
why Gage needs to get you out of here."

Megan shook her head. "No, that's why I'm not leaving."

And Gage knew that the real threat to his safety wasn't
outside. It was her—as it had always been. Worrying
about her and fighting her stubbornness would kill him
faster than any gunshot.

Penny's hand shook as she fumbled with the walkie-
talkie. It wasn't the one Gage had taken off the man he'd
killed. It was one of hers. She took another from the glass
cabinet hidden behind the bookshelf in her office. Then
she turned and passed it across her desk.

Woodrow fiddled with the one the fake waiter had
used. He was careful to not press any buttons that might
connect him with the gunmen in the chapel.

She was surprised that they hadn't called again. That
Andrea wasn't wondering why Ralph hadn't brought
Megan up to her yet.

Because he was dead.

She hadn't seen it happen, but she'd known when Gage
and Woodrow and Megan had joined her in her office
that it had. Gage had been grim. Woodrow had been relieved. And Megan...

She was in shock. Her face pale, her body trembling.
She leaned against Gage, maybe consciously, maybe subconsciously seeking his warmth and strength and protection.

Penny glanced around her office. It was big enough

that it wasn't cramped with the four of them in it. She often hosted entire wedding parties in the space, so it was spread out. In addition to the desk she had a conference table and chairs and a couch against one of the walls.

Megan sat there now with Gage beside her, hovering protectively as if he thought someone might try to take her right in front of him.

Then someone nearly had.

She didn't know how Woodrow had handled it. How he'd watched that man threaten and hurt his daughter and not only not reacted himself, but he hadn't allowed Gage to react, either. That took a kind of patience and faith she didn't possess.

When she'd heard that shot earlier, Penny had rushed upstairs without even stopping to grab a weapon. She turned back to her open glass cabinet and pulled out one now. Years ago her husband had taught her to shoot, and then she had taught their sons.

She could help Nikki. If it wasn't already too late…

She'd heard screams earlier. Just because she hadn't heard a gunshot didn't mean there hadn't been one. A gun wasn't the only weapon that could kill someone. Megan had wounded the evil Andrea with a pair of scissors. Maybe she'd avenged her injury with another pair.

Penny waited for it, for that connection she had with all her children to let her know if Nikki was hurt. Or worse…

But her connection with Nikki had never been as strong as her connection with her sons. Or even with Nicholas Rus, her husband's illegitimate son. She could feel their anxiety and fear—even now.

Especially now.

She knew they knew that the wedding guests had been

taken hostage. They were no doubt working on a plan to save them without getting them killed.

Ordinarily, Nikki would have tried to be part of that plan. The boys would have excluded her for her protection. That might have been Penny's fault more than theirs. They probably knew that she'd never wanted her daughter working as a bodyguard.

She'd wanted Nikki to work with her—as a wedding planner. But working in the chapel had put Nikki in more danger than she'd ever been in as a bodyguard.

Woodrow's hand closed over hers and gently squeezed. "We'll rescue her. We'll figure out a way to get her safely out of the chapel."

She couldn't trust him. He wasn't telling her the truth, only what he thought she wanted to hear. And maybe she did want to hear lies—empty assurances that Nikki was all right. Nikki was Nikki.

Her fearlessness and her sassy mouth were her worst enemies. They always put her in danger, and now they might get her killed. But that wouldn't be Nikki's fault. That would be Penny's. She never should have enlisted her daughter's help.

She'd meddled so often in her kids' lives that it was second nature to her. This time her meddling might have gotten her daughter killed.

Chapter 16

Nikki's arm hurt from everyone grabbing it and dragging her along. At least Andrea had dragged her down the aisle toward the wounded agent.

What the hell had the young man been thinking? He'd pulled his gun so quickly that neither she nor the minister had had a chance to draw their weapons before Derek had fired. If they'd drawn their guns then, Andrea and the other two armed guys would have shot them.

She hadn't been able to do anything to prevent the shooting. But she'd tried her best to treat his wounds. Despite her limited first aid training, she had done everything she could for him before D had dragged her back up to the altar.

She wished he would have left her near the kid, so she could make sure they didn't lose him. Not that she could do anything else for him. She'd already pleaded her case for them to get him medical attention.

Andrea had laughed at her. "Do you think I'm an idiot?"

Nikki had laughed then, which had earned her another slap across the face. She tasted blood on her lip then licked it away as if it was nothing.

And it was in comparison to what they could do, to what they would do once they had Megan in the chapel. Maybe it wouldn't come to that, though. She'd heard the outside guy on the walkie-talkie with D.

That landscaping crew that all looked alike...

It had to be her brothers. The three of them—four with Nick—could have been quadruplets. They looked that much alike. Sure, the outside gunmen had turned them away, but they would find another way inside. They wouldn't give up.

And neither would she.

Beside her the groom sniffled. Irritated, she glanced over at him. He wasn't the only one crying in the church. But he wasn't crying for the kid that had probably lost his life, he was crying for himself.

To get him to shut up, Nikki murmured, "Don't worry. We're going to be okay." Her brothers would rescue her the same way they always had. And instead of dreading it, she almost looked forward to Logan's *I told you so*.

"What about Megan?" he asked anxiously. "Do you think she's okay?"

Maybe he really loved his bride. Nikki nodded. "Yes."

"But you heard them on the walkie-talkie—the guy they sent to get her had had her."

Nikki smiled, splitting her lip open again. "If he had her, they'd already be up here."

Richard's face flushed. "But what happened?"

She could only guess. "Gage and Woodrow."

A gasp of shock slipped out of Richard's lips. Had he forgotten about his best man and the father of the bride?

Nikki hadn't. She was counting on them. But of course she knew their primary focus was Megan, as it should be.

"They would die before either of them would let something happen to her," Nikki said. "She will be okay."

For a moment Nikki envied the other woman. Unlike Megan, Nikki had no father to protect her. No old lover to jump to her defense. But she did have her brothers, and she had no doubt they would get inside the chapel. She just hoped they made it in time.

The woman approached again and swung the barrel of her long gun toward Nikki's face. "What are you talking about?" she asked.

Nikki shrugged. "I'm trying to convince him it isn't bad luck to have our wedding hijacked."

"This is not your wedding," the woman said impatiently. "You were not the one in the gown when I went into the bride's dressing room."

Nikki shrugged. "I'm in the gown now." The gown she'd vowed never to wear. But knowing what it meant to her mother, she'd been careful to get no blood on it when she'd tended to the wounded agent.

Derek had joined them, his gun trained on her, as if he considered her the greatest threat.

She felt a flash of pride. But of everyone left in the church, she probably was, and he didn't even know she was armed. The agent drawing his gun had distracted D from searching all the other guests. He had visually inspected everyone, though. But he couldn't see her weapon, strapped to her thigh beneath her dress.

"Who are you?" he asked her.

"Nikki Payne," she answered honestly. She didn't

admit to being a bodyguard. Instead she said, "My mom owns the wedding chapel."

He snorted. "I doubt providing a bride is one of her services."

Nikki chuckled. "You'd be surprised."

His eyes narrowed into cold slits, he studied her face as he had earlier. "Oh, I am…"

And he shot a glance at Andrea. He had apparently realized that he didn't know his partner any better than he knew Nikki. "Why did you really switch places with the bride?"

Nikki nodded toward his lady friend. "Because of her." A muscle twitched along his cheek as he clenched his jaw. He was angry with Andrea—maybe angry enough that Nikki could drive a wedge between them. "I know she intends to hurt Megan."

Andrea laughed. "Hurt? You have no idea."

"Why?" Nikki asked. Because of Woodrow? She doubted that or Derek wouldn't have been surprised when he had learned the father of the bride was an FBI bureau chief.

No. Whatever they wanted had nothing to do with Woodrow Lynch.

Gage?

She turned back toward the sniveling groom. Had he put his bride in danger? She nearly laughed at the thought. It was more likely the other way around. Megan must have made enemies of her own.

"They want me," Megan said as guilt overwhelmed her. She never should have agreed to Nikki Payne taking her place. She never should have put anyone else in danger like that, no matter how much Nikki had insisted she could handle it.

What would they do to her when the fake waiter didn't deliver Megan like they were expecting? Would they do to her whatever they had intended to do to Megan?

Torture her? Kill her?

Nikki wasn't the only one in danger—the other guests were, too. Just because they hadn't heard any more shots didn't mean some hadn't been fired. Andrea's gun had a silencer.

Shivering with fear for what might have already happened, she said, "I need to go up there."

The others stared at her as if she'd lost her mind. Her father shook his head.

"Maybe they would leave," she said. And then everyone else would be safe.

"They probably would leave," Gage agreed, "either with you—or after they kill you."

She shivered again despite the warmth emanating from his body so close to hers on that couch in Penny's office. Until then she hadn't realized that she'd been leaning against him. Pride had her stiffening her backbone and pulling away from him.

"We're not going to let anything happen to you," her father assured her.

"What about everyone else?" she asked. Her concern wasn't for herself, not anymore. When she'd broken up with Gage all she had worried about was getting hurt, and because of her selfishness, she'd hurt someone else.

She had hurt Gage. And even if he was able to forgive her, she wasn't certain she would ever be able to forgive herself.

"We're working on a plan," Woodrow told her.

She loved her father and appreciated how protective he'd always been, but even so, he hadn't been able to stop her and Ellen from getting hurt. They'd been heartbroken when they'd lost their mother. Maybe that was why he had gone overboard, spoiling and coddling them.

She bristled now at his almost dismissive tone. Her father had treated her like a child long enough.

"No," she told him. "I'm part of this, too. You're not excluding me."

"That's why I'm excluding you," Woodrow said. "Because it's all about you…"

Her stomach lurched. Feeling like she might be sick, Megan jumped up and ran for the door.

"Megan!" her father called after her, his voice sharp with alarm.

She didn't want him to follow her. But she knew that someone had. And she knew who before she even turned around to face him. Instead she stared down at the body lying at the end of the hallway.

Gage had done that. He'd killed a man, for her. To protect her.

It had to stop. The danger. The death. It had to stop.

"You have to let me go," she told him.

His breath shuddered out in a ragged sigh. "I would like nothing more…"

His heart pounding with fear, Woodrow started after his daughter. "Stop," a soft voice said. Penny's voice was as delicate sounding as she was delicate looking. She wasn't strong. Physically.

Emotionally and mentally he suspected he had met no one stronger than she was. Sure, he'd had to stop her from charging into the chapel to save her daughter earlier. But she'd summoned control now. Control that awed him.

"I have to stop her," he said. "She's going to run up there and offer herself as a sacrifice. I can't let her do that."

He flinched as he realized what he'd said. He heard his own hypocrisy.

"You won't let your daughter do what you let mine?" she asked, her voice sharp now with bitterness.

He turned around and reached for her, his hands closing over her shoulders. "I'm sorry."

"It's too late now," she said.

He knew she was right. It was too late—for whatever they might have had between them. He'd destroyed any chance he might have had with her, if she ever would have given him a chance. Everyone thought she'd never remarried because she was still in love with her late husband. Just like everyone thought Woodrow was still in love with his late wife.

He figured the same thing that had held him back had probably held Penny back. Fear. He hadn't wanted to get hurt again. He suspected neither had she.

But he had hurt her.

"The damage is done," she continued. "My daughter has already been taken hostage."

"Your daughter is a trained and armed bodyguard," he reminded her. "Nikki's tough. She's strong. And more importantly, she's smart." Even though she was fearless, she would be careful. "She's like her mother."

Woodrow had never met a more impressive woman than Penny Payne. She was as brilliant as she was beautiful. He'd thought so on the other occasions they'd met, at the weddings of his agents. That was why he'd reached out to her for Megan's wedding.

Maybe he'd even used it as an excuse to see her again. It wasn't as if he'd really wanted Megan to marry Richard. But he'd thought marrying her friend might keep her safer than risking her heart again.

He'd never imagined how wrong it would all go...

"Megan's not like you," he said.

"No," Penny agreed. "She's like you."

He wished she was. But she wasn't his. Not biologically. When he hadn't been around to pay attention to his young wife, she'd sought attention from other men. Blaming himself, Woodrow had forgiven her, and he loved the daughter she'd made with another man as if that daughter was his own.

Penny had to realize that Megan wasn't really his. She'd mentioned how Megan had showed her a picture of his late wife. His youngest daughter looked nothing like him or like her mother. She must have looked like her biological father, whoever he was.

"You've taught her well," Penny said. "She's every bit as strong and smart as you are. She also has your over-developed sense of responsibility."

He groaned, but he didn't argue. Even though she didn't have any of his DNA, Megan was more like him than his biological daughter. Because Megan knew they wanted her, she would go—she would give up her life for the lives of others.

He turned back to the door. "I have to stop her."

"Gage already has," Penny assured him. "He would never let her put herself in harm's way."

That was true. Despite everything he'd been through,

or maybe because of it, Gage was the best man to protect Megan. And Penny.

"When they come back," he said. If they came back…

Maybe Gage had already dragged her out through the passageway. He'd never seen a man as tormented as Gage had been, watching the fake waiter threaten Megan. He'd been more upset than Woodrow—because Woodrow had known they would save her.

"You and Megan will leave through the passageway," he said, "just like we originally planned."

She snorted. And he knew why. They hadn't stuck to the original plan.

"Gage and I will go back upstairs," he promised. "We'll rescue Nikki and the others."

She shook her head. "No. We tried your plan," she said. "It didn't work. We'll switch to my plan now." She grabbed a bag and filled it with the guns and walkie-talkies she'd put on her desk.

"Penny!" He reached for her, trying to stop her as she passed him on her way to the door. "What the hell do you think you're doing?"

He could imagine her trying to pull a Dirty Harry or a Rambo, taking on all the gunmen by herself. For her daughter, she would do anything—except trust him. She would never forgive him for not making sure Nikki stayed safe.

"I'm going to end this," she said. "It's gone on long enough. It's time to take back my chapel." Her voice cracked with emotion. "And save my child."

And his heart ached. "You intend to do that alone?"

She shook her head. Tears glistening in her eyes, she admitted, "I can't…"

He suspected it was the hardest admission Penny

Payne had ever made. She was fiercely independent and protective of her family.

"I will help you," he promised her. He only hoped that they wouldn't be too late.

What had happened to the substitute bride when the fake waiter hadn't brought up Megan as they'd ordered?

Had they already killed Nikki in her place?

Chapter 17

"I wish I could let you go," Gage admitted. But he'd held on to her since that first day they'd met in her father's house. Even after she'd dumped him and broken his heart, he hadn't been able to let her go. During all those months of captivity, he'd been tortured more by her than by anything his captors had done to him.

He'd been tortured by memories of her, of her shy smile. Of how it brightened her eyes before curving her lips. He'd been tortured by memories of her hair, curling wildly down to her shoulders as it was now that it had freed itself from the knot into which she usually bound it. He'd remembered how it had felt against his skin, how her skin had felt against his...

Like warm silk.

His body hardened and heated with desire. He wanted her. He'd wanted her then. And he wanted her now.

"You can let me go," she said.

But he ignored her comment, and despite the heavy dress, he swung her up easily in his arms and carried her toward Penny's open door. Penny and Woodrow had left, probably for the chapel. Andrea and D would be wondering why Ralph hadn't brought up Megan yet.

They would know something had gone wrong. And they might react by getting rid of the hostages.

Penny's arsenal of guns and the walkie-talkies was gone, too. She'd emptied her secret closet, which stood open like her door had. She and Woodrow had gun power. But they needed him, too. They must have thought he'd stopped Megan and gotten her to safety. He needed to bring her to that secret passage where no one could find her.

But he was torn. She felt so good in his arms, against his body that ached for hers.

"You have to let me go," she murmured as he laid her down on the couch they'd been sitting on moments ago.

He shook his head. "I tried…" And he followed her down, covering her squirming body with his.

She moved beneath him, her breasts pushing against his chest, her hips against his. But then a soft moan slipped from her lips. "Gage…"

She tensed.

He forced himself to draw in a breath. But it didn't ease his desire. He could smell her now, the sweet scent that was hers alone. He could almost taste her, too.

"I've been wanting to ask you something," she said. And the shyness he'd known and loved was back in her husky voice.

"What?" What might she want to know? She could

probably tell, from the erection straining against his dress pants, that he still wanted her.

"Did you reenlist because of me?"

The question caught him off guard, and he wasn't certain how to answer. He didn't want to make her feel guilty or bad. It wouldn't do any good. It wouldn't change what had already happened.

"You promised that you would never lie to me," she reminded him.

"Yes," he agreed. "But you didn't believe me."

"I should have," she admitted. She stared up at him with tears glistening in her eyes. "I'm sorry."

He closed his eyes, unable to bear the beauty and the guilt on her face. "Megan…"

"Tell me," she prompted him. "Tell me the truth you promised me. Did you quit the Bureau and reenlist because of me?"

He had promised her honesty, and he had broken none of his promises—no matter what she had believed at the time. He wouldn't break any now, either. He opened his eyes and focused on her beautiful face. "Yes."

She gasped as if he'd struck her. "I had hoped that it wasn't my fault."

"It wasn't," he said. "You didn't tell me to do it. It was my choice."

"To leave a job you loved?"

"I didn't love it as much…" As he'd loved her.

Hell, he still loved her. That was why he had to stay away from her. He had nothing to offer her anymore.

The tears glistening in her eyes spilled over, sliding down her cheeks. He wiped them away with his thumbs.

"I'm so sorry," she murmured. "I was such a fool. I never should have listened to what people were saying."

"People?" He hadn't realized anyone but Tucker Allison had thought that he'd been using her.

"Tucker wasn't the only one," she admitted.

"Who else?" he asked. Had his friends betrayed him? Had they doubted him like she had?

Nick wouldn't have. No one knew him better than Nick, not even his sister. Annalise knew he'd loved Megan, though.

"It doesn't matter," she said. "Nothing matters but that I believed them. And I shouldn't have. I should have trusted you. I should have trusted what we had."

Feeling as if he was the one who'd been punched now, his breath shuddered out. "Maybe we didn't have what we thought we had. Maybe it wasn't real."

That was what he'd tried to convince himself of the past several months, but he had failed.

She reached up and skimmed her fingertips along his face. "It was real," she said. "It was…" She tugged his head down to hers and pressed a soft kiss against his lips.

He'd already wanted her. He'd never stopped wanting her. But the desire intensified. He kissed her back—deeply—passionately. His lips skimmed across hers then nibbled. Using his teeth, he gently bit the fullness of her bottom lip.

She moaned and opened her mouth for him. He slid his tongue inside, and she touched it with hers shyly before retreating. He kissed her again and again.

He wanted to take her right there on the couch in his boss's mom's office. But as he skimmed his fingers over her curves, the rhinestones on the dress scraped his skin and brought him to his senses.

She was wearing a wedding gown. She was another man's bride.

Not his.

She would never be his again.

But the least he could do was protect her. From the armed gunmen. And from himself.

"Gage," she murmured in protest when he pulled away. He easily tugged her off the couch. She turned her back toward him, as if she expected him to finally be able to get those little buttons free.

But he didn't want her free. He wanted her where she could get in no trouble, where she would be in no danger. Penny's bookcase stood open yet. Gage led Megan to it, passing the desk on which the wedding planner had laid out her arsenal. She'd missed a zip tie. It might have held something together. Or she might have intended to use it as Gage did. He wrapped it around Megan's wrists and pulled it tight.

She gasped in protest. "What are you doing?" she asked.

"Protecting you from yourself." And maybe he was protecting himself from her. But he was too proud to admit that, to admit to how close he had come to losing control and taking her.

He pushed her inside the secret closet. She was small enough to fit beside the glass cabinet that had held Penny's arsenal. It was all but empty now. Just a couple of guns left inside.

The wedding planner really did think of everything. Like her daughter had said, she even had a plan for armed gunmen invading her chapel.

"Don't!" Megan protested.

But Gage ignored her and closed the bookcase, locking Megan inside. The little key charm Penny had used to open the case was still inside the lock. He left it there. It wasn't like anyone would notice it.

And from inside Megan couldn't reach it, even if she had been untied. She wouldn't be able to escape. She wouldn't be able to put herself in harm's way. And knowing that would help Gage. He couldn't afford any distractions now, not when he was about to risk his life.

But hell, he would much rather risk his life than his heart again. And if he'd stayed on that couch with Megan, he would have lost his heart entirely.

Anger coursed through Megan, heating her already hot skin. She had wanted Gage so badly, her head clouded with love and desire, that she hadn't realized he'd been tricking her. He'd tied her up. He'd hidden her away.

She strained against the binding around her wrist. But the zip tie was tight, the plastic so hard that it bit into her skin—just like Gage had nipped her bottom lip.

So seductively...

Had it all just been a ploy? A way to distract her so that he could tie her up and tuck her away? Maybe none of it had been real, the kisses or his admission.

She shouldn't have trusted him, just like Richard had warned her. When she'd broken up with him for Gage, he'd told her that they would stay friends because he knew she would need one. He knew that Gage would break her heart, that he had an ulterior motive in going after her.

She'd been hurt but realistic enough to suspect that Richard was right. She was no great beauty. No exciting lover. But with Gage, she actually had been. Making love with him had made her needy and bold. She'd touched him and kissed him. She'd climbed all over him, sliding his erection inside her, riding him…

A moan slipped out as she felt needy all over again. Her skin tingled, and her body ached. She wanted him even after what he'd done. How he'd tricked her…

Had he tricked her before? Had he just been using her like Tucker and Richard had warned her?

She had begun to doubt that. She'd begun to believe that Gage really had loved her. He'd quit his job, he'd re-enlisted—because of her. He'd admitted that now. And he really had no reason to lie to her.

So if he'd been telling the truth…

Had Richard been lying?

But what reason would he have had? He wasn't a jealous man, like Tucker Allison, who had obviously been jealous of Gage and his success in the Bureau. Richard had never been in love with her, so he'd had no reason for jealousy. Just concern because he had been her friend.

Guilt flashed through her. She'd been so worried about Nikki Payne taking her place that she hadn't given Richard much thought. He was her friend. And he was in every bit as much danger as Nikki and the other guests.

But then Richard wasn't likely to put himself in danger. He wouldn't try to play the hero like Nikki or Gage would. He probably wouldn't do or say anything at all. If he wasn't the groom, the gunmen might have never noticed him.

Derek pushed the button on the walkie-talkie. "Ralph? Ralph?"

"Where the hell is he?" Andrea demanded to know. "He should have brought her up a while ago." Her long body that he'd always found so sexy was tense almost to the point of being sharp—like her voice when she asked, "Do you think she got away?"

"I think she'd be here if she hadn't." And so would Ralph. Unless he couldn't…

"What the hell happened?" Andrea asked—as if he'd been there.

He hadn't, but he suspected he knew. "The father of the bride, the bureau chief…" How the hell had he not known that? Of course he'd been locked up in prison with limited access to the outside. Andrea had done the research. How had she not known? "And the best man… I suspect he's an agent, too."

"Not anymore," the petite brunette remarked from where she sat on the floor.

"Got fired for banging the boss's daughter?" Andrea asked with a smirk.

Nikki Payne shook her head. "Quit to reenlist. He got deployed almost immediately and then went missing for six months. But he survived those six months of captivity and torture and escaped on his own. He's like Rambo."

"Just because he survived torture doesn't mean he's Rambo," Derek replied with a glance at the groom. "Some people are just like cockroaches—hard to kill."

Sweat streaked down the groom's face.

"That's not the case with Gage," the girl said. "He's a killer. It doesn't matter how many guns or guards you have around here. He'll take them all out."

Andrea laughed.

But Derek's blood had chilled with her ominous warning. And he shivered instead.

Andrea tugged him aside. "Are you letting her get to you?" she asked. She lifted her gun. "If she is, I'll shut her up—permanently."

He pulled down the gun. "No."

For some reason he liked the young woman; he respected Nikki Payne's spunk and sass. She was the kind of woman he'd thought he'd married.

Only now he realized Andrea was a stranger to him. Just like someone else was pretending to be…

He gestured toward the profusely sweating groom. "Does he really think I don't recognize him?"

"He doesn't look the same," Andrea said. "Are you sure it's him?"

"It's him," he said. He had recognized him from his engagement notice. Seeing him in person, he was even more certain. "You confirmed it."

Andrea nodded. "Of course."

She'd found the plastic surgeon who had treated Richard's burns. Even the blowtorch hadn't been able to get Richard to admit where he had stashed the loot from their last heist. It had been the biggest.

Would he give it up if they tortured his bride instead? Andrea thought so, but Derek was beginning to doubt it. Richard was nervous but not scared. He wasn't terrified for himself or for his bride.

Derek wanted him scared, scared like he'd been years ago. Derek lifted his gun, but like he'd done with hers, Andrea held the barrel of his. "No. You can't shoot him."

"I went to prison because of him."

She shook her head. "He never testified against you. You went to prison because you were matched to the security footage on the jewelry store cameras."

"Security footage he was supposed to hack in and erase." That was why Richard had been involved. He'd been their computer hacker, their security expert. He'd never held a gun or driven a getaway vehicle. But they wouldn't have gotten into the places they had without his help. He was good—too good to have made a simple mistake like he'd claimed when the security footage had hit all the news outlets.

Derek tried to lift his gun again. He wanted to shoot the bastard—a lot of times. He wanted to take out his knees, then drill holes into his arms until he fired the kill shot right between the bastard's little beady eyes.

"I know you want to kill him," Andrea said.

Want wasn't a strong enough word. He *needed* to kill him.

"But this isn't just about revenge," Andrea reminded him. "We're here for something else."

"But where are they?" Did Richard even have them? Or had he pawned them and blown all the money already?

"We'll find them," Andrea said.

Derek sighed. They had to at least try. Without them they wouldn't be able to get away like they planned—to a country with no extradition.

Glancing down the aisle at the lifeless FBI agent, he sighed. He had already killed. He would drop a lot more bodies to find what he was looking for...

Chapter 18

Except for some rare instances usually involving her kids and Woodrow's agents, the majority of the weddings at Penny's white wedding chapel went very well. Her staff had as much to do with it as she did. She had her own caterers, waiters and bartenders in the reception area of the basement. It was where she'd brought her bag of guns and walkie-talkies.

"We knew something was up," Jimmy the bartender said. "The waiter claimed you'd hired him because you needed extra staff."

Penny shuddered, grateful that the guy hadn't killed Jimmy for asking too many questions.

"He's the only one down here who's a stranger, right?" Woodrow asked.

Penny already knew. She'd recognized everyone else in the hall.

Jimmy replied, "Yeah. But I don't know where he's gone."

"He's no longer a threat," Gage said as he joined them in the reception hall. He glanced around at the fairy lights and flowers. It was beautiful. Was he thinking of how Megan would have married another man here? Or of how she should have been marrying him?

"Where's Megan?" her father anxiously asked. "You didn't send her alone through the tunnel?"

"Of course not," Gage replied. "I stashed her where no one will find her, though."

Behind the bookcase, Penny instinctively knew. She imagined Megan was not happy in the small space. Hopefully, she wouldn't be there long.

"Who's this guy?" the bartender asked, his eyes narrowed with suspicion.

"Gage Huxton," Penny said. "He works for my son Logan."

"A bodyguard," Jimmy said with a slight sigh of relief. "And this guy…" He pointed to Woodrow.

"Father of the bride," Penny said. "And an FBI agent—he's in charge of the Chicago office."

"Okay, we can do this then," Jimmy said.

Penny wasn't so sure she could ask so much of her staff. "It's still going to be dangerous," she warned him and the waiters, waitresses and chefs who'd gathered around them.

"You said Nikki's up there," Jimmy reminded her. "That she's in danger."

"I wondered why our phones weren't working…" one of the waitresses murmured.

"Cell jammer," Penny said. "We can't call out and we can't go out. All the doors are blocked."

"So we can't call for help and we can't expect any help to get in," Jimmy said. "Sounds like we have no choice."

"You do," she assured them. "You can hide."

Like Gage had hidden Megan. There were more nooks and crannies than the bookcase in her office and the secret passageway at the end of the hall. She could find safe places for all of them.

Jimmy shook his head. "No. We can't. Nikki's in danger. She's family."

That was the way Penny had always felt, like her staff was family. That was why she struggled with the thought of putting them in danger.

Woodrow had no such struggle. "Let me tell you the plan then," he said. And like a colonel, he began directing his makeshift army of her trusted waitstaff.

But the only real soldier of the group was the most impatient. "We've got to go," Gage said. "We can't waste any more time."

He was probably eager to get back to Megan. But there was no guarantee that he would. There was no guarantee that any of them would survive. They all started off after Gage anyway. When she moved to follow, Woodrow caught her shoulders. Staring down into her face, he ordered her like he had the others, "You are staying here."

She shook her head. "I can't ask my staff to risk their lives unless I'm willing to risk mine."

"I'm not willing to risk yours," Woodrow told her.

She could have said something about his risking Nikki's. But she knew he hadn't done that lightly. Nikki had been insistent and convincing that she could handle the danger far better than Megan could.

Penny would be insistent and convincing, too. "I am going," she said. "Nobody knows this place like I do."

"We know where we're going," Woodrow said. "And we know what we're doing."

"And I know where I'm going and what I'm doing, too," she insisted as she tried to tug away from him and step around his long body.

His hands tightened on her shoulders, easily holding her in place. "You're stubborn," he said. "Do I need to lock you up like Gage did Megan?" As big as he was, he could probably easily toss her over his shoulder.

But Penny wouldn't go down without one hell of a fight. She ignored the flash of excitement she felt over a physical struggle with Woodrow Lynch.

"Your daughter is safely locked away," she said. "Mine's not. Mine is up there with that crazy woman who already tried to shoot her."

"Penny—"

She shook her head. "But she hasn't been shot," she said with a little breath of relief. "Not yet."

He looked at her as if he wanted to believe her, but he'd been in law enforcement long enough to be a cynical man. And he'd seen Nikki at her most stubborn and fearless.

If anyone would have tested the gunmen, it would have been Nikki. If anyone had been shot, it hadn't been her.

"I would *know*," she said.

Maybe Woodrow would think she was crazy—like some others did. But she had never hidden who she was. "I would *know* if one of my children was hurt."

"You're saying you're psychic?"

She shook her head again. "If I was psychic, I never would have called Nikki to help me." She would have known the danger in which she would be putting her only daughter. "But I have a special connection with my kids. I know when one of them is hurt."

He nodded. "You're empathetic."

She grabbed up one of the guns left atop the prettily set table.

"And impatient," he added.

"I am also a damn good shot," she said. Her husband had taught her when they were first married. Then she had been the one to teach their sons, because her husband had died before he could. "You need me up there."

Woodrow was beginning to think that he just needed her too much to let her put herself in danger. She was also too strong and determined for him to argue with her anymore. Before she could pass him, he caught her shoulders and swung her back around to face him.

Ready to fight, she opened her mouth. And he kissed her. His lips slid over hers, stroking back and forth. He enjoyed the friction—the sensations that he hadn't felt in so long. His blood heated; his pulse beat faster. He'd never been so excited by just a kiss. But then, Penny Payne was special. He'd known it the first moment he'd met her.

Finally, he pulled back and stared down at her.

"Why did you do that?" she asked.

He could have told her that he'd meant it just as a distraction. But he knew that was a lie. He just hoped he wasn't lying when he assured her, "We'll get Nikki out safely."

"You don't know that's possible," she said. "Don't make promises to me that you can't keep."

Another man had done that to her. He'd promised—in this very church—to be faithful. But he'd fathered a child with another woman. He'd betrayed her in the worst way a spouse could be betrayed.

Woodrow knew her pain. He'd experienced it himself. It didn't matter to him that Megan wasn't his child. And he'd been careful that no one else realized the truth. But he worried that Megan suspected. She might not have remembered her mother, but she'd seen photos. Hell, she'd seen Ellen, who looked exactly like her. Blonde. Like Woodrow had been before he'd gone gray. And blue eyed. Like Woodrow. He worried that was why Megan had always considered herself unattractive—because she didn't look like them.

But she was his. No matter that she didn't have his DNA, he loved her like his child. He loved Penny Payne, too, but in an entirely different way.

"I don't make promises I don't intend to keep," he told her. He'd promised his dying wife that he would raise Megan like his own. And he'd kept that promise. Not out of obligation. But love. He would keep this promise to Penny for the same reason—because he loved her.

He held her chin in his hand, his fingertips stroking over her silky skin, until she met his gaze. She stared at him for a long moment before she finally nodded, accepting that he spoke the truth.

He drew in a breath, heavy with the responsibility he'd just accepted. But before he could turn away, she reached up and kissed his lips.

With a smile, Gage glanced away from the older couple. He'd figured something was going on with Woodrow and Penny Payne. He hadn't known for certain what it was until he'd gone back to see what was keeping them and caught them kissing.

There was attraction between them, but it was more than that. It was deeper. It was real.

Watching Woodrow and Penny made Gage long to see Megan before they headed up to the chapel. He wanted to make certain she was all right, that she hadn't cut her wrists trying to get off the zip tie. That she wasn't panicking in the close confines of the cramped closet.

And more importantly he wanted to see her again, to look deeply into the fathomless depths of her dark eyes. He wanted to touch her again, the silkiness of her skin, the softness of her hair. He needed to be with her—just one last time—in case he didn't return from his mission.

But if he took her out of her hiding place, he doubted he would be able to get her back in. She would be like Penny, insistent on putting herself in danger.

As much as he wanted to see her again, it was better that he not risk it. It was better that he not be distracted with thoughts of her, either. With how beautiful she looked in that damn wedding gown…

With how badly he'd wanted to get her out of it, and not just so that she wouldn't marry another man. Despite everything he'd gone through because of her, he wanted her. But she wasn't his.

Even though her wedding had been hijacked, she'd intended to marry another man. Gage had to push that thought from his mind, too, or he might not try as hard to save Richard as he would the others.

And if he let her groom die, he doubted Megan would ever forgive him. She must have cared about the guy to have been his friend even before she'd become his fiancée. She wouldn't want to lose him.

Would she care if she lost Gage? She hadn't last time.

Or she wouldn't have been in this church—about to marry another man.

Gage had to remind himself of that. While he loved her, she had never really loved him. She'd said so herself.

Chapter 19

"Gage!" Megan shouted his name. She wanted to hurl obscenities at him, tell him that she hated him for tricking her.

For tying her up.

For shoving her in a closet.

But no matter what he'd done, she would never be able to hate Gage Huxton. She loved him too much.

And still she'd failed to tell him that. She'd apologized for doubting him. But she hadn't owned up to her lie. She hadn't admitted the truth. That she had loved him with all her heart. That she loved him still, even as much as he infuriated her.

Anger coursing through her, she struggled against the zip tie, wincing as the plastic cut her skin. Maybe she could rub it against something. Her wrists bound behind her back, she ran her hands over the glass case, trying to find a sharp edge. She couldn't feel one, but maybe she could find a way to break the glass.

She turned. But in the tight space, her bodice scraped against the glass. The rhinestones scratched the surface, etching deep, so deeply that the glass cracked and then fell to the floor at her feet. It narrowly missed her polished toes peeping out of the front of her white satin pumps.

A gasp of surprise slipped through her lips. How the hell had that happened?

Then realization dawned. She remembered how Andrea had looked at that dress. She must have realized what Megan just had. Those bits of sparkle weren't rhinestones.

She wasn't the one they were really after. It was the damn dress. And all this time her father and Gage had been blaming themselves. She had seen the guilt on their faces. There had also been tension between them, so they'd probably been blaming each other as well.

But this whole thing had had nothing to do with them. They weren't responsible for the danger she was in—and that everyone in the church was now in.

She was. She had made a horrible mistake. And if something happened to either of the men she loved, or to anyone else, she would never forgive herself.

Nikki strained, but she was only able to catch bits and pieces of Andrea and D's intense conversation. But she saw the way they kept looking at Richard and she filled in the blanks.

"It's you," she said. "You're the reason they're here."

He shook his head, and some of his sweat spattered

onto the marble floor. Like the young agent's blood had spattered the white runner.

Was he dead? Had a man died because of Richard?

"I thought you were just some computer nerd," she mused. She was a computer nerd, too. While Logan had refused to let her do field bodyguard work, he'd put her in charge of the Payne Protection Agency's internet security. She didn't just protect their systems, though. She'd learned to hack everyone else's. Hacking was far more dangerous than her brothers knew. "What the hell did you do?"

"Nothing," he said. But his face flashed with the lie, and his beady little eyes glanced away from her.

"You did something," she said. "You know who these people are."

She saw it in their faces now, the recognition. They knew him. She wanted to know him, too. She doubted he was who he'd claimed, because, as protective as Woodrow Lynch was, he would have checked out his baby girl's fiancé. Just like her brothers would have checked out anyone she dated, if she'd ever really dated.

"Who are you really?" she asked. She deserved to know the real identity of the man who was probably going to get her killed.

He shook his head and spattered more sweat.

A droplet landed on her cheek, and she grimaced, repulsed. Better sweat than tears.

"I'm not that man anymore," he said. "He's dead."

"He should have been," D said as he joined them, his gun pointed at Richard's face. "How the hell did a little wuss like you survive what I did to you?"

Richard sat up straighter, and it was as if his shoulders widened. As if he grew…

It had all been an act—the cowering, the slouching…

"You made the mistake of thinking just because I'm smart I'm not tough, too," Richard said.

If she hadn't wanted to kill him herself, Nikki could have commiserated with the guy. She'd battled the same prejudice.

"Oh, I'm not sure how smart you are," D said. "Putting that engagement notice in the newspaper was one hell of a mistake."

Richard stroked his fingers along his jaw. "Really. You recognized me?" He glanced beyond D—at Andrea, whose face paled.

Something was going on, something more than even D realized.

"The plastic surgeon fixed the scars," D said. "But he didn't change you enough that I wouldn't know you when I saw you again."

Richard sighed. "I never thought I'd see you again."

"I'm sure you didn't," D agreed. "Not after you left that footage on the security camera so I'd be caught."

A smirk spread across Richard's face. "I see you learned to cover up your tattoos now. Not too smart to have such identifiable ones, at least not in your business."

"What is your business?" Nikki asked.

"None of yours," Andrea answered for them. "Come on D," she said. "Let's get out of here. The cops will be coming soon."

"Yeah, because of that shot you fired," he said, and he stared at her with suspicion. "You did that because you want the cops to come. You want me to go back to prison."

"Of course not!" she said. "Why would I have broken you out if that was what I wanted?"

Nikki suspected Andrea was one of those women who didn't know what she wanted beyond attention. And she didn't particularly care what man gave it to her as long as she got it. She snorted in derision.

Andrea ignored her. But D glanced down at her. "What?"

"The police are the least of your worries right now," she said. "Those landscapers, the ones your guy said look all alike?"

D nodded. "What about them?"

"They're my brothers."

Andrea laughed now. "That's cute. You think your big brothers can come save you."

"I know they will," she said. "They'll save us all and send you two either to prison or to the morgue." She offered a pitying sigh.

Andrea laughed again, albeit nervously.

"Who are they?" D asked. "FBI?"

"One of them was," Nikki replied. "Nick worked for the father of the bride. He's the FBI agent who cleaned up the corruption in River City. My brother Cooper was a Marine. The twins were cops. Now they're all bodyguards with the Payne Protection Agency."

D flinched as he recognized the name. Even in prison he must have heard about them. Her brothers had sent a lot of criminals to join him behind bars.

"But they're the least of your concerns," she said. "Gage Huxton is the one you should fear."

"Gage?"

"The blond guy," she said.

He glanced around as if he expected Gage to pop up out of a pew. "Rambo?" He smirked as he repeated it.

Nikki laughed. "Yeah, he's a former FBI agent, former Marine and now he's a bodyguard. And trust me, protecting the bride is the assignment he takes more seriously than any of his other ones."

D shuddered as if he'd seen a ghost or feared he was about to become one.

"We need to get out of here," Andrea implored him again.

He shook her off his arm. "I'm not leaving him alive," he said as he shoved his gun against Richard's head. "And I'm not leaving without the diamonds."

It was going down now. Nikki moved her hand, shoving it beneath the skirt of her dress. But before she could reach her holster, D grabbed her arm. "You're a bodyguard, too," he said. "Just like your brothers. That's why you switched places with the bride—to protect her." He turned his gun on her now. "So who's going to protect you?"

She lifted her knee, ramming it into his groin and dropped him to his knees. She heard other guns cock and she ducked, bracing herself for the flurry of gunfire. It came—from everywhere. The balcony, the vestibule.

It was like a war, with shots going everywhere. Before she could reach for her gun, someone was grabbing her, dragging her behind the altar toward the groom's dressing room. Nikki didn't dare lift her head.

She knew she wasn't being rescued. She was being taken hostage and used as a human shield against all those flying bullets.

Help had finally arrived—for everyone else. It would do no good for Nikki.

Gunfire exploded around him with blasts of light and sound, Gage waited for the paralysis that had gripped him before. Any time he'd been in a gun battle since his escape, he'd frozen, reeling with flashbacks to those other battles lost.

But he moved now, his instincts guiding him like they had for his escape. He aimed and squeezed, taking down the gunmen guarding the doors to the vestibule. Then he turned toward the outside doors just as they opened and fired on the two guys who'd begun to rush inside. They never made it through the doors, which closed on them, leaving them outside—wounded or worse.

As the guy standing near the altar advanced down the aisle, firing on them, Gage shoved Woodrow aside and fired back. The guy dropped, but maybe he'd just fallen over the body lying on the runner. Gage advanced slowly, cautiously, his barrel pointed directly at the man's head.

D was lying on that runner, blood pooling beneath him. It turned the white fabric a dark crimson and ran across the marble tiles, too. Gage had hit him. Hell, he must have struck an artery. He dropped to his knees beside him. But there was no saving him.

"I'm dying," D said with an eerily calm acceptance.

Gage nodded. "Yes, you are. Help's coming…" After all the shooting, the police were certain to arrive.

"I'll be dead before they get inside." There were more men outside, more men fighting. Gage could hear the gunfire. He waited to flash back again, especially when he stared down at the dying man. He waited to see the faces of other men, of fellow Marines he hadn't been able to save, of enemies he'd had to kill in order to survive. But he saw only the man who lay before him.

"I think I knew you'd do it," D said. "The first time I saw you. I think I knew that if anyone was going to take me out, it would be you…"

"Am I the reason you're here?" Gage asked.

The guy shook his head, and blood trickled from the corner of his mouth. "No."

"Woodrow?"

"Who?"

"Are you here because of me?" Woodrow asked as he leaned over the dying man, too.

Derek shook his head again, and more blood gurgled out of his mouth.

"Then what do you want?" Woodrow asked. "Why did you put my daughter in danger?"

D's thin lips curved into a slight smile, and he remarked, "You have no idea who the real danger is…"

"So Megan's still in danger?" Gage asked, his heart beating in his throat. He was more nervous now than when he'd been in the gunfight.

Now D nodded, or he tried. He only moved his head slightly before the last of his life slipped away.

He was a horrible man. Gage knew that. But he felt a pang of regret that he'd killed him. Now he might never know the real reason they'd taken the church hostage. All he knew was that Megan was still in danger.

And despite their best efforts, the church wasn't secure yet.

He turned toward his former boss and mentor. He could stay and help him. Or…

Woodrow read his look and urged him, "Go. Get Megan out of here."

That was what he wanted, what his instincts were screaming at him to do.

"But we don't know if there was any truth to what he said."

Woodrow nodded in agreement. "We can't trust him. But we can't trust anyone."

No, they couldn't. Gage straightened up. He would go. He would make certain that Megan got to safety this time.

But would *she* trust him? Would she leave with him this time? Or was she already gone? Sure, he'd tied her up. But he knew about the games Woodrow had taught her and her sister when they were kids.

He knew she knew how to escape being tied up. Had she freed herself from the bookcase? If she had, she might do something stupid. She might trust someone she shouldn't.

He had to get to her—before anyone else did.

Chapter 20

"She's gone." Penny's heart sank as she realized Nikki was nowhere in the chapel. No matter how many times she kept peering around the pews for her, she could catch no sight of her beautiful girl.

Some people cowered in the pews, weeping with fear or maybe relief now if they realized they'd been rescued. Penny knew she wouldn't find Nikki cowering or crying. Even as a child Nikki had rarely cried. She probably hadn't wanted to betray any weakness in front of her older brothers.

Penny turned back to Woodrow where he crouched beside the two men lying in the aisle of her church. She didn't really want to look at them, to know that they were gone. That Nikki might have gone that way, too.

When Woodrow met her gaze, she let her resentment spill over in a glare. If he hadn't insisted that she wait in the vestibule until the shooting was over, she might have seen what had happened to her daughter.

"Maybe she ran out," Woodrow suggested.

Other guests had run out during the shooting. But Penny knew her youngest. She was every bit as stubborn as her brothers—maybe even more so. Nikki wouldn't have run away from danger. She would have run straight into it. Her foolish girl knew no fear.

Penny shook her head. "No, there's no way she would have run away."

"Then she has to be here," Woodrow said, reaching out to squeeze her shoulder. His blue eyes held such concern—and something else.

Unable to hold his gaze and acknowledge his feelings and maybe her own, Penny looked down. Then she shuddered at the sight of those bodies lying in the church aisle. She recognized D, the gunman who'd died as violently as she suspected he had lived.

"Who is he?" she asked about the young wedding guest. He had been sitting on the bride's side.

Woodrow uttered a ragged sigh. "He worked for me," he admitted. "But he shouldn't have. He had no business being an agent."

Tears stung Penny's eyes over the loss of such a young life. She suspected he'd been trying to impress Woodrow when he'd drawn his gun. Instead of getting praise, he'd taken a bullet. Or two. He hadn't died in the recent gunfire, because someone had already tried to treat his injuries.

Nikki…

Somehow Penny just *knew* that Nikki had pressed the jacket against the wound and bound it with the belt. She wouldn't have been able to not help unless she'd been too injured to help herself. Then she might be where Penny couldn't see her.

Penny stepped over the bodies on the bloody runner and hurried down the aisle toward the front. There was no blood near the altar. No bride or groom, either.

Richard was gone, too. But she cared less about him than about Nikki. There was something about him... something that had made her uneasy. She'd known Megan shouldn't marry him. But she'd thought that was just because Megan's heart belonged to another man.

Woodrow had followed her, and he peered around too. "I don't see the woman."

"Andrea." She'd left her husband to face the gun battle alone? Left him to die alone? "Doesn't anyone honor their commitments anymore?" she murmured.

"No," Woodrow said. "But maybe he told her to leave. Maybe he wanted to protect her." Like Woodrow had tried to protect her.

Penny snorted. "A woman like her doesn't need protection. People need to be protected from her, especially Megan." The woman had been insistent that the fake waiter deliver the real bride to her. Maybe she'd gone downstairs to get her herself.

Woodrow nodded in agreement. "Gage went down to make sure Megan is safe," he admitted.

She knew. Gage had passed her as he'd been leaving the chapel and she'd been entering. He'd barely spared her a glance he'd been so anxious to get back downstairs. But he'd looked pale—haunted.

"Was it Gage?" she asked as she gestured back at the gunman lying in the aisle as well as the two in the vestibule.

Woodrow nodded. "I understand now how he survived those six months. He's almost superhuman."

Nikki wasn't superhuman. She was just a very petite girl. Would she survive?

"Where is she?" Penny murmured, tears of frustration stinging her eyes. In the distance sirens wailed. Help was coming. But would it be too late?

Then something else wailed, closer than those distant sirens. Someone else, actually—it was a woman screaming. Penny wasn't certain that it was Nikki. She had never heard her daughter scream before. Every maternal instinct in her reacted, and she ran toward that scream.

The scream struck Woodrow like a blow to his heart. He wasn't sure if it was his daughter or Penny's who'd cried out in such fear. But he didn't care.

He ran toward that scream. Fortunately, his legs were longer than Penny's, and he passed her before she could burst through the closed door of the groom's dressing room.

He didn't want her getting hurt by what was happening or what she might see. She was already upset over the bodies of the strangers lying in the aisle of her beautiful little chapel. She didn't need to see her daughter if Nikki had been hurt.

Or worse.

Now more shots rang out again, echoing inside the church. Those people who'd stayed behind ran now, stumbling in their haste to escape. Falling over those dead bodies. But they had no reason to be fearful. The gunfire and the screaming emanated from the groom's dressing room.

Woodrow reached for the handle and found the door locked.

Inside that locked room, the woman screamed again. Woodrow stepped back then rushed forward, slamming his shoulder and hip against the door. Wood splintered as the frame cracked and the door sprang open.

"Nikki?" he called out for her. She had to be the one inside the room. Gage had hidden Megan away. No harm could have come to her.

Penny's daughter was the one in danger—because of him, because he'd agreed to let her sacrifice her safety to protect Megan. If something had happened to her, Penny would never forgive him.

And he would never forgive himself.

Nikki wasn't one of his agents. She wasn't even a real bodyguard. She'd had no business taking on such a dangerous assignment.

"Nikki!" he called out again.

But his only reply was the rapid retort of more gunfire. It flashed and banged, so close that he felt the burn and vibration of it. Then he realized why he'd physically felt the gunfire; he'd been hit.

Most of Woodrow's fifty-five years had been spent as an FBI field agent—some before that, like so many of his best agents, as a Marine. Despite all the dangerous missions and assignments he'd carried out, he had never been shot before. Maybe he was wrong, though. Since he had never been shot before, he couldn't be certain that he had been now. Maybe he was just experiencing shock, like the numbness the agents felt after taking a bullet in their vest. But Woodrow wasn't wearing a vest beneath his tuxedo.

He hadn't thought he would need one for his daughter's wedding. He should have known better. He should have known that bad things could happen anywhere, even in Penny Payne's beautiful little wedding chapel.

Heat radiated across his chest. Was it his blood? Or was he having a heart attack as well? He reached up and clutched his chest. And blood oozed between his fingers.

His knees began to shake, threatening to fold beneath him. He stepped back—out of the doorway—so that he wouldn't be hit again.

It might not have mattered. He knew sometimes that all it took was one shot. One shot to kill...

Locked away behind the bookcase, trapped beside the glass cabinet, Megan shouldn't have been able to hear the gunfire. For some reason it was louder inside her confined space, as if the weapons were being fired directly over her. The chapel was above the other area—the dead end of the hallway where she could have escaped through the secret passage. Or she could have run right into the arms of her captors.

That was why Gage had locked her up, for her safety. But she didn't feel safe. Each shot had her flinching as she expected the bullet to penetrate her flesh. She was safe, thanks to Gage. It was everyone else who was in danger.

Gage.

Her father.

The Paynes.

Richard? Was he in danger? Or was he the danger? She stared down at her dress. How had she not noticed? Because she hadn't paid that much attention to the dress.

She had wanted to wear her mother's dress, but Richard—who didn't care any more about fashion than she did—had insisted on designing her wedding gown. She'd been surprised, but if—as he'd claimed—he'd wanted everything to be perfect, she wasn't going to argue with him.

Of course she'd known nothing was perfect, because she'd thought Gage was dead. He hadn't been then. She had no idea about now.

He'd vowed to protect her, and that would probably prove his most dangerous mission ever. She wasn't the one everyone wanted, but she had what they wanted.

Why had Richard done it? She needed to get out and warn Gage and her dad and Nikki—if it wasn't already too late. Richard wasn't who any of them had thought he was.

They might already know that. Another gunshot drew her attention up, and she noticed the speaker above her. Mrs. Payne, who thought of everything, must have had a sound system installed so that she could stay apprised of what was happening even when she was down in her office.

While Megan could hear the shots, she couldn't hear anything else. No voices. She didn't know if someone had been shot. Or killed…

She could only imagine the worst.

The worst was Gage, his beautiful green eyes open but unseeing, lying lifeless inside the church. Gage dying without ever knowing how much she had loved him. Without knowing that she would always love him…

She couldn't lose him.

Not again…

She struggled again against the zip tie then remembered that she'd broken the case. Finding the jagged edge of glass of the cabinet, she ground the plastic against it.

The glass scratched her wrists. But she ignored the pain, and in seconds, the zip tie snapped free.

She uttered a ragged breath of relief that echoed inside the small room. She could get out now. But there was no handle inside the cabinet, no way to get that bookcase to slide open again.

Maybe if she just pushed on it...

As she pushed, someone else pulled. Someone had found her. She had no time to turn and reach for a weapon before the bookcase slid open. She had no time to protect herself from the danger that awaited her.

She was the one who had what everyone wanted, the reason people were willing to risk prison and death.

And they would have no qualms about killing her to get what they wanted. She had no time to grab a gun from the case and load it. So she did the only thing she could—she propelled herself at the person who'd found her, intent on defending herself. But she wasn't fighting for her life. She was fighting so that she could help the others.

She was fighting for Gage.

Chapter 21

Fists pummeled his chest and shoulders. Feet kicked his shins and knees. Gage grasped the struggling bundle of lace and brocade and rhinestones, clutching Megan close.

"Hey, hey, calm down," he told her. He'd had no idea how angry she could get. This was even worse than when she'd broken up with him. Then she hadn't been angry so much as cold. "I shut you in there for your protection."

And for his, too. If he'd thought she was in any danger, he would have been distracted, so distracted that D might have killed him instead of the other way around.

He felt a flash of regret, not so much that the man had died but that he'd died with his secrets. Gage still had no idea why he'd taken the wedding hostage.

Megan stilled—finally—the fight leaving her body. And she gasped his name on a breath that whispered across his throat.

So when she'd been struggling with him, she hadn't known it was him at all. She'd thought he was someone else, someone who might have hurt her. And she'd fought him. She'd fought him for her life.

He moved his hands to her face. Cupping it in his palms, he tipped it up to him. Tears glistened in her brown eyes. She must have been so afraid. He leaned down and brushed a kiss across her lips. "It's okay... it's just me."

Her breath shuddered out against his mouth, and she deepened the kiss. Her arms slid around his neck, and she clutched him closely. "You're okay!"

And he realized she hadn't been afraid for herself at all. She'd been afraid for him. "Yeah, I'm fine."

But she pulled back and ran her hands over him, as if she didn't believe him, as if she had to check for herself. If he'd been shot, he hadn't realized it. He felt no pain, or he hadn't until she touched him. But he felt a different kind of pain, the kind from desire overwhelming him. He wanted her. He *needed* her.

But he needed more to make certain that she was safe. D's words rang in his head. *You have no idea who the real danger is...*

"You're not hurt," she said.

But she was. He gently grasped her hands and lifted them. Blood smeared her skin and trailed down her wrists to saturate the cuffs of the lace sleeves of her gown.

She must have struggled so hard to break the zip tie that she'd hurt herself. Guilt and regret gripped him. "I'm sorry," he said. "I shouldn't have tied you up."

He hadn't known how determined she would be to escape—so determined that she would hurt herself.

She shook her head. "I did this on the broken glass."

He glanced behind her at the cabinet. She'd struggled even harder than he'd realized. "Why would you fight so hard to get free?"

"I wanted to help," she said.

"Help…"

"I heard all the shots—" her voice cracked with fear "—and I thought you were hurt."

He shook his head. "None hit me." He'd fired more than he'd dodged. But the gunfire hadn't stopped. It rang out now, echoing inside Penny's office.

"What about my dad? Or the Paynes…"

He waited for her to ask about Richard, but she didn't. And relief eased the tightness on his chest. He hadn't looked for Richard. He didn't know if her groom had been shot. Or worse.

Once he'd stopped D, he hadn't cared about the others, especially after hearing the dying man's warning. He'd cared only about her—about making sure she was safe.

"We have to get out of here," he said. "It's still too dangerous."

More of the men from the outside must have come into the church. It was only a matter of time before they searched the basement.

He could shoot at them like he had earlier. But he didn't want her getting caught in the cross fire. When he slid his arm around her, she tensed against him.

"No," she said. "We can't leave."

"We have to—"

And she began to struggle again. Now that she knew it was him, she didn't kick or hit. But she wriggled, pushing her hips against his groin and her breasts against his chest. He groaned as his body tensed—with desire.

"Megan," he warned her. "Be still…"

"I'm not leaving," she said. "Not until I know my dad is all right."

"Your dad told me to get you out of here," Gage said.

"You don't work for him anymore," she reminded him. "You don't have to listen to him."

"Your dad isn't the reason I want to make sure you're safe," he said.

Her face flushed, maybe from her struggle, maybe from embarrassment. "That's right. You're a bodyguard now. And protecting the bride is your assignment."

Protecting her wasn't a job to him; it was a necessity—such a necessity that he ignored her struggles and lifted her. Slinging her over his shoulder fireman style, he carried her from the office and down the hall toward that secret passage. While he kept his hand locked around hers, he had to let her down to get inside the narrow tunnel. He couldn't carry her through it. He couldn't even stand upright himself. He had to hunch over, but still his shoulders and back scraped the stone walls.

Going through it reminded him of his escape from captivity. The confined space, with its musty dankness, cut off his breath. He also knew that if anyone caught them—on either end—they just had to shoot into the tunnel to kill them both. They were more vulnerable here than they'd been anywhere else.

He'd gripped her hand to tug her along behind him. And it gave him some comfort, having the warmth and softness. This time he wasn't alone. But he'd rather be alone than risking her life with his.

"Gage," she murmured. "Are you all right?" She must have heard his erratic breathing or maybe even the crazy fast pounding of his heart. It beat so hard that his body shook with it—trembled. Or maybe he'd been gripping her hand too tightly. She was already injured. He forced himself to ease his grasp.

She squeezed his hand, offering a reassurance he hadn't had those six months. A comfort he'd been denied. God, how he'd needed her then.

Even more than he needed her now. But he was glad he'd been alone, glad he'd endured those atrocities by himself. He never wanted her to experience the pain that he had. He didn't even want her to know about it.

It was too late for the fear. She was afraid. Even though she offered assurance, her hand trembled in his. She was scared, too. She must have realized what he had.

That they weren't safe.

He'd been right to question the wisdom of escaping this way. Because there was no light at the end of this tunnel, only the dark shadow of the man who waited for them, his gun barrel trained on them. At least Gage was first. The bullets would hit him before they hit her.

Megan blinked against the brightness of the afternoon sunshine. She'd only been in that tunnel a few minutes, but it had been so dark.

She focused and turned to Gage, who knelt on the bricks of the little courtyard. He gasped, gulping in air like they'd been in that tunnel for days instead of minutes. His skin was pale, too. And she realized this tunnel had only affected him because of whatever memories it had conjured up of the nightmare he'd already endured.

"Oxygen! Someone bring some damn oxygen," a dark-haired man called out. She recognized Nicholas Rus. Fortunately, so had Gage before he'd fired his weapon at him.

Someone ran toward them, but it wasn't an EMT. Slender arms circled Megan, clasping her close. "Thank God you're all right," Ellen said. "I was so worried…"

Ellen always worried about her, like a mother hen. But this was the first time Megan had actually given her cause to worry.

"I'm fine," she assured her. But she wasn't so sure about Gage. She pulled away from her sister to stand next to him. "Are you all right?"

Drawing in a deep breath, he nodded. Then he regained his feet and his strength, his shoulders squared and his chin lifted with pride. He'd visibly shaken off the vestiges of the nightmare.

"I'm fine," he said. Then he turned to his best friend and remarked, "No thanks to you. Where the hell was the cavalry when we needed them?"

"I couldn't reach him," Ellen said. "His phone kept going to voice mail." Tears brightened her eyes. "And you'd told me not to call 911, to trust only Nick."

What had Gage gone through that he trusted no one but his best friend? Was it what he'd endured when he'd been captured? Or was it because of her? Because he'd trusted her and she'd broken his heart?

She realized now what she'd done when she'd doubted him, when she'd believed other people over him. But she'd had no idea then that she shouldn't have trusted Richard. She still couldn't believe—she had to be wrong…

"That was a mistake," Gage said. "But I didn't think he'd be irresponsible enough to shut off his damn phone—"

"I had no choice," Nick said. "Your sister would have killed me had I been taking calls while she was in labor."

"What?" Gage asked, his eyes wide with shock. "Annalise had the baby? Is she okay?"

Nick nodded. "She's just furious at you for not answering your phone, though."

"There's a cell jammer—"

"I know," Nick assured him. "Even before I listened to Ellen's voice mails, I knew something was wrong. Penny would have been at the hospital, too, if she'd been able to leave the chapel."

"They're still inside," Gage said. "She and Nikki"

"And Dad," Megan said.

Tears glistened in Ellen's eyes again. They were blue, like their dad's. Their mom had had blue eyes Megan recalled from the photos she'd seen of her. Only Megan had dark eyes and dark hair. She'd figured out in science class what that likely meant, but she'd never had the guts to ask anyone for confirmation. She hadn't wanted to know.

It didn't matter if Woodrow Lynch wasn't biologically her father like he obviously was Ellen's. He was the only parent she had ever known. She couldn't lose him. But what if it was too late?

Her heart pounding with fear as she recalled all those shots, she started toward the little white church.

Gage caught her, holding her back. "We just got you to safety. You are damn well not going back inside."

"But—"

"It's too dangerous," he insisted.

That was why she wanted to go back inside. "It's too dangerous for Dad, then." And he was alone, because he and Gage had insisted on protecting her. He had to know that she wasn't his, but he'd never loved her any less because of it. Maybe he'd even loved her a little more.

Nicholas Rus chuckled. "Nothing's too dangerous for your dad," he said. "He's the toughest guy I know."

Gage nodded in agreement. These men—warriors in

their own right—respected her father immensely. She expelled a slight breath of relief.

"He's safer than you are," Gage said. "The guy—D—"

"Derek Nielsen," Nick finished for him. "He escaped from prison just a few days ago."

Gage turned to him. "How do you know?"

"One of the guys we caught out here told us who was running the show."

Gage shook his head. "I don't think it was him."

"It's his wife," Nick said. "Andrea Nielsen."

Megan shivered as she remembered the dangerous woman.

Gage shook his head. "Just before he died, Derek told me and Woodrow that we didn't know who the real danger was."

"He died?" Nick asked but then answered his own question with a nod. He knew how Derek had died—at Gage's hand. "What did he mean?"

"That we can't trust anyone," Gage said. "I need to get Megan out of here."

"No," she protested. "I'm not leaving until I know that Dad is okay."

"If anything happens to you," Ellen said, "he won't be. It'll destroy him." She knew. She had to. As an RN, she'd taken many science classes. She understood genetics and that Megan likely shared no DNA with Woodrow Lynch. But they shared love and an incredible bond. He'd always tried so hard to protect her. That was probably why he'd never told her the truth. Hell, maybe he hadn't wanted to face it himself.

"You know that," Ellen said. "And you know that he would trust Gage to protect you." She turned to him. "I trust you," she said, but she gave him a hard stare. "Don't let anything happen to my baby sister."

"I won't," he assured her.

"Do you know where to take her?" Nick asked.

Gage nodded. "I know where the Payne Protection safe house is." His arm around Megan, he began to guide her from the courtyard.

But she dragged her heels across the bricks. She needed to tell them about the dress—about Richard. But then what Gage had said to his best friend reminded her of what was most important: "Don't worry about us," he said. "Worry about getting into the church and making sure everyone else is safe."

Nick nodded. "We will."

That was the most important thing. She would tell Gage about the dress and let Nick and the others focus on getting everyone out the church.

Before he left his friend to that job, Gage asked, "Hey, what's my nephew's name?"

Despite the situation, Nick grinned as he replied, "Woodrow Gage Payne."

He had named his son for her father. He would make sure he was all right. She didn't have to worry, but she still had that knot of apprehension in her stomach. Maybe she wasn't afraid for her father, though.

Maybe she was afraid for herself because as Gage suspected, she was pretty sure she was still in danger as long as she had the damn dress.

Nikki leaned down and felt for a pulse. There was none. She'd thought she might have killed someone before. But her brothers hadn't admitted if it had been her gun or her brother Nick's that had fired the kill shot.

They'd told her it didn't matter. They'd been protecting her—like they always had—in case she wouldn't be able to handle taking a life.

There was no doubt now. She had killed someone.

Andrea stared up at her, her last expression one of hatred and shock. Maybe she hadn't thought Nikki had it in her to take a life, either. But with the way Andrea had been wildly firing around the room, she'd had no doubt that the other woman would have killed her had Nikki not killed her first.

She glanced down at herself, looking for holes or blood in her mother's old wedding gown. Surely, she'd been shot, too. With all the bullets she'd fired, how the hell had Andrea missed her?

She heard a gasp and glanced down. Had she been wrong? Was Andrea alive yet? She reached quickly for the woman's weapon, making sure she couldn't pull that trigger again. But she hadn't been wrong. Andrea was definitely dead, but even in death, she tightly grasped her weapon.

The gasp she'd heard became a cry, one of fear and alarm. And she turned toward the doorway where her mother stood. Penny's eyes were huge in a face that had gone deathly pale.

"Mom!" Nikki exclaimed. "Are you okay?"

If Penny had showed up earlier, she might have been shot in the cross fire.

When Andrea had dragged her into the groom's dressing room, she'd closed and locked the door behind them. It was broken now.

Nikki dimly recalled it flying open. But Andrea had been standing between her and the door; she'd fired at it before swinging back toward Nikki.

That was when Nikki had shot her. She must have struck her right in the heart, which had shocked Nikki nearly as much as it had Andrea. She would have doubted that the woman possessed a heart at all.

There was no doubting her mother had a heart. Was she this upset over the dead woman? Or over Nikki firing the bullet that had killed her?

"It's okay, Mom," Nikki assured her. "I had no choice. I had to shoot her."

Penny nodded. "I know. But you didn't do it soon enough."

Nikki glanced down at her dress again. There was no blood. "I'm fine. I didn't get hit." She stepped forward over Andrea's dead body. "Did you?"

Her mother wouldn't have been able to break down the door. But then she wouldn't have needed to. Her mom had keys to every lock in the chapel. She would have just used one of them. Then dread clutched Nikki's stomach. And she knew. Someone else had been hit.

Penny shook her head and tears spilled over, sliding down her face.

Was it one of her brothers? Had they finally managed to get inside only to get shot?

"Who?" Nikki asked. She stepped closer to the broken doorjamb and peered around her mom. She saw Logan and Parker standing near the doors to the vestibule, talking to some uniformed policemen.

Garek and Milek Kozminski—Payne Protection bodyguards and brothers-in-law—were there, too. But they kept their distance from the police. They had their reasons for not trusting them. They stood in the church aisle, staring down.

Where was Cooper? Where was Nick?

She stepped closer, and her mother launched herself into her arms, seeking comfort. Nikki was stunned. She'd never had to comfort her mom, not even when her dad had died. Of course she'd just been a child then, and her mom had been acting strong for all of them. Even when Penny had been confronted with the evidence of her father's affair when Nicholas Rus had showed up in River City, she hadn't needed comfort. She'd offered it instead to Nick and to Nikki.

Now Penny trembled in Nikki's arms. Was it Nick? Was he the one who'd been shot?

She peered around her mother again. Some EMTs leaned over a body lying just outside the dressing room door.

"Who is it?" she demanded to know.

"Woodrow," Penny's voice cracked with emotion. "Woodrow has been shot."

Now regret and remorse gripped Nikki. She wasn't upset that she'd killed Andrea. She was upset that she hadn't killed the bitch sooner. She might have taken out a good man with her. A man who obviously meant a lot to her mother.

Penny had already lost too much. She couldn't lose this man, too.

Chapter 22

A_s the metal door slid closed behind them, Gage breathed a sigh of relief. The condo had been converted from an old warehouse to living space. It was all exposed brick and metal and polished concrete floors. He cared less about how it looked than about how secure it was with a security system only the Kozminskis—renowned jewel thieves—had been capable of cracking. Since they had designed it, no one else could get inside. No one else had been able to get to Gage's sister when Nick had brought Annalise here.

Gage had brought Megan for the same reason that Nick had brought Annalise: to keep her safe. But could he? Even if they rounded up all the hired gunmen at the church, he doubted she would be safe yet.

You have no idea who the real danger is...

Megan shivered, as if she'd heard his thoughts. Or maybe she was just cold. He touched the buttons on the security panel. Not only did it make sure no one would breach the doors or windows, it turned up the thermostat as well. "It'll warm up in here soon," he promised her.

She shook her head. "It doesn't matter. We can't stay here."

"Yes, we can," he said. "Nobody can get inside. You're safe." At least she was safe from whatever dangers lurked outside. She wasn't safe from him. He wanted her.

How the tunnel had affected him had proven to him that he wasn't the man he'd once been. He was getting better. He hadn't flashed back during the shoot-out. But he'd nearly crumpled in that tunnel. If not for her hand holding his, he might have.

Despite this temporary comfort, he couldn't count on her fixing him. It had been months since he'd escaped, and he hadn't been able to fix himself. Sure, he was better. But he would never be whole again. He would never be the man he'd once been. That was why he could never be with her; it wouldn't be fair to put her through that.

"We need to go back," she said.

"And get in their way?" he asked. "Every agent with Payne Protection is at the church." But for him. "They will get everyone safely out of there."

She released a shuddery breath and nodded. "I know. I know my being there would probably only put everyone in more danger." Her big brown eyes glistened with tears of guilt and concern.

"So you accept that you're still in danger?"

Biting her bottom lip, she nodded again.

His stomach tightened as need coursed through him. He wanted to bite her bottom lip—gently—to pull it inside his mouth and nibble on it. He wasn't strong enough now—after that damn tunnel—to resist the temptation. He lowered his head and did exactly what he'd just imagined.

He kissed her just as he'd wanted. Deeply. Passionately. And she kissed him back, her fingers sliding over his nape, holding his head down to hers. She nibbled on his lips, too, and shyly slid her tongue into his mouth.

And now he wanted more than kisses.

He wanted her—wanted to bury himself inside her—to feel connected with her the way they used to connect. When they'd made love, he had never felt closer to anyone than he had to her, so close that they'd been part of each other.

Her hands slid away from his neck and she stepped back until his arms—that he hadn't even realized he'd wound around her—dropped back to his sides. He drew in a deep breath as he fought for control. He couldn't connect to her as he once had. He wasn't the same man.

And she was engaged to someone else. If the gunmen hadn't laid siege to the chapel, she would have been married to Richard. She would have been leaving for her honeymoon.

The thought struck him like a blow, nearly doubling him over with pain. She wasn't his.

"I'm sorry," he said. He shouldn't have kissed her. He had no right. Not anymore.

While that hadn't stopped him at the church, he'd known then that he couldn't go beyond kissing her. There had been too much going on.

Too much danger…

The danger wasn't over yet, but it couldn't get to them here. The only danger was Gage acting on the desire he felt for her.

"Don't be scared," he told her.

She glanced at the heavy steel door. "You said we're safe here."

"We are," he agreed. "I don't want you to be scared of me."

"I'm not," she replied—too quickly.

"You should be," he said.

She'd seen him snap a man's neck. Had been there when he'd freaked out in the tunnel. And she had to know that he'd taken out more than one man with his gun during the shoot-out. She would be crazy to not be afraid of him.

Her lips curved into a slight smile, a sad smile. "I used to be afraid of you," she admitted.

"When?" he asked.

She had never betrayed any fear. But then she was far braver than he'd ever known.

"The first time we met," she said. "At my father's house, you terrified me."

"Then?" He laughed at the thought of anyone fearing him then. Compared to the man he was now, he'd been a clueless kid then. Harmless. "Why?"

"Because of how you looked at me," she said.

He could imagine how that had been—like he'd wanted to eat her alive. He suspected he was looking at her that way right now, because he wanted her even more now than he had then.

Even though the condo had begun to warm up, she shivered again. "No one had ever looked at me that way before." Her throat moved as she swallowed. "Or since…"

Gage finally let himself ask the question that had been burning him up with jealousy. "Then why did you agree to marry Richard?"

"Because I was afraid of you," she said. "I was afraid of how you made me feel, of how easily you could hurt me."

He shook his head. "I never would have hurt you." Not then. He wasn't sure what he was capable of now; he wasn't the same person he'd once been. That was why he couldn't risk getting into a relationship with her again, even if she was interested.

"And I felt safe with Richard," she continued, "like he couldn't hurt me…"

He heard the doubt now. "You don't believe that anymore?"

As if bracing herself, she sucked in a breath. "I need to tell you something."

Nerves clenched his stomach muscles again. "What?"

"I'll tell you," she said. "But first you have to get me the hell out of this dress!"

Megan's heart leaped like the passion in Gage's green eyes. His pupils dilated. And he stepped closer to her. He must have thought she wanted out of her dress in order to be naked with him. She opened her mouth to explain. But as much as she wanted the dress off, she wanted Gage even more.

His arms remained at the sides of his tense body, and he shook his head. "This is a bad idea…"

It was. She knew that for all the reasons she'd just told him. She was afraid of him, not of what he would do to her but of how he made her feel. Too much.

"I can't stay in this dress," she said.

He drew back as if she'd doused him with a bucket of ice water. "Of course. Yeah, you've wanted out of that dress all day."

And that was before she'd realized what it was all

about; she'd never wanted to wear it in the first place. "Please," she implored him. "Help me get it off."

He reached into his pocket and pulled out a knife. With a flick of his thumb, the blade popped out. "Turn around," he told her.

She immediately spun around, presenting her back to him. He tunneled his fingers into her hair and lifted the heavy weight off her neck. But that left him with only one hand to wield the knife, so she replaced his hand with hers, holding her hair up and out of his way.

"I wish I hadn't lost all of my pins earlier," she remarked.

"I'm glad you did," he said.

Heat flashed through her as she remembered all the times he had pulled down her hair. He'd preferred it curling wildly around her shoulders, had claimed that it was incredibly sexy.

"It's in your way," she pointed out. That was why she'd always bound it, to keep it out of her way. And because it made it so clear to her that she wasn't genetically related to her father.

"It's fine," he said, and his fingertips skimmed along her spine.

Even through the heavy material, she could feel his touch. But it wasn't enough. She wanted the fabric gone. She wanted nothing between his skin and hers. But most especially not this dress.

"I'll cut through these little loops around the buttons," he said.

"You should have used that knife earlier," she said.

The buttons pinged as they dropped onto the wooden floor. And she sucked in a breath. "Wait!"

What if the buttons were like the rhinestones that

weren't really rhinestones? They spun away and rolled across the floor, disappearing beneath the leather sofa and chair.

"Did you change your mind?" he asked. "Do you want to keep it on?"

She could finally breathe again without the tight bodice squeezing her breasts. Expelling a ragged sigh of relief, she vehemently replied, "Hell, no!"

He chuckled, or at least she thought that was what that rusty sound was. But maybe she'd been mistaken, because when the dress dropped away and she turned back to him, he wasn't laughing at all.

His face was tense, a muscle twitching along his tightly clenched jaw. He stared at her in that way that only he had ever looked at her—with desire. But it was more than desire. It was need.

She recognized it because she felt it herself. She had to tell him about the dress. When he reached for her, she forgot all about it and the diamonds on it. He lifted her out of the mound of material. Sweeping her up in his arms, he carried her through a doorway off the living room.

He didn't release her, not even when he laid her down on a bed. Instead he joined her, his hard, long body pressing hers into the mattress. And he kissed her. His lips pressed against hers, deepening the kiss.

She lifted her hands, clutching at him. Holding him to her, she kissed him back and rubbed her breasts against his chest. While she wore only the white silk bra and panties she'd had on beneath her gown, he wore a tuxedo. The black jacket, the loosened tie and vest. It was too much. She needed to feel his skin against hers. Wishing she had his knife to undo the buttons, she reached between them and pulled his shirt loose.

But he caught her hands.

"Gage," she murmured in protest. He couldn't leave her like this, wanting him so badly that she trembled with need.

He groaned and leaned his forehead against hers. "I don't think I can stop..."

"I thought you were."

He shook his head. "I was just getting rid of this." He pulled off his jacket, dropping it to the floor beside the bed. He was more careful with the holster and gun inside it, laying them on the table next to the bed. His other clothes followed until he was completely naked.

The blinds were drawn in the bedroom, so the only light spilling in was from the living room. But despite the shadows, she could see the scars on his body.

As he caught her staring, he tensed. "I'm sorry," he said. "I forgot." And he reached for his shirt.

She caught his hand, forcing him to drop it back onto the floor. "I'm glad," she said.

"That I got hurt?"

He hadn't just been hurt. He'd been tortured.

"I'm glad that for a few minutes you were able to forget what you've been through," she said. Because she didn't think she would ever forget what he'd endured, how she'd nearly lost him.

As she stared up at his face, she wondered if he was really back. Or if the Gage she had loved was gone forever.

"I won't ever really forget," he said. "I won't ever really get over what I went through—what I saw—what I had to do to survive."

She shivered.

"I'm not the man you remember," he said. He reached

for his shirt again, intent on putting it back on to hide his scars. And maybe to hide his injured soul from her.

She stopped him again, her hand on his. Then she leaned forward and kissed him. "You're not the same," she agreed. "But neither am I."

His lips curved into a slight smile. "But you don't know me anymore."

"I know that you're the man that I want." Not just tonight but always.

He nodded. "We both need this," he said, as if he was trying to convince himself. "We've been through hell today." And he closed his arms around her, drawing her body against his scarred one.

But even with the scars, he was still beautiful—all straining muscles. She rubbed against him.

He unclasped her bra and pushed down the cups until it fell away from her. Her nipples rubbed against his chest until he pushed her back. Then his tongue rubbed over her nipples, teasing them.

Heat pooled between her legs. "Gage…"

"It's been so long," he murmured. "I'm not going to last."

But he took his time with her. He pulled off her panties and made sure she was ready for him, his fingers moving in and out of her. She shuddered as she came.

It had been a long time. She hadn't been with anyone since him. She'd told Richard she wanted to wait for their wedding night. But she knew now—even if she'd still believed Gage dead—that she wouldn't have been able to make love with him. She hadn't loved him.

She'd loved only Gage.

He pushed her back onto the mattress and parted her legs. Then he was there, nudging against her core. She arched and stretched, trying to take all of him. She bit her lip as he thrust inside her.

He tensed. "Did I hurt you?"

She shook her head. "No, it's just been a while."

His brow furrowed, and he stared down at her with surprise. And hope.

"There's been no one since you," she told him.

"You don't have to lie to me," he said.

"I only did that once," she said. "When I told you I never loved you. That was the only lie I've ever told you."

He closed his eyes as if overwhelmed and murmured her name. "Megan…"

He'd said he wasn't the same man he'd been. But he felt the same to her—felt as perfect as he always had—as if they'd been made for each other.

She moved beneath him, the tension building tightly inside her as the passion—the passion she'd only felt with him—overwhelmed her.

He moved slowly, sliding in and out of her while he kissed her lips. And her neck. And her shoulder. As he kissed her, he touched her. He teased her breasts with his fingers, making the nipples tighten and tingle.

"Gage…" She was so close—to losing her mind.

Then he moved his hand between them, flicking his thumb over the most sensitive part of her. And she came, screaming his name.

His body tensed, shuddering, as he filled her. He moved so that he dropped onto the bed next to her.

She shuddered in the aftermath of the orgasm. Because she felt cold suddenly—separate—where a moment ago they had been so close they'd felt like one.

Then his arm slid under her shoulders, and he rolled

her up against him. His other hand reached across his body to wrap around hers, his palm against her hip.

"Gage?" she whispered. She peered up at his face. His eyes, those beautiful green eyes, were closed. And his jaw, shadowed with stubble a few shades darker than his hair, was clenched yet but not nearly as rigidly as it was when he was awake.

She suspected that after what he'd been through during those long months he'd been missing, this was as at rest as Gage ever was anymore. So she didn't have the heart to wake him up—to tell him what the rhinestones on her dress really were.

Megan settled her head on Gage's shoulder. She knew she was still in danger because of that damn dress. But here—in his arms—she felt safe. Her only wish was that everyone else was, too.

The mother of men who routinely put their lives on the line to protect others, Penny had spent more than her share of time in hospital waiting rooms. She'd never paced the floor over a man who hadn't been a relative. Nick didn't count. She hadn't given birth to him, but he was her son, same as Logan and Parker and Cooper. The Kozminskis, Milek and Garek, were her boys, too. They all waited with her, their eyes full of concern for her. And confusion.

They had no idea why she was so upset. Neither did she. It wasn't as if she knew Woodrow Lynch that well. They'd met a little over a year ago, but he lived in Chicago and she in River City. They'd never even been out on a date.

He'd never asked. But if he had, she wasn't sure she would have accepted. She hadn't wanted to be in this position again. She hadn't wanted to love a man that she risked losing because of what he did, of who he was.

She'd never had the chance to pace a waiting room for her husband. He'd died before he'd ever made it to the hospital, like Derek Nielsen had. So she'd been spared this nightmare of waiting, of worrying.

Losing her husband had been fast, like ripping off a Band-Aid. That could be why it hadn't hurt like this. And even though she'd forgiven him his betrayal, she'd never completely trusted him again, not enough to love him freely anymore.

Not that she loved Woodrow Lynch. She couldn't. She hardly knew him. Sure, he was a great father. That was obvious with how much his girls loved him. Ellen wasn't pacing like she was. She was too weak from morning sickness. She slumped in a chair with her husband's arm around her shoulders. They'd brought their kids to her mother-in-law earlier, when Gage had turned them away from the chapel.

It wasn't just family in the waiting room, though—his and hers. All of Woodrow's agents had come to hospital, too. They not only respected their boss, they loved him.

No agent loved him more than Nicholas Rus did. Actually, it was Nicholas Payne now. He had finally done what she'd asked. He'd taken his father's name. And he'd given his new son Woodrow's name. Nick stepped into her path so that she had to stop pacing. But the minute she stopped, the fear caught her, overwhelming her. Nick's arms closed around, holding her as she fell apart.

She couldn't lose Woodrow—just as she'd realized she loved him, too.

Chapter 23

Something soft brushed against Gage's chin and his neck and his chest. He opened his eyes and glanced down to find Megan's head on his shoulder. His heart swelled in his chest, love overwhelming him. He loved this, loved waking with her in his arms. This was how they used to sleep whenever he had convinced her to stay over at his place. It had always felt so natural to him—so right—to sleep with her in his arms, her head on his chest.

Maybe that was why he'd struggled so hard to sleep since his escape. It hadn't been because of the nightmares but because she hadn't been with him. He couldn't remember the last time he'd fallen asleep so quickly or slept so soundly. Glancing at his watch, he realized that it had only been a couple of hours. That much uninterrupted sleep was a big deal for him.

He couldn't get used to it, though, couldn't get used

to having her back in his arms. Even if she wanted to be
with him again, he wouldn't let her make that sacrifice.
Because he loved her, he couldn't put her through life
with a man as broken as he was now.

It wasn't as if she really wanted to be with him again.
She had just been through a lot today and had needed
someone. He'd been there for her.

Where had Richard gone?

Had he made it out of the chapel alive? Had everyone else? Gage reached for his phone, which was in the
pocket of the tuxedo jacket lying on the floor on her side
of the bed. So he had to roll across her. His body tensed
as she stirred beneath him. He wanted to bury himself
inside her, wanted to feel as close to her as he had just
those couple of hours ago.

Her thick lashes fluttered just before she opened her
eyes and stared up at him. At first she looked surprised,
like she hadn't expected to find him in bed with her.
He studied her, waiting for disappointment. After all, he
wasn't the man she had really wanted, the one she had
agreed to marry.

Why had she agreed to marry Richard?

She'd admitted they'd never had the passion that she
and Gage had. That passion flared now in her eyes, and
her skin flushed. She reached up and linked her arms
around his neck, pulling his head down for a kiss.

Like before, he couldn't resist her, not with her naked
body lying warm and soft beneath his. She was already
wet and ready for him, so he slid inside her. She lifted
her legs and locked them around his waist, matching his
rhythm as he thrust inside her.

She moaned then screamed his name as she came. Her
inner muscles clutched at him as her body shuddered with

release. The tension that had been gripping him snapped, and he joined her in ecstasy.

He tried to pull back, but she held on to him, as if unwilling to release him. Being connected with her was all that he'd remembered: so right, so humbling…

Love filled his heart, and he wanted to tell her how he felt. But it wasn't fair. He couldn't ask her to take a risk on a man like him, one who'd been so damaged not just physically but mentally as well.

He drew in a steadying breath and pulled away from her. He grabbed up his jacket from the floor and found his phone. Seeing the dark screen, he cursed. The cell jammer had drained his battery. Fortunately, a charger had been left next to the bed. He plugged it in.

"It's so dead that it's going to take a couple of minutes before I can get it to power up," he said. "Then I'll call Nick and find out what all happened at the chapel."

She nodded then drew in an unsteady breath. "That's good. I need to tell you something before you talk to Nick."

"What?" he asked. Somehow he didn't think she was going to profess her love for him.

"I know why the gunmen showed up at the church."

He tensed. There was something about her tone that raised his suspicions. He and Woodrow had been blaming each other for the gunmen showing up at the church. But what if it had been because of her?

"Why?" he asked. "Why did they want you so badly?" Not that he could blame them. He wanted her badly, too, so badly that even after making love with her twice, he wanted her again. "What did you do?"

"I didn't do anything," she said with a trace of defensiveness. "It wasn't really me they wanted."

"I heard—"

She pressed her fingers across her lips. "They didn't want *me*. They wanted my dress."

He snorted. "That thing?"

She had looked beautiful in it. But she would look beautiful in a gunnysack as well. The dress itself had been ostentatious and gaudy, not something she would have chosen to wear at all.

"Yes, that thing," she said. "I thought the rhinestones were tacky."

"Then why did you pick it?"

"I didn't pick it," she said. "Richard did."

His stomach knotted with anger. Gage never would have told her what to wear, especially not for her wedding day. All he would have wanted was for her to be comfortable and happy.

"And those rhinestones," she said. "They're not rhinestones at all."

"What are they?"

"Diamonds."

He snorted again. "Yeah, right."

"How do you think I broke that glass cabinet in Penny's closet?" she asked.

"Kicked it—hit it, I don't know," he admitted.

"With the rhinestones."

"But rhinestones…" Then he realized she was right. Only diamonds could have cut the glass. He cursed. "What the hell—how did they get there?"

He glanced through the open bedroom door to where the dress lay on the hardwood floor of the living room. It sparkled in the late afternoon sun shining through the skylight above it. There were a lot of rhinestones sewn into the heavy fabric. If they were all diamonds, a fortune lay there.

No wonder the gunmen had laid siege to the church. The risk they'd faced would have been worth it had they gotten the dress. But to get the dress, they would have had to get Megan, too.

He'd managed to protect her at the chapel. But she was still in danger because she had the dress. He had to keep her safe. So he reached for her again, wanting to wrap his arms around her and hold her close so no one could get her.

But she pulled away from him. Taking a sheet with her as she left the bed where they had made love, she wrapped it around herself. She could be shy like that, even after they'd made love. He suspected there was something more to her wanting to cover up.

She felt exposed. Or foolish.

She had been such a fool. Would Gage ever forgive her for all the mistakes she'd made? Instead of trusting him, she had trusted the wrong man, and it had nearly cost her life as well as the lives of other people she cared about.

"Is your phone charged yet?" she asked. She needed to know for certain that her father was all right and that the Paynes were, too. Nikki had risked her life taking Megan's place. But fortunately she hadn't taken her dress.

If she had...

Who knew what the gunmen and Andrea would have done to her? Of course given Andrea's disposition, she might have hurt Nikki anyway, just out of spite.

Gage glanced at his cell and nodded. "It's charged enough to power up now." But he didn't reach for it.

"Are you going to tell me how the diamonds got on your gown?"

His green eyes were narrowed with suspicion as he stared at her.

And Megan shivered. "I didn't put them there," she assured him.

He sighed. "Richard..."

She nodded. "It has to be. He had the dress designed. He found the seamstress. It had to be him."

"How the hell would he have gotten his hands on that many diamonds?" Gage mused aloud. "Unless he stole them..."

"He must have," she agreed.

"The danger is not from who you think." Gage muttered the words.

She shivered again. "What?"

"Those were D's last words," Gage said. Regret flashed in his green eyes.

"He died."

Gage nodded. "He said he knew that I would be the one—" He cleared his throat. "That if he died, I'd be the one."

"I'm sure you had no choice," she said.

"Like the guy who was trying to bring you upstairs to the chapel."

She narrowed her eyes and studied his face. Was he worried about what she'd think? He was nothing like the men he'd killed. "You had no choice," she said again. "He would have killed me."

Gage nodded and released a ragged sigh. "Yes, he would have."

"And D must have realized he'd given you no choice,

either," she said. "Or he wouldn't have given you a warning."

"That was a warning," Gage agreed.

"It must have been about Richard."

A muscle twitched along Gage's tightly clenched jaw, and he nodded. "It must have been. So they knew each other."

"And I didn't know him at all," she said. "He's not at all who I thought he was…" She'd thought him a harmless nerd, not a thief.

But what if that wasn't all he was? What if he was a killer, too?

"Never thought I'd see *you* in a wedding dress," Logan remarked as he joined Nikki in the corner of the hospital waiting room.

She glanced down at the gown, surprised she was still wearing it. She had forgotten all about it. "I never thought I'd wear this dress, either," she admitted. But despite her reservations, it had brought her luck.

If she had switched dresses with Megan, she doubted she would have gotten out of the chapel alive. Because she'd figured out where the diamonds Derek wanted were.

Those weren't rhinestones on the real bride's wedding gown. "Where are Gage and Megan?" she asked.

Logan glanced around the waiting room. "I don't know."

"I couldn't reach him on his cell phone," Nick said as he joined them.

Nikki looked around for her mom, whom Nick had been comforting earlier.

"Ellen told the hospital that it was fine for Penny to

go see Woodrow." They had only been allowing family members back since he'd come out of surgery. They'd gotten out the bullet, but he'd lost so much blood that it was still touch and go. He might not make it.

Regret struck Nikki's heart. If only she'd taken down Andrea earlier…

But Andrea wasn't a threat anymore. Richard Boersman was, though.

"We need to get a hold of Gage," Nikki said.

"Yeah," Nick agreed. "He would want to be here. And of course Megan needs to be here, too. She doesn't even know about her dad."

Nikki shook her head. "They can't come here. They're still in danger."

"We rounded up everyone at the church," Logan said. "How could they still be in danger?"

"The danger is not from who you think," Nick murmured.

And Nikki shivered. "I will never get used to you having that same freaky sixth sense Mom has."

"It's not that," Nick said. "Gage said those were the escaped convict's last words."

"He warned him." She wasn't surprised. While the guy had obviously had no qualms about killing, he'd also had a warped sense of honor, too. If not for him, Nikki would be dead. His wife would have killed her when she'd stormed into the chapel after he'd untied her.

If only he hadn't untied her…

"So Gage knows she's not safe yet," Nikki said.

"That's why he got Megan out of there," Nick said. "He got her to the safe house."

Nikki expelled a breath of relief. "That's good." But it

wasn't enough. "We still need to talk to him. Warn him about Richard."

"Richard?" Logan repeated the name.

"The groom," Nikki said. "Didn't you meet him at the church?"

Logan shook his head.

"You didn't see another guy in a tuxedo? Short, nerdy-looking guy?" she asked.

Parker stepped up and shook his head. "There was no one wearing a tuxedo but Woodrow."

And he'd been lying on the floor, bleeding. Nikki shuddered as she remembered. She'd been so busy consoling her mother and worrying about Chief Special Agent Lynch that she hadn't even thought to look for Richard.

"Gage was wearing a tux, too," Nick said. "But nobody else that we saw inside the church."

Nikki cursed. "He must have gotten away." Or worse yet, he'd followed Gage and Megan. "Until we catch him, Megan isn't safe."

She had what he wanted. His diamonds.

He had endured Derek torturing him and hadn't given them up. He wouldn't let anyone get between him and his fortune. Not Megan and not Gage.

Chapter 24

"They already knew about Richard?" Megan asked as Gage clicked off the cell phone.

Fortunately, he'd taken the call in the living room while she'd been getting dressed in the bedroom. Since Payne Protection often used the condo as a safe house, the closet was stocked with clothes in an assortment of sizes.

He'd found a pair of jeans and a black sweater that fit. He turned to where she stood in the bedroom doorway. She wore a red sweater dress with tall suede boots. She looked so damn sexy.

He forced himself to focus on her question and nodded. "Yeah, they already knew about Richard and the diamonds." He glanced at where the wedding dress spilled out of a box sitting on the leather couch. But they'd shared with him something he hadn't known, something that made him feel physically ill.

Woodrow was hurt. Badly.

He wasn't certain how to tell Megan that her father might not make it. He wasn't certain if he should even tell her at all. Because if he told her, she would want to go to the hospital.

And it wouldn't be safe for them to leave until Richard was caught.

"How did they know?" Megan asked.

"Nikki overheard an argument between Richard and Derek Nielsen in the church," he said.

"Derek Nielsen?"

"D," he explained. "Remember, Nick told us his name outside the church." He was surprised that he'd remembered, though. He'd been so shaken from going through that damn tunnel. "Derek just recently broke out of prison. He was serving a fifteen-year sentence for armed robbery."

"Let me guess," she said. "Of a jewelry store?"

He nodded.

"I don't understand how Richard was involved."

"Nikki figured he was the one who bypassed the security system so that no alarm went off. There were actually several robberies where someone hacked the security systems and the stores were robbed."

"Richard?"

He nodded. "The Kozminskis—they're bodyguards with Payne Protection, too—recognized D at the church. They knew he was responsible for several more jewelry store robberies than the one for which he was serving time."

"How do they know?" she asked.

"Have you heard the saying it takes a thief…"

She nodded. "But you said they're bodyguards."

"They are."

"And thieves, too?"

"Not anymore," he said. "But they keep a foot in that world. It's a good thing, though. It gives us information we wouldn't be able to get without them."

"Did they know anything about Richard?" she asked.

He nodded. "Not by name. But they knew Nielsen recruited some college kid several years ago and had him hacking the stores' security systems. But then there was a glitch with Derek's last robbery. Some security footage of him showed up, and he was arrested."

Megan gasped. "Richard betrayed him."

"There's another saying," Gage began.

"There's no honor among thieves," Megan finished for him.

"Except the Kozminskis," he quickly added. He would trust those guys with his life, and he might have to if they were the backup bodyguards Logan was sending to the safe house.

"What is it?" Megan asked.

"What's what?" he asked, stalling for time.

He wasn't sure how to tell her what he needed to. She loved her father so much; she would be devastated if he didn't survive his gunshot wound.

She narrowed her eyes and studied his face. "What are you not telling me?"

"Megan…"

"I know there's something you're not telling me," she insisted.

He still needed to stall for time, at least until his backup arrived at the condo to see if Richard was lurking outside. Gage had whisked her away from the church quickly, and he hadn't noticed anyone following them. But he had underestimated Richard once. He wouldn't make that mistake again.

So to stall, he asked the question that had been bothering him. "If you can read me that well," he said, "how could you not know that I was telling you the truth about how I felt about you?"

She sucked in a breath. "You want to talk about that now?"

He nodded.

"I told you that I was wrong," she said. "I shouldn't have doubted you. I shouldn't have listened to Tucker or Richard."

He flinched.

"What?" Annoyance pulled her full lips into a frown. "What is it?"

"Tucker..."

"What about Tucker?"

"He died." Gage couldn't believe it. But his name had been on the list of casualties Nick had run down for him. "He arrived early, so he made it inside the church. Then Nikki said he tried to draw his weapon when Derek had ordered all the guests to be searched." He must have gotten scared, or he'd been trying to play the hero he'd always wanted to be.

Stupid kid...

Megan's lashes fluttered over the tears brimming in her eyes. Then she stalked over to the dress and pounded her fist against the side of the box. "He didn't deserve to die, especially not over these damn things."

Seeing how upset she was about Tucker, Gage dreaded telling her about her father. But he needed to let her know. She would never forgive him if Woodrow didn't make it and she didn't get to see him again.

One last time...

* * *

No one had ever scared her like Gage could. When he'd started flirting with her, she'd been afraid because she'd never had a man like him—so handsome and sexy—interested in her before. She hadn't trusted his attraction to her was real. He'd scared her even more when he'd reenlisted and disappeared during his deployment. That had nearly scared her to death.

But this—the fear she felt now because he kept avoiding her gaze—scared her nearly as much. He had information that he knew would upset her so much that he was reluctant to share it with her.

"What is it?" she asked again, as she had so many times before. "Just tell me!"

"Megan..." The reluctance was there in his deep and raspy voice. He really didn't want to tell her.

So she started guessing, knowing that when she hit on it he would betray himself. "Did Richard get away?"

He nodded. "Yeah, nobody even saw him at the church. He must have escaped during the shoot-out."

She grimaced as she remembered all the shots she'd heard emanating from the speaker in that small closet in which Gage had locked her. "Tucker died and Derek," she said. "Was anyone else killed or hurt?"

The look on his face chilled her blood. "There were more casualties!"

He nodded. "The woman—Andrea."

She gasped. She'd been afraid of the woman. But she hadn't wished her dead. She hadn't wished any of them dead. "That's too bad."

"Nikki had to kill her."

"That's even worse." She couldn't imagine how Nikki felt. "Is she okay?"

He expelled a breath but nodded. "*She's* fine."

Panic clutched her heart. Someone else obviously was not fine. He wasn't willing to come right out and tell her. So she had to keep asking questions. "And Mrs. Payne? Penny?"

He nodded again.

Realization dawned on her, making her sick. "My dad!" she exclaimed. "He got hurt."

Gage nodded yet again.

Tears stung her eyes. Everybody had kept telling her that he was so tough, that he could handle anything. That was the only reason she'd left with Gage before knowing if everyone had survived the shoot-out inside the chapel.

"I shouldn't have left the church," she said, berating herself. She'd thought her staying there—when all everyone had actually wanted was that damn dress—might put other people in danger. But she shouldn't have left until she'd known everyone else was out of trouble.

"How badly is he hurt?" she demanded to know.

Gage flinched as if it hurt him just to think about it. He had always thought so highly of her father. All Woodrow Lynch's agents respected and loved him. He wasn't just a boss to them. He was a friend—a mentor—a *father*— to them as well.

"How badly is he hurt?" she asked again.

Was he just hurt or was he dead?

"He was shot," he said. "Andrea shot him before Nikki killed her."

And now she wished Nikki had killed the woman earlier. Or that Megan had. Maybe she should have plunged those scissors into the woman's cold heart instead of her shoulder.

Megan trembled with both anger and fear. How dare she…how dare she hurt Megan's father…

"He's been through surgery. They removed the bullet. It was close to his heart, did some damage to one of his lungs," Gage said. And now he spoke almost too freely.

She felt sick thinking of the physical damage that had been done to her father. He'd always been so strong, so invincible.

"And he lost a lot of blood," Gage continued.

"Is—is he going to make it?" she asked.

He fell silent again, and his green eyes looked down. He was unwilling to meet her gaze.

"Gage!" she yelled. "Tell me!"

"They don't know," he admitted, his voice ragged with his own emotions. She saw it then. He hadn't just respected her father. He'd loved him, too. He had loved working with him.

If not for her, she doubted Gage would have quit the Bureau. He would have kept working with her father. She had put this all in motion.

If she hadn't broken up with him…

If she hadn't agreed to marry a man she hadn't loved…

It was all her fault. She'd already lost Gage through her stupidity. She couldn't lose her father, too.

Images played behind Woodrow's closed lids. The flash of the gunfire as the bullet fired. He waited for the pain he'd felt, but he was numb.

Was he dead?

Had he died?

What about Penny? She'd been right behind him. Had she been shot too?

Megan was safe. Gage would make certain of that.

He'd promised to get her to a secure place. He would protect her with his life.

Woodrow would have done the same for Penny—if he'd had the chance. He struggled to move, but something lay against his side, something warm and soft that lulled him into a feeling of security himself. But he wasn't safe. He'd been shot once. Even though he'd tried to stay awake, consciousness had slipped away from him.

He had no idea if he'd been shot again. Or if anyone else had...

"Penny..." he murmured her name as he fought to regain consciousness.

"Shh..." a soft voice soothingly replied. "I'm right here. I'm right here."

And when he finally dragged his lids up, he saw that she was. She was the warmth and softness he'd felt as she lay next to him in the narrow hospital bed. He'd never been as comfortable as he'd been with her lying beside him.

He was sure it had nothing to do with the drugs that were pumping into his veins through the IV in his arm. It was all her: Penny Payne.

Her face was flushed as if she was embarrassed he'd caught her in his bed. Her curls were rumpled like her bronze dress, and her makeup slightly smeared beneath her eyes, making dark circles look even darker. But she had never looked more beautiful to him.

"You're all right?" he asked.

She nodded. "Yes. Are you?"

"I'm alive?" It was a question; he wasn't sure. His body still felt curiously numb but for his heart that swelled with love.

For her...

He wanted this, wanted to go to sleep every night with Penny in his arms, wanted to wake every morning with her lying beside him.

Her lips curved into a smile, one full of relief. And she blinked back tears. "Yes, you're alive."

"You sound surprised," he mused.

She shook her head. "No, I never had any doubt you'd survive."

"Liar."

Her lips curved into a bigger smile. He couldn't resist; he leaned forward and kissed those lips. Her breath escaped in a ragged sigh against his mouth.

"I was so scared," she admitted. "I hoped but I didn't know."

"Like you always know everything," he teased.

She shook her head. "Not everything…"

Panic clutched his heart. "Is Nikki okay?"

"Yes," she said. "You were right about her. She's far tougher than I ever realized. She shot and killed the woman who shot you."

"Did she get hurt?" He remembered all those flashes of gunfire.

"Not a scratch on her."

"She's not just tough then," he remarked with surprise. "She's damn lucky."

Penny's lips curved into a smile again. "She thinks it's the dress."

"The dress she was wearing?"

"My old wedding dress."

"Then it is lucky."

"I'm not so sure," Penny admitted. "I didn't have the storybook marriage I thought I'd have."

"Neither did I," he admitted.

"I know."

And she would. She must have realized that Megan wasn't his. It didn't matter, though. He didn't love her any less. He didn't blame her for what her mother had done. Hell, he didn't even blame her mother. He'd never been there for Evelyn, not like she'd wanted or needed him to be. His job had always mattered more to him than she had.

Now Penny...

If she wanted him to quit, he would do it in a heartbeat. He knew now that nothing mattered more than love. But maybe he'd only realized that because he was truly in love for the first time in his life.

Before he shared his feelings with her, he had to know. "Did everyone else make it out all right?"

She nodded. "Yes."

He released a ragged breath of relief. "So it's over..."

Her eyes—those beautiful warm brown eyes—squeezed shut, as if she didn't want him to see the truth in them.

"You said everyone made it out all right."

"Yes, but it's not over," she said.

Then he remembered what Derek had told him and Gage. *The danger is not who you think...*

He groaned.

She sat up and looked at the machines hooked to him, monitoring his condition. "Are you okay?"

"Yes." But he wouldn't be able to tell her what he wanted to tell her until he knew this was over. "Physically, I'm fine. But if something happens to one of my daughters..."

She squeezed his IV-less arm. "I know."

No parent knew better than she did, not with the danger her kids routinely faced.

"Nick and my other boys," she said, claiming her husband's illegitimate son in the way he had claimed Megan—wholeheartedly, "they're working on finding Richard."

"Richard?"

"Yes, he worked with Derek and double-crossed him. That was how D wound up behind bars and Richard wound up with the fortune in diamonds Derek had stolen."

He sucked in a breath.

And she touched his chest.

He couldn't feel her fingers though through the heavy bandages wrapped around his torso. Now he knew where he'd been shot. He expelled that breath in a shaky sigh of relief that he'd survived.

"Are you sure you're all right?" she asked.

He nodded. "I'm just shocked. I checked Richard out. And he has no record."

"He'd never been caught," she said.

Woodrow shook his head. "I don't understand…"

"What?" she asked. "You couldn't have known. No one suspected what he was capable of."

"But why wouldn't Derek have turned him in?" he wondered. "If he'd given up his partner, he might have gotten a reduced sentence."

"From what Nikki overheard, Derek thought he was dead. Apparently, he tortured Richard to find out where he'd stashed the diamonds. He'd thought he'd gone too far and Richard had died."

"But he survived." Woodrow regretted that after all the fear the man had caused Megan and might still cause her. Realization dawned as he remembered what he had discovered about the man who could have been his son-in-law, probably would have been had Derek not broken out of prison and hijacked the wedding.

"I know he had a lot of plastic surgery five or so years ago," Woodrow said. His hacker had hacked the hacker's medical records. "It was due to burns, though. I figured they were just from the fire Megan had mentioned Richard had been in."

Instead he had been tortured. Derek Nielsen must have been determined to get those diamonds. But Richard had been even more determined to keep them. He'd been willing to give up his life over them.

"Nikki figures Andrea helped him," Penny said, "that she was playing both of them."

But she was dead and so was Derek Nielsen. And hopefully Richard was long gone.

"I'm sure he left the church and headed straight to the airport," Woodrow said.

Penny shook her head. "I doubt it. He won't leave without the diamonds."

"So he'll retrieve those from wherever he stashed them, and he'll leave."

Her face, which had been flushed with color when he had awakened, grew pale now.

"What?" he asked. The numbness was beginning to wear off because he felt a pang of fear now—in his heart.

"The diamonds were on Megan's wedding gown."

He knew what that meant. Richard wouldn't leave without the diamonds and probably not without Megan, either.

"Gage will protect her," Penny assured him.

Woodrow trusted Gage. But Richard Boersman was

more dangerous than any of them had realized. And even more desperate.

He had been willing to give up his life once for those diamonds. He would definitely be willing to do it again. And Woodrow suspected that for those damn diamonds, Richard would have no qualms about taking a life or two.

Chapter 25

Gage had been through some epic battles in his life. But no one had ever fought him as hard as Megan was. He tightened his arms around her, lifting and carrying her away from the security panel.

"You can't keep me here," she shouted at him as she pummeled his shoulders with her small fists. "You can't treat me like a prisoner."

He had said those same words himself before, so he knew exactly how she was feeling. His heart ached with sympathy for her. He didn't want to hurt her—like he'd been hurt. He only wanted to protect her. "I can't let you leave until we know where the hell Richard is."

"Richard won't hurt me," she said.

Gage wasn't so sure.

She must have seen the doubt on his face because she insisted, "He won't. He just wants the diamonds."

"Why did he sew them on to your dress?" Gage wondered.

"What was the reason?" Megan shrugged. "I don't know. And at the moment, I don't care. I just want to see my dad." Her voice cracked with emotion, and tears shimmered in her dark eyes.

"You will see him," he promised. "We'll leave as soon as my backup bodyguards arrive." But even then he wasn't certain it was a good idea to take her out of the safe house. Nobody had any idea of what Richard was capable. And Gage couldn't figure out why the hell he'd had the diamonds sewn on to Megan's dress. What was the purpose of that?

No, it was too risky, and Gage wasn't willing to take any chances with Megan's life. Refusing to bring her to see her father would be taking a chance with his life, though. She might kill him.

"You're lying to me," she accused him. "You have no intention of bringing me to see him."

"It's too dangerous," he told her.

She shook her head. "No, it's not. But what does it matter if it is? Why do you care?"

She was asking something else—something else he couldn't answer honestly. He couldn't tell her how he felt. He couldn't burden her with his feelings because there were too many now—too many nightmares—too much damage.

So he reminded her instead, "It's my job. Protecting you is my assignment."

She sucked in a breath. "That's all I am to you?" She glanced over his shoulder to the bedroom where they'd made love.

"That was a mistake," he told her. "I crossed the line. I shouldn't have."

"Do you do that on all your assignments?" she asked.

He thought of his first one, of the elderly lady with Alzheimer's and nearly smiled. "No..."

But he couldn't let her think that it meant something that he had with her. He couldn't let her think they might have a future together. After what he'd been through, he couldn't offer anyone a future.

"It didn't mean anything," he said. "I could *never* be with you again." Because he had nothing to offer her... but nightmares and uncertainty.

She flinched and nodded. "I knew that. I knew that you would never be able to forgive me."

"Megan..." She broke free of his grasp and ran to the control panel again.

He gave her a moment to figure out she couldn't escape, just like his captors used to give him...until the day he'd proven them wrong. But security in the Kozminskis' condo was high. You didn't need the code just to get in; you needed it to get out, too.

When she began to type in numbers without hesitation, Gage realized she'd watched him enter the code and she'd remembered it.

Cursing, he rushed forward just as the metal door began to open. She slipped through the narrow space and ran out. What the hell did she think, that she was going to walk to the hospital? Hail a cab? She had no car keys, no money for a cab.

"Megan!" he called after her. "Come back here! You can't leave."

She ran faster, turning the corner of the warehouse without so much as a glance back at him. Even if she had money for the fare, there were no cabs or buses running in this area of town. Once industrial, it was mostly abandoned now but for the warehouse Milek Kozminski had converted into the condo and art studio space.

"Megan!" he yelled.

But she didn't answer him. He figured she was just being stubborn until he turned the corner. Then he saw why she hadn't answered.

There was a hand clasped over her mouth and a gun pressed to her head. Richard had caught her—right next to the open door of a black sedan.

Gage hadn't drawn his gun, but he wore his holster. All he had to do was reach for it. But would Richard shoot before he could?

"Let her go," Gage advised him.

"You'd like that, wouldn't you?" Richard asked, his voice full of resentment. "You stole her from me once, but you're not stealing her again."

"You love her that much?" Gage asked hopefully. Richard wouldn't hurt her if he loved her.

The other man laughed. "Love? I leave that for fools like you. I don't love her."

"Then let her go." Because Gage loved her. Losing her once had nearly destroyed him. Losing her again…

He couldn't imagine it. It would be a nightmare beyond any he'd endured.

"I need her!" Richard said.

"But you said you don't love her." Then Gage realized why the other man claimed to need her—because he needed what he thought she had. "She doesn't have the diamonds anymore."

Richard's face flushed. "What? Where are they?"

"In the condo," Gage said. "Or they were."

"What do you mean?"

"I left the door wide open. Anyone could have walked off with them now." And Gage couldn't have cared less. Money mattered nothing to him.

"You better hope not," Richard said. "Or I will pull this trigger."

Megan's eyes widened with shock. Obviously, she had never considered her fiancé capable of such violence. But then neither had Gage.

"You don't want to hurt her," Gage said. "Or you won't live to see those diamonds again."

Richard's face flushed an even darker shade of red. "You tough guys…" He shook his head. "Like Derek. He thought he was tougher than me, too. He thought he could break me. But I broke him. I sent him to prison and he didn't even know."

"Because you did it behind his back," Gage said. "You were underhanded, just like you were with Megan, hiding who you truly were from her."

Richard chuckled. "It was easy to fool her, thanks to you."

"Me?"

"You distracted her for me so she didn't ask too many questions. Then she felt so guilty about dumping me for you that I could manipulate her into doing whatever I wanted," he boasted.

"Like wearing that ugly damn dress."

"That dress is worth millions," Richard said. "Maybe even billions!"

"Then let her go," Gage said. "And get your damn diamonds."

"Oh, I'll get them," Richard assured him. "But first I need to do this."

Gage didn't know what he was going to do, but that it would be bad. So he reached for his weapon. But he couldn't draw it fast enough.

Richard pulled his trigger first, firing the bullet right into Gage. Then he chuckled and asked, "Was that straightforward enough for you?"

Megan screamed so loudly it either penetrated Richard's hand or knocked it away from her mouth. Gage lay facedown on the sidewalk in front of her. Richard had just shot him—in cold blood.

How had she never realized how cold-blooded he was? She'd thought the reason she had felt no passion with him or from him had been her fault. Now she knew. He was a heartless monster.

"Should I make sure he's dead this time?" Richard asked as he lowered the barrel of his gun toward Gage's head.

She screamed again and did what she should have moments ago—she grabbed his arm. He fired anyway, but the shot missed Gage. Or at least she hoped it did. She saw no blood spread across his back. But his sweater was black. Maybe he had been struck.

Richard was stronger than she'd known. He easily pulled free of her grasp and turned on her with the gun. "You can't help him," he said. "But you can help yourself."

She didn't care about herself, not if she lost Gage. And she might have already lost her dad. "You're crazy if you think I would help you!" Then she saw the madness in his eyes and realized that he was crazy.

"You were going to help me," he said, "before *he* came back from the dead." He pointed his barrel at Gage again.

"No!" she shouted at him, to draw his focus back to her. "I would have never helped you with anything illegal."

He grinned, a mocking grin. "By marrying me, you were going to help me get those diamonds out of the country."

"But I didn't even know you had them."

"You had them," he said. "And you would have worn that dress through airport security."

She never would have worn that dress on a plane. The minute she'd put it on she had changed her mind about marrying him at all, even before Gage had appeared in her dressing room. "They would have found them then."

"You think airport security would have searched the daughter of an FBI bureau chief?" And he would have made damn certain they knew she was. He chuckled. "Never."

"That's the only interest you had in me," she realized. "My father."

He didn't even bother denying it. In fact he uttered another mocking little chuckle that confirmed it.

"He might be dead," she said. "Andrea might have killed him."

He cursed. "That stupid bitch. She's an idiot. She screwed everything up with her petty jealousy. She just had to see the woman I was marrying." He shook his head in disgust.

"She's dead," Megan informed him.

"The cute little brunette killed her?" he asked.

Megan nodded.

"Figured Andrea was too stupid to let that go."

"Let *me* go," Megan urged him. "Just get in your car and drive away." Then she could get help for Gage.

Maybe he hadn't been injured too badly. But he lay so still on the pavement.

"Not without the diamonds," Richard said. "We're going to get those and then maybe I'll think about letting you go."

She didn't believe him. Finally, she recognized when someone was lying or telling the truth. Too bad she'd figured it out too late to listen to Gage. If she hadn't left the condo, they would be safe inside it. Together. He wouldn't be bleeding on the concrete. This—like everything else—was all her fault.

Actually, it wasn't all hers. It was Richard's. He had manipulated her long enough. If only she could get to Gage's gun.

But it must lie beneath him. She couldn't see it. There were other weapons back inside the condo, though. Payne Protection had an arsenal there.

"Then let's get the diamonds," she urged him.

His hand on her arm, he jerked her forward so that she nearly stumbled over Gage's body. Her heart lurching, she stepped over him. Richard kicked him as he crossed his body. Gage didn't move or even grunt in pain.

Tears stung her eyes. She'd lost him again and this time for good. She wanted Richard to pay for that, for taking the life of a good man.

He dragged her along the sidewalk back to the condo. The metal door stood open, how Gage had left it. He hadn't cared about the diamonds lying just inside on the couch. He'd cared only about her, about keeping her safe. Of course it had been his job to protect her. It was her fault that she'd kept making it so hard for him.

But that was really the only thing that was her fault. Everything else was on Richard, on his treachery and greed. It gleamed in his eyes as he caught sight of the wedding dress spilling out of the box on the couch.

"There they are, just like he said." He turned back and pointed the gun at her face.

"You need me," she reminded him. "You need the bureau chief's daughter to help you out of the country."

A smirk spread across his face. "Yeah, right. Like you'd help me…"

"I would," she said. But she had never been a very convincing liar. Why had Gage believed her when she'd told him she'd never loved him? Maybe he'd had some of the same insecurities she'd had.

"I can't fly out of the country," he said.

"Why not?"

"That little brunette, she overheard me and D talking," he said. "She knows."

"Then you're trapped."

He gave her another condescending smile. "With this much money, I can get my hands on anything I want. You were only my plan A."

He *would* have a plan B. He was brilliant. It was one of the things she'd admired about him, his intelligence and how understanding he'd been when she'd dumped him for Gage. But he was so smart that he'd intended to manipulate her the entire time.

"I don't need you anymore." He turned the gun barrel toward her.

"Richard…"

"I'm doing you a favor," he said. "This way you don't have to mourn Gage Huxton all over again. You can be with him—for eternity."

Megan squeezed her eyes shut just as the shot rang out.

* * *

No matter how many painkillers they'd pumped through his IV, Woodrow had found no relief. He couldn't sleep, not without Penny by his side. She had been gone too long.

He was only allowed one visitor at a time, so she'd been giving everyone else a turn. Ellen. His son-in-law. The only exception had been Nick. He'd been allowed to bring in his newborn son with him.

"Why the hell did you saddle him with a name like Woodrow?" he'd teased his best agent as the guy had cradled his baby in hands that were nearly as big as the infant himself.

The only man who could have been a better agent had quit before he'd had the chance to prove himself. He'd proved himself at the church, though.

Where the hell was Gage?

Hopefully, keeping Megan safe. He knew Gage would give up his life before he'd let anything happen to the love of his life. Fortunately, he'd found her when they were young. They would have a long life together.

It had taken Woodrow too long to find Penny. And getting shot had proved to him that he couldn't waste another minute. Sure, he'd been hesitant to say anything to her until they knew everyone else was safe. But it didn't matter.

It wasn't like he was going to wait until Richard was caught. The guy was smart. He could elude the authorities for years. And Woodrow wasn't willing to wait years. Not now that he'd finally found his true love.

His door creaked open, and he turned toward it with a reassuring smile. He'd presented that face to every worried visitor. As if thinking about her had conjured her from his dreams, Penny stepped through the door. His smile widened into a grin of delight.

Her curls were still tousled. The circles beneath her eyes might have grown darker. She was still the most beautiful woman he had ever seen. She didn't smile back. In fact her brown eyes were dark with worry and regret.

She didn't have good news for him.

Pain jabbed his heart as he realized that. He shook his head and implored her, "Wait!"

She paused half in, half out of his hospital room.

He gestured her inside, and the door closed behind her. "I want you," he said. "I just don't want whatever you have to tell me."

She gasped. "Woodrow..."

"Just wait," he told her. "Before you tell me whatever it is you have to tell me, I want to ask you something first."

"But..."

He gestured her closer until she stood right next to his bed. Then he pulled her down beside him, like when he had awakened and found her pressed against his side. "I think you brought me back," he said.

"What?"

"The surgeon and doctors are all surprised that I made it," he said. "They said I lost so much blood that they didn't expect me to wake up."

She gasped again and trembled against him.

"But I had to come back," he said. "For you..."

Tears glistened in her eyes.

"It took me fifty-five years to find you," he said. And he lifted and pressed her small hand against his heart. He couldn't feel it through the bandage, but he knew it was there. More importantly, he knew she was already inside it. "I wasn't going to give you up without a fight."

"I'm glad," she murmured. And her lips curved into a slight smile. "I was worried that I'd already lost you."

He shook his head. "Not a chance."

"That's why I told myself I couldn't fall for you," she said. "Because you're too great a risk. I could lose you like I lost…"

"Your husband?"

She shook her head. "I lost him before he died. I lost the illusion of what I thought we had. It wasn't this. I know that now."

"Me, too," he said.

She nodded. "Megan…"

"She's not mine. Biologically."

"It doesn't matter," she agreed. "With the child…"

But with the spouse, the trust was irrevocably broken. He had forgiven, but he'd never forgotten. Just as he imagined she had.

"I will never betray you," he promised. "I would never put you through what I was put through."

"I know."

"And this bullet thing…" He sighed. "That was a fluke. My first gunshot wound in all my years with the Bureau and the Marines."

"Maybe I'm bad luck," she suggested with a smile.

"You're good luck," he said. "I doubt I would have survived if I hadn't wanted to be with you."

She snuggled against his side, clutching his shoulders. Then she lifted her face and pressed her lips to his. "I didn't want to fall for you," she said. "But I did."

"I love you," he said. "And I want to marry you."

The regret was back in her dark eyes. "Woodrow, I need to tell you—"

He pressed his mouth to hers and then his fingers. "It doesn't matter. Nothing matters except you becoming my wife. I want to be with you through good times and bad. If the bad starts now—" and he had a sick feeling that it had "—then I want to go through it with you. Please, Penny, say that you'll marry me."

Tears streaked down her face. Any other woman might be too afraid after all she'd lost to risk her heart again, especially on a man like him. But she was the bravest woman he knew. And she nodded. "Of course I will marry you."

His breath shuddered out in a sigh of relief. And he kissed her again—deeply. "I love you. I want to marry you as soon as we can get a license."

"I can see to that," the wedding planner assured him.

"But first you want to tell me what you came in to say." He braced himself. Whatever it was, no matter how bad, he would be able to handle it with her love and support.

"Richard found Megan and Gage at the safe house," she said. "He got there before any other Payne Protection bodyguards arrived for backup."

He sucked in a breath. "And?"

"There was a shooting."

He cursed and clutched his arms around her, holding her close.

"Who did we lose?" he asked. Because he knew that someone had died.

Chapter 26

The young doctor gasped as Gage pulled off his sweater. "Oh, my God, what happened to you?"

Gage glanced down at the blood trickling from the wound on his shoulder. It had nearly stopped bleeding now. "It's just a scratch," he said. "The bullet barely grazed me."

Fortunately, Richard was a lousy shot, but Gage had played dead to buy himself some time. He might have wound up dead for real if Megan hadn't prevented Richard from shooting him again. She'd saved his life, which had enabled him to save hers.

He shuddered as he remembered Richard pointing that gun in her beautiful face. Shooting him had been a risk, though. Richard could have squeezed the trigger out of reflex as he went down.

So Gage hadn't given him the chance to even get his finger on the trigger. He'd fired as soon as Richard had lifted his gun.

While Megan hadn't been shot, she wasn't all right. She'd barely said anything since the shooting. Nick and the other Payne Protection bodyguards who'd showed up at the condo had asked her questions, but she'd either nodded or shaken her head. She hadn't said anything to them after she'd asked them about her dad.

"I'm fine," he said, dismissing the doctor's concern for him.

The only reason he'd agreed to come to the hospital had been for her, so she could see her father. And for a doctor to see her and make sure she was all right. Gage's gunshot wound had gotten them back to the ER faster than her shock would have, though.

"You need to check her out."

The dark-haired doctor glanced at Megan, who stood near Gage's gurney. Her skin—usually such a warm honey tone—was unnaturally pale except for the droplets of Richard's blood that had spattered across her face. The doctor noticed the blood and asked, "Was she shot as well?"

"No," Megan replied. "I wasn't."

But Gage flinched as he remembered how close she had come to getting shot—to getting killed. Damn Richard. But he couldn't hurt her ever again.

"I think she's in shock, though," Gage said.

She shook her head and tumbled her curly hair around her blood-spattered face. "I'm fine."

She wasn't. And they both knew it. After what she'd seen, she might never be fine again. Too bad she'd opened her eyes right as the bullet had struck Richard. Gage had had to take the kill shot—or risk Richard killing her.

"She's been through a lot."

The doctor looked from Megan back to Gage, his smooth dark brow beginning to furrow with confusion.

"She was at that wedding chapel that armed gunmen invaded earlier today," Gage explained.

The doctor's eyes widened. "There was a shoot-out there. Is that where the blood came from?" He gestured at her face.

Gage wasn't going to waste time explaining about the second shooting. So he simply replied, "She was the bride."

She was supposed to marry the man Gage had killed. How did she feel about his killing her groom? How did she feel about him now? He could tell nothing from her face.

The doctor looked at her with more concern now. "Your father came through the ER just as my shift started early this afternoon." His face was easy to read; he didn't think Woodrow had had a chance when he'd seen him.

"He made it," Gage said.

Nick had assured him of that when he'd showed up at the condo with Garek and Milek Kozminski. They'd been so sorry for not getting there sooner. But Gage had brushed off their apologies. They'd brought good news.

"He's tough," Gage said and offered Megan a reassuring smile. He suspected she was still worried. She wouldn't believe her father was okay until she saw him for herself.

"I don't need stitches or a tetanus shot," Gage told the doctor as the young man probed his wound. "Just stick a bandage on it."

"Looks like you've been through a lot, too," the doctor remarked as he swabbed the injury with alcohol, cleaning it before taping on the bandage Gage had requested. "Where did all the scars come from?"

Gage didn't answer. Hell, he wasn't even sure where he'd been.

The young man peered closer at the ridges of healed flesh along Gage's torso, shoulders and arms. "Looks like you were tortured." Then as he glanced up and met Gage's gaze, his face flushed with embarrassment at his lack of tact. "I'm sorry…"

Gage shrugged. "It's fine."

"He was a Marine," Megan said. He heard both her pride and her regret.

One was *always* a Marine. Even her father. That was how he'd survived getting shot. But Gage didn't explain that to her. He didn't say anything.

The doctor spoke again. "Thank you for your service."

Gage glanced at Megan and murmured, "The worst wounds leave no marks…"

The worst wounds leave no marks…

"You're never going to forgive me, are you?" she asked as they rode the elevator up from the hospital lobby to her father's room. He'd been moved from ICU to a private room. While she was relieved about that, she was still scared over how close she'd come to losing him. And scared that Gage was still lost to her…

"Forgive you for what?" Gage asked, as if he truly had no idea.

"For breaking your heart."

His lips parted in a soft gasp. "Do you know what that means?"

"You were talking about me," she said, "when you talked about the worst wounds…"

He grinned. "Well, that, too. But it means that you actually believe I loved you. Or how else could you have broken my heart?"

Loved. Her heart cracked at the past tense. He didn't

love her anymore. And after what she'd put him through, she doubted he ever would again.

"I was stupid," she said.

"You were not stupid," he said—as if he needed to defend her to her.

"Yes, I was," she insisted. She had been so stupid. How could she have ever considered a cold-blooded con artist like Richard a friend?

"You were insecure," Gage corrected her. "That's how people like Tucker Allison and Richard got to you. You never saw yourself as you really are."

"How am I really?" she asked, because she felt like a fool.

"Beautiful…"

She snorted.

Then his hand shot out, hitting the stop button on the elevator control panel. The car jerked to a stop, launching Megan into his arms. Gage caught her and held her tightly, kissing her with such passion. His lips moved over hers, gliding first before sucking her lower lip into his mouth. He nipped it lightly before sliding his tongue over the sensitive flesh. He groaned, and his arms clutched her closely against him, molding her soft curves to his hard muscles. His erection pressed against her.

The passion and need were real. He was attracted to her. But was it just attraction?

When he finally pulled back, she panted for breath, and her heart pounded erratically.

"Do you get it now?" he asked.

She smiled suggestively. "No, but I'd like to…"

He laughed. And whatever torment he still carried with him appeared to lighten as his green eyes twinkled.

"Oh, I'd also like to," he agreed. "But I have to do something else first." He restarted the elevator.

"See my dad," she agreed as the doors opened. But once he returned her safely to her father, would he consider his mission completed, and would he leave, never to see her again?

Before she could ask him, he stopped at the nurses' station. "Woodrow Lynch?"

An older nurse looked up from her computer monitor and uttered a weary sigh. "Yes. But he's had too much company and not enough rest. We need to cut off visiting hours for him early."

"I'm his daughter," Megan said.

The nurse pursed her thin lips as if she didn't believe her.

"She is," Gage insisted in a gruff voice that brooked no argument. They had never discussed it. But he'd been to her house. He'd seen photos of her mother and of her father when he was younger. He had to know she couldn't biologically be Woodrow's child. But he also knew that they were family no matter what the DNA.

"Are you Megan?" another, younger nurse asked as she joined them at the desk.

Megan nodded.

"And you're Gage?" she asked.

He nodded. "Yes."

"He's been waiting for them," this nurse told the other one.

The older woman, with her brush-cut short gray hair, glared at her. "But he's had too much company and is only supposed to have one visitor at a time."

"He was shot at her wedding," the younger nurse said. "He won't rest until he knows they're all right."

The older nurse pursed her lips again disapprovingly but nodded her agreement. Like it mattered. Megan had been through too much to let anyone keep her from her father.

And the same went for Gage. If he tried to walk away, she wouldn't let him. She'd persist until he gave her another chance. She would never give up on them again.

The younger nurse gestured at them to follow her, and she led them down the hall to a closed door. "Sorry about her," she said. "I think she's jealous."

"Jealous?" Gage asked.

"Of the love…"

And when she opened the door, they saw the love— Penny curled up against Woodrow's side in his narrow hospital bed. Penny tensed and tried to ease away, but Woodrow kept his arm around her shoulders. Despite having been shot, he looked happier than Megan had ever seen her father.

Tears of joy and relief stung her eyes. She rushed forward to hug him. "I'm so glad you're all right!"

He clasped her head in his hand, holding it against his, as his breath shuddered out in a sigh of relief. "Me, too, my beauty. I'm so glad you're all right."

"What?" Gage asked with his arms outstretched. "I gave you my word that I would keep her safe. Did you doubt me?"

"He wasn't the one doubting you," Penny said. "You've been doubting yourself."

Gage chuckled, and it sounded a little less rusty than when Megan had heard it before. "Damn you," Gage cursed her with a wealth of affection in his gruff voice. "For always being right!"

"It's a pain in the ass, isn't it?" Woodrow said. "Don't

know what I was thinking to propose to this woman. It's going to be a hardship to have a wife who's always right."

"You're engaged!" Megan uttered a squeal of pure delight. No wonder her father looked so happy. He was going to marry a wonderful woman. She hugged Penny, too.

Penny touched her cheek, tipping her face to hers. "Are you sure you're okay with this?" she asked. "This feels like horrible timing after what happened at your wedding."

"I'm so happy something good came out of such a horrible day," Megan said.

Penny nodded in agreement then she glanced up at Gage. "Is our engagement going to be the only good thing?"

Gage shrugged. "I guess that's up to Woodrow."

"Me?" Her father tried to mimic Gage's gesture of stretching his arms out but winced. He was going to be okay. But it was going to take him a while to heal completely. "I already proposed."

"Yes," Gage said. "But will you let me?"

Megan's pulse quickened. Could he be asking what she thought he was asking?

Her father grinned. "Convince me you're worthy of my daughter."

"I love her," Gage said. "I've always loved her."

Megan turned to him, unable to believe what she was hearing. "Loved—you said," she reminded him. "Past tense—as in you did once but don't anymore."

"I never stopped," he said then uttered a ragged sigh. "God knows I tried…"

She flinched. "I'm sorry," she murmured. "Sorry for everything…" If only she hadn't been such a fool… "You quitting the Bureau—reenlisting—it was all my fault." How could she expect him to forgive her when she couldn't forgive herself?

Gage pulled her into his arms, his hands smoothing over her back. "I'm the one who's sorry," he said, and he leaned his forehead against hers, staring deeply into her eyes. "I acted like an idiot with wounded pride. I shouldn't have run away. I should have stayed and fought for you."

She nodded and lightly tapped his chest with her fist. "Yes, you should have."

"I will," he promised. "I won't give up on us again."

"Neither will I," she said.

"It won't always be easy," he warned her. "I'm not myself yet. But with you, I'm more myself than I've been since we broke up. And for you, I will work on getting completely whole again."

How had she ever doubted his love, even for a moment?

Then she remembered. "But you were going to let me marry Richard…"

"That's why," he said. "I thought he would be the better man for you. I thought I was too broken, that the sleepless nights and my nightmares, the flashbacks… I thought it would all be too much for you. I didn't want to put you through what I'm going through."

"That was noble," her father said, as if he agreed with Gage's reasons for not wanting to be with her again.

Megan snorted. "That was stupid. And rude…"

Gage stepped back as if she'd slapped him. "I thought—"

"You thought I wasn't strong enough to help you through this," she said.

He nodded. "You're right. I was stupid and wrong. And you proved that to me. You proved to me how strong you are."

Until today—her wedding day—she hadn't even realized how strong she was. That she was capable of stabbing someone with scissors or tricking armed gunmen…

But she knew not thinking her strong enough hadn't been the only reason for his hesitation.

"You probably also thought I didn't love you enough," she said. "And that is my fault."

He shook his head. "I never should have believed you that day. I should have known that you were just saying you never loved me to protect yourself—that you were scared."

"Not anymore," she said. "Back then I was so afraid of getting hurt. But I had no idea what pain was until I thought I'd lost you forever. I don't want to ever go through that again."

"So you'll marry me?"

"You haven't asked," Penny pointed out, but there was amusement in her voice. She pointed to the floor, apparently wanting Gage to drop to his knees.

"And I haven't given my permission," Woodrow said.

Gage turned to his former boss. "Sir? I promise you that I will spend the rest of my life doing everything in my power to make your daughter happy."

Her father nodded. "You have proven to me over and over again that you're a man of your word, Gage Huxton. Your word is good enough for me. You have my permission."

Gage nodded, too, and there was a hint of moisture in his green eyes. Megan knew her father meant a lot to him.

Woodrow reached out and squeezed her hand. He stared up at her and asked, "What about you, Megan? Is his word good enough for you?"

Like they had, she nodded. She would never doubt Gage's word again. "Yes."

Her father released her hand—as if letting her go. She turned back to Gage, who had dropped to his knees as Penny had directed. Tears rushed into her eyes; she had to blink them back to focus on his handsome face.

"Will you marry me?" he asked. "Will you be my wife?"

She opened her mouth to reply. But he pressed his fingers over her lips.

"I promise that you will never doubt my love again," he said. "I will make sure that you always feel secure and safe with me."

"I do," she told him. "And I will marry you, Gage Huxton. I will be your wife." She threw her arms around his neck and held him closely while Penny and her father cheered.

"What the hell's going on in there?" Nikki Payne asked of the nurses who stood near the door of Woodrow Lynch's hospital room.

The younger nurse smiled. "More love."

The older one snorted but blinked back tears as she hurried away, as if embarrassed at getting caught either at the door or with tears in her eyes. The younger one pushed the door open a little farther so that Nikki could see inside to the two couples embracing.

"Two engagements today," the younger nurse said as she closed the door again. She glanced down at the diamond on her own hand. "My fiancé could have learned something from these two guys about romance." She blinked back tears of her own and hurried off.

Nikki was happy for her mother. So happy...

While Penny had always had all of them—and whatever other kids she'd emotionally adopted as her own, like the Kozminskis—she had still been alone. She had been the only parent. She had been the one offering comfort and never receiving it.

Woodrow had apparently been the same, raising his daughters alone as both father and mother. He'd also been a father figure for all of his agents. Like Penny, he had been there for everyone else while no one had been there for him with support, with comfort, with love…

That was all in the past now for both of them.

Just like all Gage and Megan's pain was in the past. After all they'd been through, they would never break up again. Their love was stronger now—unbreakable—like Gage had been in captivity.

Wrinkling her nose and blinking against the sting in her eyes, Nikki turned away from the closed door. She would be back—with a bottle of champagne so they could really celebrate.

She was happy for them even though this wasn't what she wanted for herself. She had never been the girly girl. She'd never wanted to play Cinderella or Sleeping Beauty. She'd never needed a prince to rescue her. She'd never wanted to marry and have kids. She'd just wanted to kick ass like her brothers.

She hadn't wanted love for herself, but she'd at least believed in it—until she'd learned of her father's betrayal. Then she'd doubted that it was ever real.

Until now…

She blinked harder, fighting back the moisture blurring her eyes. She had no doubt that Megan and Gage were truly, deeply in love. And she had no doubt that her mother had at long last found her true soul mate in Woodrow Lynch.

Real love existed.

For other people…

Just not for Nikki. Not just yet, but maybe someday soon.

* * * * *

Look for the next thrilling installment in the
BACHELOR BODYGUARDS *series, coming soon!*

Don't forget the previous titles in the series:

BODYGUARD'S BABY SURPRISE
BODYGUARD DADDY
HIS CHRISTMAS ASSIGNMENT

And if you love Lisa Childs,
be sure to pick up her other stories:

RED HOT
TAMING THE SHIFTER
THE AGENT'S REDEMPTION
AGENT TO THE RESCUE
AGENT UNDERCOVER
THE PREGNANT WITNESS
CURSED
BRIDEGROOM BODYGUARD

Available now from Harlequin!

REQUEST YOUR FREE BOOKS!
2 FREE NOVELS PLUS 2 FREE GIFTS!

ROMANTIC suspense

Sparked by danger, fueled by passion

YES! Please send me 2 FREE Harlequin® Romantic Suspense novels and my 2 FREE gifts (gifts are worth about $10). After receiving them, if I don't wish to receive any more books, I can return the shipping statement marked "cancel." If I don't cancel, I will receive 4 brand-new novels every month and be billed just $4.74 per book in the U.S. or $5.49 per book in Canada. That's a savings of at least 12% off the cover price! It's quite a bargain! Shipping and handling is just 50¢ per book in the U.S. and 75¢ per book in Canada.* I understand that accepting the 2 free books and gifts places me under no obligation to buy anything. I can always return a shipment and cancel at any time. Even if I never buy another book, the two free books and gifts are mine to keep forever.

240/340 HDN GH3P

Name	(PLEASE PRINT)	
Address		Apt. #
City	State/Prov.	Zip/Postal Code

Signature (if under 18, a parent or guardian must sign)

Mail to the **Reader Service:**

IN U.S.A.: P.O. Box 1867, Buffalo, NY 14240-1867
IN CANADA: P.O. Box 609, Fort Erie, Ontario L2A 5X3

Want to try two free books from another line?
Call 1-800-873-8635 or visit www.ReaderService.com.

* Terms and prices subject to change without notice. Prices do not include applicable taxes. Sales tax applicable in N.Y. Canadian residents will be charged applicable taxes. Offer not valid in Quebec. This offer is limited to one order per household. Not valid for current subscribers to Harlequin Romantic Suspense books. All orders subject to credit approval. Credit or debit balances in a customer's account(s) may be offset by any other outstanding balance owed by or to the customer. Please allow 4 to 6 weeks for delivery. Offer available while quantities last.

Your Privacy—The Reader Service is committed to protecting your privacy. Our Privacy Policy is available online at www.ReaderService.com or upon request from the Reader Service.

We make a portion of our mailing list available to reputable third parties that offer products we believe may interest you. If you prefer that we not exchange your name with third parties, or if you wish to clarify or modify your communication preferences, please visit us at www.ReaderService.com/consumerchoice or write to us at Reader Service Preference Service, P.O. Box 9062, Buffalo, NY 14240-9062. Include your complete name and address.

HRS15

*Texas Ranger Jake McCord is undercover to investigate
Alanna Colton's involvement with her father's
disappearance. He never expected to fall for the wild
beauty. Will she ever forgive him for posing as a horse
whisperer at her beloved family stables?*

*Read on for a sneak preview of
HIGH-STAKES COLTON,
the next book in THE COLTONS OF TEXAS
continuity by Karen Anders.*

Fully dressed, they crossed the stable area with no one
but the horses to see their progress. Up the back road to
the quiet and dark house, they climbed the stairs to the
back patio, skirting the pool to her suite of rooms. "How
did you know which room was mine the other day?"

"I didn't. I took my chances. I knew you were housed
in the left wing. I'm just lucky I didn't knock on Fowler's
door."

She laughed at that, finding it extremely funny. "You
would have had some 'splaining to do," she said, wiping
her eyes.

They stopped outside the door. "I had a good time,
Jake. I will admit rubbing ointment into your shoulders
was just a ruse to get inside to talk to you."

Hooking his thumbs in the front pockets of his jeans,
Jake watched her, his expression light. "Sassy and
underhanded."

"Guilty." The longing on her face made his heart trip a little.

"Come here, sweetheart," he whispered.

She didn't hesitate and went right into his arms. He shifted, widening his stance, when she slipped her arms around his waist and turned her face against him. Resting his jaw against her head, he began slowly massaging the small of her back. Alanna tightened her arms around him and Jake could detect a light quivering in her, as though she had been braced for pain that hadn't materialized. Shifting his hold, he cradled her head firmly against him and brushed a gentling kiss against her temple, his expression unsettled.

He didn't know what in hell was going to happen to them. And if he'd realized anything during the past few days, it was that he wasn't sure what kind of future they had, if any. He suspected when she found out about why he was there and who he really was, that would be it.

Was he a fool to hope for a different outcome?

Don't miss
HIGH-STAKES COLTON by Karen Anders,
available September 2016 wherever
Harlequin® Romantic Suspense
books and ebooks are sold.

www.Harlequin.com

HRSEXP0816